The Great Pretender

Cesar A. Perez

ISBN: 0692820582
ISBN 13: 9780692820582
Library of Congress Control Number: 2016921130
Aragon Books, Greer, South Carolina

To my wife and children. You fill my life with meaning and purpose.

Chapter 1

THAT DAY, LIFE was an inescapable curse. The same dreadful memories haunted him faithfully as soon as he awoke, and they seized any chance of going back to sleep. After trying unsuccessfully to escape the thoughts that had first chased him into exhaustion and then crudely lured him out of sleep, he rushed up from the bed like an animal escaping its cage. But he already knew that any attempt to enjoy a single moment would be bullied away by guilt, because the peace that once had been so real to him was now permanently out of his grasp. Hell was an actual place, he was convinced, because he had a taste of it on Earth.

His anger at himself was rising, and the four walls of the most expensive hotel room money could rent in Charleston were getting darker and closing in on him. He threw an unpacked suitcase across the room, furious with himself for not being able to snap out of the reality he had created. The lamp light reflected brightly on the nickel-plated Smith and Wesson revolver that fell out of the suitcase when it hit the floor. He picked up the revolver, sat on the bed, and verified that there was a round in the chamber. *One quick pull of the trigger,* he thought, *and it could all be over.*

He put the gun back in the suitcase, for now, and decided to get out of there. A quick glance at the clock on the unfamiliar nightstand revealed it was almost four in the afternoon. Not trusting the hotel clock, he checked the time on the Rolex watch his father had given him when he graduated from Stanford. But it really didn't matter what time it was; he figured today would be as meaningless as any other.

Not really caring what he looked like, he grabbed a hairbrush out of his duffel bag and haphazardly brushed his hair as he looked out the window. He despised the man in the mirror and avoided him whenever possible. The door slammed behind him as he rushed outside, hoping for a change of scenery, a smell, anything that might bring some temporary relief.

The temperature outside was a perfect seventy degrees. He noticed the beauty of spring in the South all around him. Everywhere he looked, the scenery was like a masterpiece portrayed by a skillful painter with a unique knowledge and understanding of the intrinsic beauty of life. Countless colors looked as if they were about to burst out of flowers and trees. It was impossible to miss this kind of beauty, but he couldn't enjoy it. The thought came to mind that this must be what heaven is like. It was so beautiful, so peaceful, so unattainable. *Does heaven even exist?* he asked himself for the thousandth time. He wasn't sure about anything anymore. All the good things he'd been so certain of at one time now seemed utopic and out of reach.

He slowed down his steps, finding himself drifting into the same haunting memories. As people walked by, he looked at their faces, and somehow they all looked happy—peaceful, as if they had perfect lives. An older couple ahead of him walked hand in hand, their pace tranquil. He didn't have to see their faces to know they were smiling, and he wondered how they'd been able to do life right, at least well enough to enjoy the freedom and happiness that had eluded him for good.

As he watched the elderly couple walk away into the breathtaking background of spring, he felt himself go back to what seemed to be his rightful place in the world. This place existed in his mind only, and there he was not free to enjoy anything beautiful or good. The world was so full of wonder, but the once-promising Nathan Berkley was now a washed-up shadow of his former self who no longer felt a part of it. He couldn't see the chains that bound him, but they were mighty and powerful—unbreakable. He desperately needed to see a glimmer of his old self, but the guilt that imprisoned him was cruel and persistent.

Chapter 2

Nathan couldn't remember the last time he had eaten, and he really didn't care, but he knew he needed to eat something. He looked around to see where he was, and a couple of blocks over, he spotted a sign for a place that brought back a flood of memories. He shook his head and smiled. "How did I get here?" he muttered to himself. "I can't believe this. Nawlin's, of all places."

He was greeted with the customary southern hospitality South Carolina was well known for. The restaurant staff seemed tired from taking care of the after-church crowd that Sunday, but somehow they still found a way to smile and be courteous. Nathan knew it was something to be thankful for, and he made every effort to respond in kind.

The place hadn't changed at all. It had the same unique decor that allowed it to pass as both a seafood restaurant and a country-style buffet. Right away he felt himself go back in time as he took in the smells and ambience. Most people went there because they wanted a country-style meal. But to him it was so much more than a restaurant. It was where life really had begun, where he had discovered that it was meant to be an incredible journey.

From the corner of his eye, Nathan noticed someone approaching him. He turned to see if his suspicion was right, but before he had a chance to see who it was, he found himself in a tight squeeze. He had been sure no one would recognize him because very little about his appearance resembled what he looked like when he lived in Charleston. He had aged at twice the normal rate, and he was well tanned from the last few months in Costa Rica. But Sarah had recognized him nonetheless.

"Nathan? It's really you, isn't it?" she exclaimed, looking astonished as she pulled back to look him over. "Oh my, it's so good to see you. I can't believe you're here! How you been, hon?"

There had been no doubt in his mind that anyone he knew in Charleston would want nothing to do with him. Her reaction made him feel good, and for the first time in days, he felt a slight, much-needed dose of contentment.

"I'm doing okay, Sarah. And you?"

"Fine. Just fine," she responded with a kind smile. "Come on in! Your favorite table is empty, and Jack just finished up a batch of that fried chicken you used to like so much. I'll go get you a plate right now. Unless you want something else, of course..."

Nathan nodded and started walking to the spot she had mentioned. She patted him on the shoulder while looking him up and down. He looked discouraged and was much thinner than before. There was no trace of the energy he'd always exuded. His hair was longer, but he still had that sophisticated yuppie look about him.

"How about some mashed taters to go with them biscuits?" Knowing her southern accent would get a chuckle out of him, she exaggerated it as she used to years ago when he would poke fun at her.

He laughed. "No, thanks, Sarah, the chicken alone will do."

"Well, you're gonna get some anyway, and I expect you'll be eating them?"

Nathan knew it would be of no use to tell Sarah no, so he nodded and sat down. He could tell she wanted to sit down and catch up, probably find out how he had been, where he had been, but the restaurant was too busy, and she left to help other customers once he was settled. That suited him because he wasn't in the mood to talk.

Well into his plate of fried chicken and mashed potatoes, he realized he still had not tasted the first bite. The place brought back so many memories, and his mind had been racing from thought to thought since he sat down. His gaze shifted from table to table, and he wondered about each person, once again feeling they all must have perfect lives. He wished he could trade places with any of them. It didn't matter who, just as long as he could experience some degree of peace and joy. He knew the thought was absurd, but escaping reality every once in a while made the next moment possible.

A fork dropped a few tables over, and he looked in that direction. He watched a well-dressed woman get up from her chair to retrieve it and sit back down. The place in front of her was empty, and he figured she must have been eating by herself. Strangely enough, seeing her sit by herself made him feel a little better, as if he wasn't the only person in the world who was alone.

An elderly man walked up to the dessert bar with a little girl, and Nathan watched them walk hand in hand. It was hard to tell which one was more excited to pick a dessert. They looked over the choices and giggled at each other. Their joy felt so real to Nathan, and he longed for the family he once had. He put his fork down and lowered his hat as he fought hard not to cry.

Sarah came to the table and offered him more to drink.

"I'm fine. Thanks. But I'll take a cup of coffee," he said, trying to look upbeat.

"Sure, hon. Listen, my shift is over, and I have to scoot. It sure was good to see you again, Nathan," Sarah said with a sincere look in her eyes. "Now, you make sure to go get you some dessert. Okay? We've got some great stuff tonight."

"Sure, Sarah. Thanks. I might just do that."

She hugged him and walked toward the door.

It was getting dark outside, and his first impulse was to leave a tip, get up, and go back to his hotel room. But the thought of being in that room, any room, with just him and all the memories and regrets was terrifying. The decor and attention to detail in the upscale hotel where he was staying were second to none, but the place felt impersonal and far from home. Every place felt far from home. Nathan didn't need nice and upscale. Those things had lost their allure a long time ago. He needed to recover what he'd lost, but he was convinced it was too late.

A laugh from the table in front of Nathan caused him to lift his gaze. A boy about three years old was pushing his half-eaten plate to the side as he made his case to go to the dessert bar. His dad was laughing while trying to wipe the macaroni and cheese from the boy's mouth. But his son didn't seem to have time to wipe his mouth—the dessert bar was much more important. His entire body twitched, making sure his dad knew that getting to the desserts was a matter of life and death.

Nathan looked on as the scene unfolded. It brought back such sweet memories of his son when he was about that age, and as the overwhelming weight of all his regrets crushed his heart, he winced, knowing those days were long gone.

In his fight for justice and everything that was right in the world, the little boy worked to wiggle away from his daddy, who was trying hard to wipe off as much cheese from his mouth as possible before he got away. With all the commotion, his drink was pushed off the table, and it landed with a loud noise on the floor.

The boy's dad looked up and noticed Nathan sitting at the table next to them. "I'm so sorry, sir. I hope we didn't startle you."

Nathan looked at the young man with a half-hearted smile. "Oh, no. It's okay. I understand. I know what it's like."

The young man smiled and started to clean up the mess. "Thanks. Again, I'm sorry if we disturbed you," he said. His son sat quietly in his seat, not making a peep, realizing he was probably in trouble.

"I'm fine, really."

"Tell this man you're sorry, Jamie!"

The little boy looked embarrassed. He hesitated but then complied, figuring he had better do this so he might have a chance to go to the dessert bar. "I'm sorry," he said, looking at a fictitious object on his lap.

"It's okay, buddy! I get pretty excited about dessert myself, and I have spilled my share of drinks," Nathan responded in a fatherly tone he'd not used in years.

The young man smiled gratefully and took his son to get some ice cream from the bar. As Nathan watched them walk off, the memory of the look on his own son's face in a similar situation came to mind. His son had been about the same age as Jamie at the time, and in an excited attempt to get some chips, he had picked up the bag from the bottom and they had spilled all over the floor.

"Oops! Sorry, Daddy." The sweet words replayed in his mind. Nathan remembered the moment as if it'd just happened. He could still see the chips spread out all over the kitchen floor with his son standing right in the middle.

"It's okay, buddy. Don't you worry about it. We'll clean it up together, and it will be like it never happened. Come on! Let's clean this up before Mommy sees it." He could still see the look of relief on his son's face. But more importantly, he remembered the expression of love and admiration that made him feel as if he was doing his job as a dad.

Back then, Nathan had a clear purpose with a simple path forward. To everyone around him, he appeared to be the guy who had it all together. But he'd messed up and thrown it all away. *How did it all go so wrong so fast? And why wasn't I able to stop it?* he asked himself for the millionth time.

Father and son came back to the table, and Jamie seemed perfectly happy as he attacked his double scoops of ice cream. The little boy looked at Nathan but then quickly glanced away after they made eye contact. But something seemed to catch Jamie's attention, and he turned back to look at Nathan again.

"Where did you get that hat? Is it really old? Is it a real John Deere hat?" he asked.

His dad took a quick peek at the hat and then looked back at Jamie. "Son, don't ask that. You know better." He looked embarrassed, but he also had a trace of a smile on his face. From the dad's reaction, Nathan could tell Jamie had asked a similar question to someone else before, and he smiled back at the boy, letting him know it was okay.

"Why, it sure is a John Deere. And you're right, the hat is a little old now," Nathan responded.

"Then buy you another hat! My daddy has a lot of hats. Some are from really cool places. He'll give you one."

"Jamie!" the dad said firmly.

Nathan laughed and said, "I couldn't get rid of this one, Jamie. This one is pretty special."

"What's so special about it?" the boy asked curiously.

"That's enough questions, Jamie."

Jamie looked at the hat, then back at Nathan, and without any expression he got back to his ice cream.

Nathan couldn't help but envy Jamie's father. He wondered if he realized what a gift he had in that little boy—what it meant to get to be with his son.

Unfortunately for Nathan, he had learned that lesson the hard way. In his case the warnings had been clear, and he'd sensed the danger of taking his blessings for granted. He had foreseen the consequences that would follow his actions if he didn't change course and chart in the right direction. But one day it was too late, and he found himself trying to swim against an irreversible tide he had failed to avoid.

He looked toward the window as sweet memories of his wife and kids, when life was happy and whole, filled his heart with inescapable melancholy. Forgetting where he was, Nathan became a spectator of the greatest story he'd ever known—the life he'd once had.

Chapter 3

Seventeen years earlier...

With college under his belt, Nathan decided to get away for a couple of weeks before life got too serious with a career and all the responsibilities that seemed to chase adults. Technically, at twenty-two he was an adult, but he wasn't ready for a life ruled by a daily routine just yet—something he'd regularly explain to his parents. But the real reason Nathan wanted to get away was the deep disdain that had ripened in him for his father, who'd always put his career before his son. Nathan had long ago given up trying to get his father's attention. He hated the man John Berkley was, but even more so he hated the thing that had been the focus of his father's life.

As a college student, a young John Berkley had heard a very eloquent and articulately delivered lecture on postmodern philosophy. He was quickly captivated by the lecturer's perspective and charisma and hypnotized by his passion. The lecture had become to him a commission to advance the cause of liberating the mind and oneself from the shackles of traditional beliefs in an American culture he felt was stuck in the past. He felt a sense of purpose and energy he'd never felt before, and from that moment on, he devoted his life to champion the cause.

Circumstances in his life had fueled a passion for knowledge and a quest for answers. He had an insatiable need to find meaning in life and answers to the questions that haunted him. This drove him to follow up his undergraduate degree in sociology with a master's in psychology and a doctorate in philosophy. John anchored much of his belief and thought in the theory of evolution. He felt that the explanation of natural selection provided a strong base to the building blocks of his deductions. A staunch defender of evolution and a trailblazer in thought, he unofficially gained the title of "the Missing Link." His dedication and thought inspired many and soon propelled him to the national spotlight, and he began appearing on talk shows and cable news programs to help interpret and explain the world.

Although it wasn't his intent, many soon began to see him as a sort of post-modern spiritual guru. He didn't subscribe to any specific religious belief system but did borrow from some of them to offer explanations through which many people in a postmodern society found comfort. To his pleasant surprise, John was soon regarded as a liberal bastion who could bring people out of the captivity of the past and into the promised land of progress and free thinking.

People from all over the world traveled to the school where John taught to interview him, to hear lectures about his theories, and to study under him. Having Dr. John Berkley as a speaker at a conference on postmodern worldviews was a rare treat, and it was sure to draw large crowds of people who needed an authoritative voice to give them permission to explore more freeing definitions of truth. The invitations to address large crowds and give keynote speeches came regularly and often involved lucrative speaking fees.

John married Sandra Cardenal, his college sweetheart, while he was working on his doctorate at Yale. They were attracted to each other at first sight, but their common worldview made them irresistible to one another. Sandra's affluent upbringing in Spain had been saturated in postmodernist views that reflected a part of the culture that was pushing God away and putting people at the center of everything. To her, life was like everything else, relative with no ultimate truth in which to anchor her views. In her and John's minds, life was a coincidence—nothing had any real meaning or supernatural relevance. But they were convinced John was at the verge of finding the key that would unlock the meaning of life and satisfy the most gnawing questions in the human experience.

Little Nathan was born within a year of their wedding amid a whirlwind of activity. Growing up, he couldn't remember a time when they were not in a hurry. Their lives felt perpetually busy.

As the years passed, the Berkley family did the best they could to keep up with the activity generated by John's successful career. From jet setting to Europe one week and Asia the next to having a house full of cameras during a

TV interview, they found that life was never dull. And even though at times all the attention was fun, Nathan always had a feeling that something was missing.

When Nathan was about eight years old, John and Sandra decided it was probably best not to take a young boy on trips with them. His presence was distracting to John and not much fun for Nathan. From then on, the more trips his dad went on, the more Nathan longed to spend time with him. As any little boy would, he grew up admiring and wanting to be like his dad. But as the years went by, the adoration for his hero turned into dislike for someone whom he saw as more concerned with himself and his legacy than with his family.

As Nathan matured, he became more convinced that his dad had chosen the life and recognition his career brought above anything else. And although John wouldn't admit it, not even to himself, in his heart the work he was doing was worth the sacrifice. His passion and drive had, years ago, overshadowed any feelings of guilt he felt for not being the family man he knew he should be.

The only real interest John had shown in Nathan was when he'd pushed his son to follow in his footsteps to continue the Berkley dynasty and further advance his own field of study. But Nathan's great disdain for his father had led to a complete lack of interest in what he did. He had made it clear that he would not dedicate his life to the same cause. It had caused a lot of tension between them, and he wanted nothing to do with it.

Now, as a young adult, Nathan was fed up with everything and everyone who had any relation to his father. His world seemed to always be closing in and trying to suppress who he was. He needed a break from it all, to take a deep breath and figure out what he wanted to do next.

Chapter 4

NATHAN HAD ALWAYS heard good things about the South. Most people spoke about its beautiful places and friendly people affectionately, so he decided it would be his getaway destination. Dr. John Berkley cast a big shadow, and Charleston seemed like a distant enough place for Nathan to get out from under it and just be himself for a few days. Before analyzing the whole thing too much, he bought a plane ticket to Columbia, SC. There he would rent a car and drive to Charleston. He wanted enough time away, so he made the return date two weeks later.

That afternoon, with plane ticket in hand, Nathan walked excitedly into the living room, where John was fussing with his computer. E-mail was a new thing for John, and he was trying to figure out how to use it.

"This darn thing is going to be the end of me. Life was just fine with letters and fax," John yelled as he tapped on the keyboard without aiming at any one key.

"Do you need some help?" Nathan offered.

"No, thanks. I think I have it now." He paused, the look on his face more frustrated. "Never mind; no, I don't have it!" He shook his head and pretended not to be bothered. "So your mom says you decided to visit the South, huh?" he said with a somewhat disapproving tone. Nathan nodded and offered no explanation.

"That's fine, I suppose. But are you sure you don't want to go to Europe? When you start working, you'll have less time for a leisurely getaway, and this may be your best chance to go there."

"Maybe someday. For now Charleston it is," Nathan answered abruptly. His destination wasn't up for discussion.

"Well, that is a beautiful part of the country, and I think you'll really like it. I went there once for a conference, and although I didn't get to see much, what I did see was nice."

"Yes, I remember when you and Mom went down there while I was at summer camp. You guys seemed to like it from the way you talked about it." Nathan never missed a chance to remind John of his track record as a dad.

"Uh-huh! I got it!" John said, ignoring Nathan's comment. "These darn things! They're supposed to make our lives easier, but you spend half of your life trying to get along with them. Anyway, here it is."

Nathan looked perplexed but said nothing, wondering what his father had found.

"Dr. Livingston lives in Charleston. I've known him for many years, and I wrote the foreword for one of his books. He'll be able to find you a nice hotel and show you around. I can also make calls to other acquaintances in Charleston who will know just where to take you. They'll be great people for you to know anyway. Let me see if I can figure out how to find their names and phone numbers in this darn thing."

Nathan appreciated what John was trying to do, but at the same time, he was annoyed by his father's arrogance. Why couldn't he just let this happen without having to be the hero? This trip was not John's to plan. Besides, Nathan couldn't care less to meet anyone that might enhance his résumé.

"I appreciate the intention, but that's not what I'm looking for," Nathan said, and he paused, feeling his anger rising and remembering exactly why he needed to go away. "I just want to go, to see where the wind takes me, that sort of thing—completely unplanned, no hotel reservations, no appointments to keep. I just want to go!"

"Never mind, then, Nathan," John replied with a look of disappointment Nathan had seen all too often. "As always, have it your way. Good luck to you down there."

Nathan didn't bother to respond. He walked out of the room.

As he packed a suitcase in his room, Nathan caught his reflection in the mirror and was, once again, reminded of how empty he felt inside. He longed for purpose and meaning, for knowledge of who the real Nathan was. He tried to understand what he felt, but he didn't even know where to start. The world around him was a growing mystery. He craved answers to the questions in his mind, and he wasn't getting those answers in the world he lived in, full of knowledge, academia, theories, and fake smiles and handshakes. Even if he couldn't get answers, at the very least he needed a change of scenery.

On the outside, Nathan Berkley had it all—good looks, a well-known family name, a top-notch education, and money. But he was sick of a life that seemed perfect on the outside when, just under the surface, it was constantly falling apart; it had become nonsensical. He couldn't help but wonder what the point of it all was, and the deeper he reached within himself to figure it out, the emptier and more hopeless he felt.

Nathan couldn't put a finger on what was missing from his life, but he knew it was critical. He hoped that getting away would help him find it, and he was bound and determined to give it his best shot.

Chapter 5

AFTER A QUICK check to make sure Nathan had packed everything he might need, he and Sandra got in the car and started their drive to Bradley International Airport in Hartford County. His mother wanted to visit some friends in Hartford, so she'd volunteered to drive him there.

Nathan noticed Sandra had not been very talkative. She usually wasn't much of a talker, but he could tell something was bothering her. She tried to avoid confrontation at any cost. But there were two sure signs this was something she had to let out: she was nervously fidgeting with the controls in the car, and she was looking over at him every few seconds. He tried the sleepy, groggy act, but there were certain things Sandra Berkley just had to speak out about.

"Nathan, why didn't you let your father call some of his acquaintances in Charleston?" she said with a more pronounced Spanish accent, which came out when she was upset or very tired.

Nathan didn't want to talk about it, so he just shrugged his shoulders and said nothing. But Sandra's gaze fixed on him, and she probably wouldn't look forward again until she had an answer. He made quick eye contact and pointed at the road ahead with his index finger.

"Mom! The road?"

She looked ahead, the frustration growing on her face. Within seconds, he could tell she was looking at him again. He smiled and then started laughing, partly out of frustration but mostly because he thought she was funny when she got this way.

"Mom, I'm not going to play this game. I'm going away for a few days, and I really don't want to have a fight right before I leave." He paused and shook his head as he leaned back. "I just want to go, to have nothing planned. My whole goal is to just be!"

Sandra looked ahead without much expression, obviously thinking about what Nathan said. "Well, he was upset with you, Nathan. He was just trying to help."

"This is my trip, my time, not his to control. He doesn't get to determine what I should be doing."

Sandra glanced over at Nathan as if to check the emotion on his face and then looked ahead. Neither said anything else for the next few miles. As they rolled past the first sign for Bradley International Airport, Nathan felt a double tap on his hand.

"You just have fun, Nathan. Okay?" She had a peaceful, reassuring smile on her face. "And be careful. Please?"

He smiled back and gave her hand a small squeeze before he reached for the plane ticket in his bag to check on the flight details. Nathan was proud of her because this was one of the few times she was reacting to her own emotions, not to his father's expectations. To the world, she was more Mrs. Dr. Berkley than Sandra Cardenal. And for as long as Nathan could remember, she had seemed okay with living in Dr. Berkley's shadow and basking in his glory. Because of that, he'd always found it hard to respect her. She and their environment had created a persona for her, and often unbeknownst to her, she had spent her best energy to fit it. She'd never wanted to do anything that might make Dr. Berkley look bad, and that had often meant not doing the things she needed to do as his mom.

"Okay, Nathan. Have a good trip. Call us if you need something, and be careful," Sandra said, initiating a quick good-bye at the airport.

"I will. See you in a couple weeks," he said, with no intention of calling home.

She looked at her watch and realized it was time to go meet her friends. They hugged briefly, and she was off.

⊶⊷⊛ ⊛⊷⊶

As soon as Nathan took his seat in first class, he felt a sense of relaxation he couldn't remember experiencing in a long time. It was as if all the expectations and demands on him were suddenly lifted off his shoulders. He no longer felt like a Berkley under the world's microscope, and he welcomed the sensation. He felt no need to perform. *The trip is already a success*, he thought.

His cell phone suddenly jolted him from the moment of peace. "Argh," he muttered out loud as the elderly gentleman sitting beside him watched. The man stared at him for a few seconds and then turned away, saying nothing. Nathan shrugged it off and looked to see who was calling. It was John.

"Nope! Not now," he said as he looked over to the man sitting beside him. This time, the man didn't even acknowledge him. Nathan shrugged with pride. He wanted to bask a little longer in this unexpected time of peace and independence.

Not wanting anything to interrupt this great moment, Nathan turned down any form of entertainment offered by the flight attendant. After a few minutes, he closed his eyes and fell asleep. His mind quickly made the transition into another reality, and the fast sequence of dream events placed him on a porch swing.

Two large white columns came in and out of sight as he swung back and forth between them. The creaking of the swing was as real as anything he'd ever heard, and the warm breeze was almost palpable.

The most vivid green grass he'd ever seen overloaded his senses. Rows of colorful flowers burst out around tall maple trees whose leaves seemed to dance to the tune of a gentle wind. He couldn't get over the beauty of the place. Never before had he seen or experienced anything like it.

He noticed a woman sitting beside him. She looked happy and peaceful beyond words, needing nothing more than what she had at the moment. He knew he didn't know her, but at the same time, he felt as if he'd known her a long time. She looked over and smiled at him, and he knew she was the most important person in his life. A little girl was running through the grass. Every few steps she yelled, "Daddy, Daddy," making sure his eyes stayed fixed on her. She had the sweetest and purest voice he'd ever heard. Her words hung in the air, and he had no doubt she was talking to him.

The young woman looked over at him again, and he turned to her. He knew she was beautiful but couldn't really define her features. Her gaze felt as if it went through him, and he got the sense that she knew him better than he knew himself. She adored him unconditionally with her eyes, and her smile captivated him. He was overwhelmed by the feelings of love and devotion he felt toward them. In his dream, all was well and nothing else in the world mattered.

He looked over at the little girl, who was now busy playing in a sandbox. She turned to him and said something he couldn't make out. The breeze picked up, and the tree leaves flapped loudly in response. He heard the little girl say something to him again, but he still couldn't make it out. He leaned forward to listen attentively, squinting his eyes as if that might help him hear her better. As she patiently repeated her words, he stood up and started walking toward her. With every step, he could notice more of her features. He got close enough to see her eyes. They were hazel just like his, and something inside him burst with an unexplainable joy.

The little girl repeated herself once again, and he felt himself almost running toward her. The faster he went, the farther she seemed to be from him and the fainter her voice became. He could feel his arms stretching to her, longing to touch her. A strong wind swung the tree branches violently, and the sound from the leaves drowned the girl's voice.

She was now fading away quickly, and everything around him was changing. The trees and flowers were disappearing into a blur. He turned back, trying to get one last look at the young woman, but he could see only a faint trace of the porch now. The picture faded in his mind, as the view of the plane cabin and the sound of revving engines replaced the wind and leaves.

Nathan saw someone standing over him, quickly coming into focus as he struggled to open his eyes. The little girl's voice was just an echo in his mind now. He closed his eyes, hoping to see her again, but she was gone. His eyes darted back and forth, and he willed himself to go back to sleep, to drift back into the dream for just another moment.

"Sir, you need to put your seat back in the upright position. We're about to land, sir!"

He looked up at the flight attendant, frustrated and heartbroken, and nodded as he searched for the lever to adjust his seat. The flight attendant tried to hide her frustration with a smile as she walked off.

Nathan felt as if he had just gotten off an intense roller coaster and was trying to find his footing on the ground. The dream had been so real, the most endearing thing he'd ever experienced. The beauty was so vivid in his mind, and the amazing peace he experienced still felt real. He wasn't sure what had just happened to him, but there was no doubt it had been extraordinary. Sitting back and enjoying the moment, Nathan looked out the window to get his first peek at South Carolina.

Chapter 6

It was a clear day, and Nathan had a great view of the city as the plane began its preparations for landing. The white church steeples poked out of a thick span of green trees, and the sun glistened off Lake Murray, turning it into a sea of gold. "It's definitely green here," he said in a low voice. He glanced over at the man beside him, figuring he would be shaking his head if he had heard him, but the revving engines were loud enough that he hadn't heard him.

Nathan felt a deeper sense of liberation the further he got from his life in New Haven. He felt less watched, less tied to the expectations of others. He could hardly wait to get out of the plane and see where the day might take him.

After he got his baggage, he started walking toward the car-rental area. Something caught his attention as he passed by a bookstore, and he stopped in his tracks when he realized what it was. *I just can't get away from him. Can I?* he thought to himself as he shook his head. Dr. John Berkley's last book was prominently displayed at the front of the store. The title, with which he was all too familiar, was a vivid gold-lettered attention getter: *Finding Purpose in Chance*.

Nathan had completely forgotten about the new book John had published. Growing up, he'd tried to show interest in his dad's work in order to get close to him, but John often put Nathan's questions on hold until he finished whatever he was doing at the time. The task would usually take longer than expected, so they almost never got to have a meaningful conversation. Over time, Nathan's attempts turned to rebellion and rejection of anything John valued.

He picked up a copy of the book and smiled. The weight and thickness of it reminded him of the vast amount of time John had spent researching and writing it. He shook his head as he pictured his dad basking in his glory as he always did on release day. He worked hard and was very successful. And whether one agreed with him or not, the magnitude of his accomplishments was impressive. Nathan was proud of his dad from that standpoint, but he'd always felt like he hadn't experienced his father in the way he needed most. As a result, Nathan thought more of him as Dr. John Berkley than as his dad.

He was glad not to be home today, glad to miss the zoo everything turned into when a new Dr. Berkley book came out. The media would certainly go to their house to interview him. Prior to the interview, John would pace around rehearsing complicated responses to simple questions, and he would be in the best mood he'd been in all year. As John orated his answers, reporters would nod in unison, most of them only half understanding what he was talking about.

He shook his head at the thought of Sandra gloating with her friends before rushing back to New Haven to be with John. Her need to hurry away after dropping him off made more sense now.

Finding Purpose in Chance was John's attempt at providing a magical ten-step formula to find happiness in a world where, as far as he thought, no absolute truths existed. In John's world, there was no moral guide or predetermined guiding principles. Everything the eye could see was there by chance, and chance, coupled with the decisions one made, controlled a person's fate. This book was his attempt to give the world a guide to taking control of one's destiny and making the best of life. Nathan had not planned his trip to start on the same day the book was released, but he also had not avoided it.

A store attendant walked up to Nathan. "I hear that's a great book," she said, partly as an attempt to get him to buy it. "I think it will help a lot of people. I want to get it for my dad. He could use some good advice."

"Is that right?" replied Nathan.

"Oh yes…I hear Dr. Berkley is brilliant. He must really know what he's talking about. Have you read any of his stuff before?"

Nathan felt a sudden rage surge through his entire body, and he struggled with how to respond. "I really want to just throw this book across the room and see it bust when it hits the wall, but then I'll have to pay you twenty bucks for it, and I really don't want to waste my money."

He knew he was supposed to feel bad, but he didn't. The girl looked shocked and embarrassed, as if she might have said or done something she shouldn't have. Nathan gently put the book back on the stand and forced a smile as he walked off. Right there and then, he decided to extend his trip. He was not going to return to the Berkley circus any sooner than he had to.

He knew he probably owed the girl at the store an apology, and although at the time he didn't really care, he looked back and made eye contact. She was still standing on the same spot with her jaw dropped. He smiled at her apologetically and kept walking toward the car-rental area.

Chapter 7

MEDIA CREWS SWARMED like hyenas in front of a priceless three-story Victorian home, ready to pounce to get the exclusive with Dr. Berkley when the door opened. The release of a new book was not a big news item, but John's publicist had set up a news conference assuring the worthiness of covering the book release by highlighting some of the controversial material in it, which pitted John's arguments against the best contemporary Christian thinkers. The news outlets responded, but the publicist's ploy was not the bait. Because of John's popularity, anything might turn into a hot topic. And with his bombastic personality, he always put on a good show, which made for entertaining television.

Sandra had purposely stayed longer at her friends' gathering so the interviews on TV would come on while she was with them. John was alone at home, peeking through the window shades as the media trucks pulled up to the house and tried to find a place to park. Reporters chatted with one another as they prepped their equipment, hoping to get the first question in as soon as John opened the door. His chest was about to burst with pride, and he couldn't wait to get out there and start talking to the reporters.

John composed himself and took a slow look in the mirror to make sure he was camera ready. Acting as if this happened to him every day, as if it was no big deal, he opened the front door casually and looked almost surprised to encounter someone at the door. Within a split second, he could hardly see the reporters' faces for all the microphones that were placed close to his mouth. Several reporters asked their questions at the same time. The more seasoned reporters waited, knowing they would get the nod from John to ask their question.

"Dr. Berkley, sir! The critics are already saying that your book will be on the New York Times best-seller list in its first week. How does that make you feel?" a reporter bellowed her question.

"Sir, Dr. Berkley!" Another waved, trying to get his attention. "How do you account for—"

"Wait! Please, one at a time," John interrupted, loving every second of the attention.

"Josh?" John pointed to a reporter in the group as another tried to jump in with a question.

"Yes, thank you, Dr. Berkley," responded a calm and well-dressed reporter. "What did you write about this time?"

John paused before answering, wanting both to set the mood for his answer and to evoke silence from the reporters.

"Thank you, Josh, for your question. *Finding Purpose in Chance* is personal, the catalyst for writing it being my lifelong journey to find answers to my own struggles as a human being. While I've always believed we're all here by mere chance, I couldn't shake the feeling that there's some kind of purpose for each of us. There's a potential we can all reach that makes life worth living, but we must know how to find that purpose. In *Finding Purpose in Chance*, you will find answers as to why you are the way you are, why you think the things you think, and why you feel as you do when different things happen. It's full of practical advice so you can be happy and successful in a world full of riddles."

The reporters hung on every word he spoke.

"Where did you get all the insight for the book?" asked another reporter.

Glad to get the question but not wanting to seem too eager, John paused as he quickly scanned the crowd of reporters. "Thanks...Wade, is it?" The reporter nodded.

"That's a great question, Wade. I've been very lucky in that I've had the chance to study under some of the top minds of our time and have been exposed to great thinking available through books and research findings. I'm also no spring chicken, meaning I've been around a few years longer than most of you. Except for maybe you, Dennis." With a joking smile, he pointed at a reporter toward the back. The group laughed, some of them turning their heads toward Dennis. The reporter smiled back at John, shaking his finger at him.

"Anyway," John continued, "I've been alive long enough to have learned a few valuable lessons. So I took the knowledge I acquired over the years, coupled it with what I validated through my own research, and deducted what I believe to be valuable insights for living. I believe every person has some amount of wisdom to live by, but we should always strive to become better by continuing to learn. And yes! We may have different beliefs, but that's okay! That's what makes us unique and special. We should celebrate that. It expands our fields of thought and widens the array of possibilities for humanity. My goal is to dare the reader to reach deep within and find the real self. The potential to awaken the inner self, to make more sense of the here and now, to become better, is available to all of us!"

As John finished his thought, he looked at the group of reporters and knew by the expressions on their faces that the interview was going well. This energized him, and he was ready for any question that may come his way.

A woman John had never seen at one of these interviews piped above everyone else and got her question in. "Dr. Berkley, how would you respond to what some evangelical leaders are saying about your theories? They say we should look to God for guidance, based on His truth, not on what we decide truth is. Who is right, sir, you or them?"

The reporters poked their heads around, wide-eyed, looking for the person asking the daring question. Some had perplexed expressions on their faces, as if wondering why anyone would ask something so bizarre. Others readied their pens, knowing this would for sure change the mood of the interview. They were ready to note the change in John's facial expressions and body language, anything that could make their articles more sensational.

John hid his irritation at having to share his spotlight with the Bible thumpers, as he called them, and managed to crack a smile.

The upscale street was so quiet the crowd could have heard a mouse walk. Everyone waited on John's response. His answer was calm and collected, but the smile was gone.

"These so-called evangelicals, they know that the way to control you and your purse is to make you think there's something wrong with you. That you can't trust in yourself to make good choices. They use the concept of God to try to instill fear in you so they can manipulate you and your emotions."

"Sir," the reporter responded, taking a step toward him, "I'm going to need a little more than that. Your response is a little vague."

"Look," John replied, his frustration showing. All the other reporters were happy to stand by quietly and listen. "I'm not going to get into those arguments right now. I won't waste my time addressing half-formed thoughts from a bunch of religious zealots who have nothing better to do than to attack me for no good reason."

⤙▱◼⤚

As Nathan walked through the airport, he noticed a group of people gathered around a TV monitor. He wondered what might be so interesting and decided to take a peek. Before he could see what was on the screen, he recognized an all-too-familiar voice. Because of who his dad was, and since there wasn't anything more newsworthy happening, the interview was live on a cable news channel. *What are the odds that the day I get away from him, I have to see him all over this airport?* he thought, wanting to throw his backpack at the monitor.

A young couple with a baby joined the group to see what was going on as the camera panned to the reporter asking the questions that were obviously pushing John's buttons.

She pressed on. "But, sir, with all due respect, is it not enough to look at the world around us and see we need a little help? You'll have to admit we've made a mess of things."

"I choose not to live in an imaginary world," John responded more forcefully. "I argue my points and write while keeping my feet planted in reality." He scanned the group of reporters, apparently reading their expressions to see if one of them was ready to ask another question. But to his obvious disappointment, everyone was looking at the reporter asking the questions. The interview had taken a wrong turn for him, and there was little chance he could bring the discussion back to anything that would help his book sales. The only thing he could do was end it as quickly and gracefully as possible. Before the reporter had a chance to ask a follow-up question, John addressed the crowd.

"I think it's good to discuss and debate different ideas. Being exposed to different ideologies helps us validate what is true." He paused before he continued, showing that he was in control of the conversation. "Separate what is real from what is not…I welcome any discussion that may challenge my viewpoints, but it will have to be another time. I have to tend to my students now. Don't want to be late for class. Yale may fire me!" He flashed a smile, and the group laughed. The reporter that had asked the challenging questions smiled back at him and closed her notebook. John looked back at her. He could see from the expression on her face that she knew why the interview was ending early.

The small crowd looking at the monitor dispersed quickly and went about their business. Nathan stood there for a moment as the newscast went back to an anchor who eagerly began to recap what had just happened. He looked around, slightly concerned that someone might recognize him and ask him to comment. But a sudden relief came over him. Nobody knew him there, and that was a very good thing. He walked away from the monitor, glad to be just another person there, and went about his own business.

This trip was already paying off. Nathan wanted to find out who he really was, and being just another face in the crowd was a great start. What he didn't know was how to go about his journey of self-discovery, but he had a feeling deep inside that there was a way. And John's approach was not it.

Chapter 8

BOTH TIRED AND excited to hit the road, Nathan walked up to the car-rental counter. "Good morning. I have a car reserved for Nathan Berkley. A convertible?" The attendant started to answer, but Nathan went on. "Also, I'd like directions to Charleston."

The attendant was at the end of a long shift and looked annoyed at the rapid questions and demands from some kid who obviously came from money. Although casual and comfortable, Nathan's clothes screamed department store with valet parking, and he spoke and carried himself in a way that made it hard to miss.

"Well, we don't have a convertible, but we do know where Charleston is." The attendant seemed to have no patience for the yuppie with a northern accent.

"Okay. I did reserve a convertible, though."

"Sir, it is a little chilly out today. So it's probably good that—"

"However, I did reserve a convertible," Nathan interrupted, showing a little irritation. He was still frustrated by the reaction to the book from the lady in the bookstore and the TV interview, and he was operating on a short fuse.

"I can put you in a nonconvertible car with two doors, sir," the attendant responded tersely.

"Fine!" Nathan said, refusing to let this guy get to him.

Within minutes, the attendant processed the paperwork and handed Nathan a set of keys.

"So, how do I get to Charleston?"

"Oh yeah, how do you get to Charleston, right," the attendant responded with a subtle sneer. "Follow the signs to Interstate Twenty-Six heading west.

When you run out of interstate, voilà! There you are! Charleston." He paused, as if taunting the yuppie to get more irritated, but Nathan ignored him.

Nathan headed for the car-pickup area. After a few minutes of waiting, he saw another attendant pull up in a minivan, get out, and start walking toward him.

"Nathan Berkley?"

"Um…yes," Nathan responded.

"Wonderful, sir. This is your vehicle. Please allow me to help you with your bags, and you'll be on your way."

"I was supposed to get a two-door, not a minivan. There must be some type of mistake."

The attendant didn't make eye contact and instead said, "I'm sorry, sir. There was a computer error, and we just gave the last two-door to another customer. We can get you in a Camry. That would be closer to a two-door, but it just got here, and we think it may have a problem, so we'll need to check it out before it can leave the lot. This van is very nice, though, and we won't charge you for the additional cost to rent it."

"You're serious?" Nathan asked, ready to pounce on the guy. Enough was enough. "How long will that take?"

"Maybe an hour? Can't know for sure until we take a look."

"Never mind the Camry; I'll just take this thing." His initial reaction had been to go inside and ask for the manager, but he was tired of wasting time. He decided to take the van and be on his way.

"Certainly, sir. And again, we're sorry for the inconvenience. Here is your paperwork."

Nathan didn't feel as sporty as he had hoped, but he couldn't wait to get away from the airport. He put the van in gear and started out slowly. Out of the corner of his eye, he caught a glimpse of the rental-car desk inside the building. From what he could see through the glare of the glass doors, the attendant and the guy who had brought him the van were laughing and watching him drive off.

He hit the brakes and started to put the van in park as his first reaction kicked back in, but he quickly collected himself and thought about whether it was really worth it. He looked inside and saw that the two guys had seen him stop. They were still laughing but now looked concerned. Nathan was right at six-foot-tall and had a considerable build from all his years of swim competition, so they didn't want him to come in upset with them. Knowing they would just deny everything and he would waste precious time talking through all the details with the manager, he put the van back in drive. He was ready to get to Charleston, and he didn't want to delay any further.

Just as the guy at the rental counter had said, Nathan quickly saw the sign to Interstate 26 West, but he didn't get too comfortable until he confirmed it went to Charleston. "What a couple jerks!" he said out loud. Back at home, these guys would have gotten under his skin and stayed under it. He had never been one to back down from a fight, but he had decided to let this one go and get to his destination.

To his surprise, being far from home allowed him to put things in a more positive perspective. It helped not to be around all the people and expectations that made life seem meaningless. He hated all the expectations that he measure up to a father who meant nothing to him, and he needed a new start—a real path forward. Nathan had a strange feeling that this trip might help him see life in a new, more realistic way, and in the process get a chance to find himself. He felt as if the person who had escaped him all his life, and whom he was so desperate to find, was lurking in the shadows and taunting him, waiting to be found.

Nathan hit the gas, Charleston bound. He took a deep breath and lay back against the headrest, welcoming a sense of excitement he had not experienced in a very long time.

Chapter 9

KATE JOHNSON LIFTED her head as her dad finished praying in front of the congregation. It was so good to finally be home. She couldn't believe two weeks had already passed since her college graduation. She would always remember the last four years at the University of South Carolina in Columbia as some of the best in her life. But she was ready to get back home to Charleston, especially under the circumstances.

This was a time of transition for the Johnson family. Austin, the baby in the family, had left a year ago to go overseas on his first tour of duty. Not having him around was hard, but the fact that he was in a very violent part of the world with a lot of unrest made it unbearable. Kate and Austin had always had a special connection growing up, and not having him around had been an adjustment neither she nor anyone else in the family had wanted to make. She was ready to be home and give back to a family that had done so much for her.

Her dad, Warren Johnson, was a Baptist minister with an amazing gift for public speaking. A decade earlier, he had become well known for his work in Christian apologetics. Because of his thorough research and ability to explain everyday life from Bible teachings, he was regarded as one of the top people in his time to defend the Christian faith. His books were widely read in the Christian community, as well as by many in secular society. He always had an invitation to speak somewhere in the United States and abroad, which had given Kate the chance to go places most people could only dream of seeing. A few years back, Warren had accepted a senior pastor position at a church in Charleston, which allowed him to be at home and get much-needed rest. He was her rock, and she was so thankful to have him at home now.

His closing remarks were heartfelt, and Kate sensed heaviness in his words. She knew where it came from because she felt the same burden. Sundays seemed especially hard without Austin around. There had been many years she'd wished he was anywhere but sitting in the pew beside her, irritating and getting her in trouble. But today, there was no one else she would rather have sitting beside her.

She looked up at her dad, and they made eye contact as he spoke. They each knew what the other was feeling, and this somehow brought comfort to both of them. He and Austin had always been very close, and she knew his absence was as hard on her dad as it was on her. Warren smiled at her with his eyes and looked back at the congregation. She couldn't help but think about how much he reminded her of Austin, especially when he smiled.

The day Austin announced he would put college on hold to join the military had come as a surprise to Kate and her family. But his conviction was strong and real, and they knew it was the right thing to do. Seeing her young brother, all dressed up in his United States Marine Corps uniform, board that plane was the hardest thing she had gone through.

Warren had seen the relationship between her and Austin grow strong through their childhood, and he knew how hard this was on her. On their walk to the car, he put his hand on her shoulder and tried to make her feel better.

"Kate, we are all called to do something we know is right but don't completely understand. We just know that not doing it would be wrong. We are called to do things that fit into a master plan of which we are not in control. Austin understands that, and we need to support him no matter what. It will all work out for the best."

She knew he was right, and she trusted him. It still came natural to want things to go her way, but she had learned that results that came from faith and patience were always better, no matter how hard and long the wait may be.

The night before Austin left, Kate and her brother had been rocking on the front porch—something they had done through the years when one of them had something on his or her mind and needed to talk. Kate had been very quiet, and

32

Austin knew that meant she was upset. He wanted to see a smile on her face, and he was determined to do whatever it took to make that happen.

Their mom, Rachel, called them to dinner, and they came in to take their place at the table. Austin couldn't wait to dig in to his last southern home-cooked meal. Rachel had fixed all his favorites: fried pork chops, mashed potatoes, fried okra, sweet peas, made-from-scratch biscuits, and sweet-potato pie. He savored every bite, knowing it would be a long time before he would get to eat his mom's cooking again.

Everyone was enjoying the meal and having casual conversation. They had a lot of questions for Austin: where he would be first, what he would do there, how safe things would be at each stop, etc. As he answered them, he looked around the table and thought about the many times they had eaten together in that room. This was the home where he had grown up, and every nook and cranny triggered a memory. The love he felt for everyone sitting at that table overwhelmed him. But he had decided there would be no tears that night, so he fought back every urge. Austin knew they needed to remember him as being upbeat and confident.

He looked at the floor as if searching for something. Their older sister, Edee, who never missed a beat, noticed it and asked, "What are you doing?"

Austin looked up with a sheepish expression. "Bully. I'm trying to find Bully. Where is that guy? Bully, come here, boy!" he called out for the family dog, an English bulldog who still didn't answer to his name even though they'd had him for two years. Everybody briefly looked around the room for Bully and then continued to eat.

"I saw him earlier in the back porch, doing what he does best," Warren said, looking at Rachel. "Laying around half asleep and making snorting noises. I'm telling you, that thing looks like a slobbery, grumpy Santa Claus more each day."

Rachel cocked her head forward with a warning look that suggested he say no more. Warren smiled at his plate, saying nothing else. Kate and Edee laughed. They knew their dad liked Bully, but he loved to pick on Rachel about him because she had been the one to pick a bulldog when they decided to get a dog.

Austin took advantage of the diversion to stuff some mashed potatoes in a napkin. "Well, Bully needs to hang out with us tonight. I'm going to miss that lazy, no good mutt," he said, pretending to be serious as he got up, looking at Rachel from the corner of his eye.

"Don't talk about our Bully that way, son!" Warren said, unable to hide the fact that he wasn't serious. Rachel and the girls laughed.

"I'm just going to ignore y'all, because y'all don't know what you're talking about. Right, girls? And he does not look like a grumpy Santa Claus! He's cute." Rachel glared at Warren to reprimand him and then turned to Kate and Edee for agreement.

"Right, Mom!" Edee answered as Austin walked out of the room laughing.

Within seconds, they heard some commotion coming from the back porch. They couldn't really tell what was going on, but they could make out Austin calling Bully's name repeatedly. The dining room got very quiet as they tried to figure out what was going on. Rachel was the first to see Austin come in. She dropped her fork and erupted in laughter; Warren, Kate, and Edee looked at her, alarmed. Rachel's right hand covered her mouth as she looked toward the doorway. They all turned to the same direction, and their eyes popped wide open.

In the doorway stood Austin, holding Bully, whose face was covered in mashed potatoes. He had tried, half successfully, to make Bully a beard, mustache, and eyebrows. There was a Santa Claus hat on top of Bully's head, which Austin tried to keep in place to no avail. Austin was covered in mashed potatoes from trying to fix Bully up, which explained the earlier commotion. Bully, his permanent grouchy look intact, was grunting, enjoying the taste of mashed potatoes as he flung his tongue all over his face. Everyone laughed—not just because it was funny, but because it was Austin and the kind of strange thing only he would try to do.

Austin sat down and put Bully on the floor, and the dog took off running for his life. Austin asked Rachel, "Bully runs?" Rachel shook her head and smiled. He glanced around the table, still laughing but stopping long enough to get a good look at each person, as if taking mental pictures of his family.

He was holding a white laundry bag on his back; he had been unable to affix it to the dog. "Well, Bully doesn't make a very good Santa. I guess I'm not that good of a Santa's helper either," he said, wiping mashed potatoes off his shirt.

"That did not go as planned. Dad, it was perfect you brought up the Santa thing, though."

Austin was struck by how much he hated to leave his family, and he got more serious as he thought about the days ahead. He looked down at the bag for a few seconds and fiddled with the tie strings. The laughter around the table was dissolving.

"You okay, son?" Warren asked.

With a sober expression on his face, Austin nodded. "I've never been better." He looked down at the bag again and then back to Warren. "There is so much I would like to say to all of you. I can't even begin to tell you what y'all mean to me...what you've done for me through the years. I could never do what I'm about to do had it not been for what I've learned from each of you." He glanced over at Kate, and she smiled at him.

Austin stood up and went to embrace each of them, whispering something to remember him by. "I love you so much, Mom. You and Dad always knew how to make me feel loved and safe. I won't forget all the nuggets of wisdom you've spoken into my life."

"Thank you, Edee, for being such a great example to Kate and me. You were a real pain at times, but nobody's perfect."

"We love you, Austin," responded an emotional Edee. "Please come back to us in one piece."

"It's what I have to do," he said to Kate. "I'll be back when you least expect me."

After a few minutes, everyone left the room except for Austin and Warren. Austin looked at his dad and smiled. "You've been a one-of-a-kind father. Had it not been for your example all these years, I don't think I could have really understood who God is and why I needed Him in my life." He paused for a moment to fight back the emotion he could feel rising up in him. "You've always been my best friend," Austin said as he started to take a hammer out of the bag.

"I want to give you something before I leave tomorrow," he continued. "You gave me this when I was eight years old. Do you remember it?"

Warren nodded and smiled, holding the hammer as if it was his most precious possession.

"It's just for safe keeping until I get back. The day you gave me that hammer has always stuck with me. We went to Lowe's that morning on a mission to build that birdhouse for Mom. I can still remember how excited I was as we walked through the store together gathering the materials. I couldn't wait to get home and start. It was your brand-new hammer, and I was dying to use it. Do you remember how all I wanted to do was get my hands on it and start banging on something?"

Warren nodded.

Austin looked at the hammer and smiled. "I didn't have a clue what I was doing, but you still let me use it. That made me feel like there was nothing I couldn't do. I felt like you trusted me, and somehow I knew you would always be there for me. Of course, I busted every board I tried to nail, and it took us three times as long to build the birdhouse…"

Warren laughed as the memories played in his mind.

"I was so proud when you gave me this hammer the next Christmas."

Austin pulled from his wallet a note Warren had included with the gift. "'Son, mistakes are only bad if you allow them to hold you back. You learn from them, pickup your tools again and continue to build.' I still carry this with me."

Warren said, "And you have, Austin. I've seen you do just that all these years. We are all so proud of you. God has made all my dreams come true in allowing me to watch you, Kate, and Edee grow up into who you are today. I love you, son."

Overcome with emotion, Austin cried on his father's shoulder as they embraced. "I love you too, Dad."

⊷⇒ ⇐⊶

Being a preacher's daughter was often stereotyped as if it were some kind of curse, but in Kate's case, she would not have had it any other way. She had seen her daddy's imperfections through the years. He had as many or more than most people. But his humility and desire to be true to himself and others had influenced those around him the most. Those characteristics made him both vulnerable and strong at the same time, and they were the reason that others trusted him and were willing to follow him.

The congregation stood to sing the closing song. Kate knew the words to it well but didn't join in singing it. Instead, she reflected on the past and wondered about the future. She reminded herself that life was a journey. And her journey, like everyone else's, was like a train ride that the passenger couldn't control. Some stops along the way would bring grief and pain. But on the next stop, someone else might just get on and change a person's life in the most unexpected ways.

Chapter 10

AFTER AN HOUR and a half in the car, Nathan was convinced he had chosen the right place for his introduction to the South. All he had really seen of South Carolina was the Columbia airport and the interstate. But it all felt right, and he was having fun. He had grown tired of always feeling as if he was in a hurry, overwhelmed by the demands of life. For a long time now, his life had felt like a never-ending vicious cycle of always being late and never accomplishing everything that needed to be done. And by the look of things, it seemed as if everyone around him had the same problem. At the moment, it felt good to have no one to report or answer to—it was just him, a cup of coffee from a gas station he had stopped at, and the open road.

The highway extended to four lanes, and he could tell he was getting close to the city of Charleston. Within minutes of getting off on the wrong exit, Nathan found himself in James Island. He couldn't believe he had made the error, when all he'd had to do to get to Charleston was stay on I-26.

He tried to find his way back to I-26, but it seemed as if every turn he made was the wrong one. In an attempt not to wander out too far, he took a left at an intersection so he could turn around and start tracking his moves back to the highway. He looked at the name of the road. "Riverland Drive. You can remember that, dummy," he said out loud to himself. There were a few small driveways on the right side of the street, so he drove on a little farther to find a bigger place to turn around.

Spring was more advanced in the South than in New Haven because of the difference in temperature. Flowers were already bursting out of bushes and small trees in a multitude of colors. Nathan found himself mesmerized by the beauty that seemed to embrace him as he drove under tunnels of oak trees' long branches that had formed over the road. He was awestruck by the majesty of the sun's rays as they broke through to accentuate the Spanish moss that draped the oaks' branches. He opened the sun roof and instantly the van filled with the scents of flowers and of freshly cut lawns. Everything seemed intently and carefully designed to make the senses burst.

"Where am I? This place is beautiful," Nathan exclaimed as he drove on, no longer caring that he was lost.

Nathan's parents had never been the stop-and-smell-the-roses type, and neither was he. They were more concerned with reaching the destination than with enjoying the journey. But the beauty around him was enchanting, and today, the journey felt more important. He was struck by how free flowing it all was, but at the same time, everything seemed to be meticulously ordered and organized.

He took a left turn and soon spotted the Saint James Church on the left side of the road. The white church sat back about a hundred yards from the road, behind decorative azalea bushes and perfectly framed by overarching oaks. The first thing that came to Nathan's mind was "movie set." It reminded him of several movies he had seen set in the South, with its large white columns and tall steeple rising above the trees.

He slowed down and stuck his cell phone out the window to take a picture of it, making a mental note to send the image to his friend Jake back in New Haven, who had all but invited himself to come on the trip with him. But Nathan had not wanted the trip to become a multiday party scene, so he impolitely turned him down as one could do only with a best friend.

Sitting at a stoplight, he noticed a sign to the far right. The sign read "Nawlin's." It wasn't very ornate, just simple dark red letters on a white background. He thought about the last time he had eaten, which had been early that morning before he and Sandra left for the airport. He had wanted some southern food, and the name on the sign gave him every indication that this may be just the place for that, so he decided to give it a try.

Nathan parked the van out of sight, walked into the restaurant, and took in the ambience. It was simple but done in good taste. The restaurant had the country look he expected but with its own personality. The walls were covered with brown cedar paneling, and on display were cooking utensils and pictures of buildings from years gone by. The angler's motif was nicely blended with the ambience, indicating that although their specialty was country-style cooking, this was still Charleston.

"Hi, hon!" someone greeted him from behind. He turned around to see a young waitress standing beside him. "Just you, sweetie?"

"Yes," he answered, feeling somewhat embarrassed that she kept addressing him so personally.

"Come on with me. I'll get you our special VIP table." She led him toward the main seating area and pointed to a table for two. He noticed the buffet bar as they walked by and took a peek at what it had to offer.

"Excuse me," he exclaimed, kidding with her as she sat him at a regular table, "but how is this a VIP table?"

She laughed. "Everybody here is a VIP to us. That work for you?"

"I guess. Thank you."

She took out a small pad, practically threw it on the table, and leaned over as she clicked her pen. "So now that we have that settled, how about something to drink?"

"I'll have some iced tea."

"Sweet?" she asked.

"Sweet what?" he asked.

She stepped back as if to take a full look at him. "Do you want sweet tea? We have both, sweet and unsweet."

"Unsweetened, please," he responded as he remembered that people in the South drank their iced tea sweet.

"You ain't from around here. Are ya, hon?" she asked, her southern accent intensified to throw in a hint of playful attitude. Her hands were on her hips, and her head was tilted down, staring him down and demanding a response.

"I'm from New Haven," Nathan replied without the need to fake a northern accent. He smiled, appreciating her taking the time to joke around with him.

"What brings you down here?"

"Hanging out. Just finished college a few weeks ago, and I wanted to come check out the South."

"Well, then let me be the first person to officially welcome you."

Nathan nodded in acknowledgment.

"So what do you think so far?"

"I love it. It's really beautiful down here. Can I ask you a question?"

"Sure!"

"Do you call everyone 'hon'?"

"I sure do...*hon*!" she exclaimed with a smile. They both laughed as she poured his tea.

"Do you like fried chicken?" she asked as if the only right answer was yes.

"You can call me hon. I was starting to get used to it."

She nodded.

"I haven't had it much, maybe once in my entire life. My parents are real health nuts, so we didn't eat much fried food at home."

"Well, you can't come to Nawlin's and not eat our fried chicken. Oh boy, are you in for a treat! Take this plate to the buffet and get you a couple of pieces. Don't worry. We won't tell Mama." She winked and walked away.

Chapter II

AFTER A BUSY Sunday morning in church, Warren, Rachel, and Kate got in the car to head home. They typically ate at home after church, but they hadn't prepared anything ahead of time, and Warren suggested they go out to eat.

"Kate, it's your choice today, honey. Where would you like to go?" A short pause. "I know just the place!" Warren bellowed before she could answer, with a mischievous look on his face. "We haven't been there in a long time, and Nawlin's never disappoints. What do y'all think?"

Rachel and Kate looked at each other, knowing full well that once Nawlin's was mentioned, there was no point in bringing up other choices.

"I think I've lost a pant size here lately anyway," Warren kidded, looking at his waist and patting his belly. "I'm sure I'll find it in one meal at Nawlin's. How about it, girls?"

Kate shrugged and smiled. "That's fine, Daddy. Whatever y'all want to do."

"Great! Now let's go put some meat on these bones!" he replied.

Warren managed to get them there in record time. As soon as they walked in the door, they were greeted by a waitress they knew well.

"Hi there. Long time no see. How have y'all been doing?"

Warren hugged her and said, "Hi, Sarah. We're good, just couldn't stay away for another week. How's your mom doing?"

Sarah put her head down and averted her eyes for a moment before she regained her smile. "Not good, Dr. Johnson. She's not doing good at all. The last surgery she had just about did her in."

Warren kept his arm around her. "I know, hon. I know. You just keep loving on her and taking care of her. The Lord knows what he's doing. And," he said with a reassuring smile, "please call me Warren!"

Sarah smiled and nodded. As she led them to their table, she looked at Kate and asked, "Have you guys heard from Austin?"

Kate nodded and said, "He calls us about once a week…seems to be doing okay. He'd be really upset if he knew we're here without him."

Sarah laughed and kept walking. "Well, here's your table, right by the buffet bar, just like Doctor"—she paused as she caught herself—"as Warren likes."

"Good save," he said.

"Thanks! Help yourselves to the bar, guys, and I'll bring you back the usual for your drinks."

Within what seemed like seconds, Warren had gone to the bar and returned with a plate full of food. He was tall and slender, and his family had wondered often where he put the food he ate. "I just come from good stock," he would always reply.

Kate went to the bar to see what she might eat. She knew that if she came back to the table with nothing on her plate but salad, Warren would tease her about needing to "put some meat on those bones." Their shrimp and okra was good, so she filled her plate with that and some mashed potatoes. She wasn't really paying attention as she rounded the corner, and suddenly she felt someone's foot under hers. Losing her balance, Kate spilled the entire contents of her plate all over the foot's owner.

Grease and mashed potatoes trailed down a blue shirt. Startled and panicked, Kate looked up to see a man with dark brown hair and hazel eyes. "Oh my gosh. I'm so sorry. Are you okay?"

The surprised young man just stood there staring at his clothes, too shocked to say anything. He was well dressed, a few inches taller than her, and he looked out of place in that restaurant.

"I really am so sorry. I just wasn't paying attention. Here, I'll get some napkins so you can get cleaned up."

He said nothing as he bent down to pick up the food from the floor. Kate didn't know if he was mad, so she apologized again as she reached over to the nearby table to get some napkins.

"You really need to wa—" he started to say as he looked up to get the napkins from Kate. They made eye contact as she pulled her sun-kissed sandy-blond hair from her face to reveal stunning blue eyes, and in a split second he went from looking annoyed to captivated. Stopping in midsentence, he said the first thing that came to mind. "It's okay. Really! It's fine. I really wasn't paying attention either. Are you okay?"

"Of course. I'm fine. It's you I feel bad about," she replied.

He stood up, wiped gravy off his hand and extended it to her. "My name is Nathan...Nathan Berkley."

Kate shook his hand as she gazed at the mess on the floor. Nathan looked down too. His plate had fallen on the ground when they collided, and he was embarrassed that she could see he had three pieces of fried chicken on it. She looked back up, smiling, and right away he knew she'd noticed.

"You like that chicken, don't you? How do you stay fit, eating like that?" she asked, hoping to lighten up the mood.

"Do I like it?" He paused, trying to play on his charm to hide how embarrassed he was. "Not only do I like it, but I'm on my second plate. That waitress over there suggested it, and I almost wish she hadn't. I don't eat a lot of this kind of food in Connecticut."

"Sarah?" she asked, pointing at the person who had greeted her and her family when they came in.

"So that's her name?" he replied.

"Yep, that's our Sarah. She's a good friend of the family. Where in Connecticut are you from?"

"New Haven."

"So did you come down here to eat fried chicken?"

"It'd be worth it if I had," he replied, all matter of fact, and she laughed.

He couldn't keep his eyes off hers. Wondering if she might notice that he was staring, he elaborated more on his answer. "The chicken was a nice surprise. I just finished school, and before I got too serious about finding a job and doing all the grown-up stuff, I wanted to get away. The South just seemed like a cool place to visit."

"So what do you think so far?"

"It's all right, I guess." Nathan shrugged as he said this, trying to get a reaction out of her.

"Yeah. It ain't that bad," she responded, shrugging too. They laughed, and she knelt to scoop the food off the floor and onto her plate.

"Please don't do that. You really don't have to," Nathan exclaimed.

"Oh, come on," she responded. "I caused this mess."

Right at that time, Sarah walked up.

"What in the world did y'all do? Gosh! This is why we can't have nice things," she joked.

Kate smiled at her. "Sorry, Sarah. It was all me on this one."

"I've got this, sweetie," Sarah responded with a warm look.

"Okay. Thanks, Sarah. Well, I guess I've done enough damage here," Kate said and smiled at Nathan. "I better get back to my table now."

"Oh, okay," Nathan responded, disappointed this was the end of their conversation.

Kate extended her hand to shake his. "By the way, my name is Kate Johnson. I'm sorry again. It was nice meeting you."

"Likewise," he responded as she started to walk toward her table.

"Enjoy your time in Charleston."

"I will. Thank you."

Nathan sat down at his table, and his eyes followed her as she went to hers. Warren and Rachel asked her where she'd been, and she quickly recounted the story. Nathan could see from his table that they were laughing. After a few bites of dessert, he paid for his food and said bye to Sarah. As he walked toward the door, he and Kate made eye contact and waved good-bye. She said something to Warren and Rachel, who turned around looking for Nathan and waved from the table.

As Nathan got in his van, he wished he had a good reason to go back in and talk to her, but he didn't. So he put it in drive and left.

Chapter 12

OVER THE NEXT couple of days, Nathan went into tourist mode. He visited some of the plantations and fell in love with walking through the history-filled streets. He loved the southern and sophisticated feel of the streets and the people. There was no question in his mind he had picked the perfect place to visit.

After two days of heavy walking, Nathan decided to relax. He found the ideal place close to the harbor. Within a few minutes of his sitting on a swing in front of a large fountain, some children began playing nearby. It was not long before they noticed the fountain and started running through the water jetting out of the ground.

The fresh breeze and the smell of the ocean seemed to blend with the excited voices of the children, creating a feeling of calmness. Nathan was surprised at himself. He had always thought of kids as loud, obnoxious, and sticky. In his mind, they just seemed to cause trouble and break stuff. But somehow, sitting there that evening with nothing to do but just be, he found himself actually enjoying them.

Nathan could see how carefree and happy the children were. He thought about how it was they who seemed to get the point of life, much more so than most adults he knew. The children seemed to genuinely enjoy the moment and to feel free to make the most of it. He remembered times as a child when he had experienced that kind of freedom, doing something as simple as kicking a soccer ball around with his friends. But his parents had never really understood the importance of nurturing him through play and validating him as child, and as a result Nathan became an early adult, hoping they might want to be around more. Adult-sized expectations, however, were impossible for a child to meet, and the inevitable failures led to disappointment for John and Sandra and resentment of his parents for Nathan.

The past was in the past, though, and Nathan wanted to make the most of the present. Everything around him—from the excited voices of the children to the ocean breeze and the sound of the waves in the distance—seemed to harmonize, to transcend the moment. Nathan loved how much more clearly he was able to think away from home. He thought about how he wanted his life to be more like this. He could see more clearly than ever how he'd allowed himself to get too wound up in life, and because of it, he had missed so much without even knowing it.

The oversized swing groaned as it traveled back and forth, almost resembling what he felt inside. He knew, although he couldn't explain how, that there was a purpose to his life. There had to be more to life than what he had made it, and he yearned to know what his purpose was and who he was.

Nathan leaned his head back and closed his eyes as a simple but unanswerable question threatened to extinguish the mystery of the moment. *But how can I know?*

Chapter 13

WITH ONLY A week and a half left in Charleston, Nathan was already starting to miss it. Something about the place and the people made him feel more alive. Life just made more sense to him there. As different occurrences from his time there came to mind, he thought about the one that had most impressed him—his experience at Nawlin's. He chuckled as he thought about the girl who had run into him and knocked both of their plates all over the floor. He still remembered her name. *Kate.*

He also remembered the way Kate and her family had interacted at the table when she'd gone back. Although he'd only seen them for a few moments, the scene had made an impact on him. They looked happy to be with one another.

The strangest thing to him at the time was seeing them bow their heads to pray for their meal—most shocking to him was that they were so comfortable doing it in public. That was something he had never seen anyone do before. To him, it was something that only happened in the movies. It was strange to say the least. He knew a lot of people who talked about being Christians, but he'd never seen them bow their heads in public and say the blessing. Although it had been strange, and definitely not his thing, something about it had felt noble.

He decided to take a stroll by the water as he formulated a plan for what he might do that day. It was about ten in the morning, and the ocean breeze he'd gotten so spoiled by the last few days was blowing faithfully. Ahead of him, he could hear the waves beat against the concrete levee. People posed for pictures with the ocean as their backdrop, and the seagulls seemed to linger above the water as if purposefully trying to sneak into pictures.

To the left he could see a large cruise ship, with hundreds of people boarding it. And even though he couldn't see their faces, he figured they were smiling from ear to ear. He wondered where they might be going, although it really didn't matter. At the time, he was right where he wanted to be. He leaned against the rail that separated him from the water and stared at the ship for a few minutes.

"You wouldn't want to get on that thing. Those ships only serve fancy food—no fried chicken."

The voice sounded familiar, and although there were other people around, Nathan knew the comment was directed at him. When he turned around, looking at him was the face he had not been able to get out of his mind the past couple of days.

Not wanting to be outwitted, he replied, "Well, I hear people in those boats wear pretty fancy stuff to eat their fancy meals, and they may not appreciate someone running into them and dumping their food all over them."

Fighting not to laugh, she pretended to be offended. "Is that how you greet people in New Haven?"

"You started it...Have you been following me?" he responded, amazed that Kate was standing in front of him.

"Yeah. You wish. I've got a lot more sense than that," she replied as she took her headphones out of her ears.

Seeing she was wearing exercise clothes and running shoes and was breathing a little heavy, Nathan asked, "Have you been running in this heat?"

She nodded.

"Which way did you come from?" he asked, somewhat impressed.

She pointed at the Ravenel Bridge to their left.

"Really? That thing is like three miles long...you just ran over that?"

She nodded and smiled, looking surprised it seemed like such a big deal to him.

"And you're not dying?"

"No. I'll live, but thanks for the concern."

"Impressive!" he exclaimed. "I couldn't run a mile to save my life."

"I think I heard a little southern twang in that last sentence, Mr. New Haven. What's up with that?"

"I guess you could say the South becomes me."

"You've still got a long way to go, buddy. But you're showing some progress."

"Hey, just a few blocks from here, there is an ice cream joint. Do you want to go put on a couple pounds with me?" Nathan had thought about her a lot since they had met at the restaurant. He didn't want this to be just a quick conversation that would let her get away again.

Kate tilted her head, her blond ponytail falling to the side, and squinted her eyes at him. "What kind of girl do you think I am? Do you think I'm going to go with you just because you offer me ice cream?"

"It's Ben and Jerry's," Nathan said matter-of-factly.

Kate laughed, impressed with his quick wit. "Oh, then I'm in."

They began walking toward the ice cream place, and Nathan hoped he could remember how to get to it. She would no doubt have a great line if he couldn't find his way. But he liked that. To his relief, they made it to Ben & Jerry's without getting lost. They got their ice cream and found a corner table to sit at.

"So, does an accomplished runner like you come to a place like this often?" he asked as he took a draw from a thick cookies-and-cream milkshake.

"I used to, actually. But I haven't been back since Austin left. He worked very close to here, and I would come and meet him here sometimes." Kate thought about the last time she and Austin had met there, and she smiled, remembering what a goofball he had been. He couldn't help himself sometimes, especially when there were kids around.

Nathan didn't say anything right away, suddenly feeling awkward and almost out of place. He felt the pit of his stomach drop as all his hopes dashed away because of this Austin guy. *Man*, he thought to himself. *Of course! It makes sense. A girl like this couldn't be alone.*

Kate felt the awkward silence and glanced over at Nathan, who looked a little disappointed and shocked. "What is it?" she asked, realizing she hadn't specified who Austin was. Then, without waiting for an answer, she smiled and tapped his arm. "Austin is my brother."

Nathan felt dumb but tried not to show it.

"A little worried, were you?"

He looked away before speaking, trying to come up with something witty and play it cool. "Don't flatter yourself. I was just having a quiet moment and taking in the scenery."

"Got it," Kate said with a look that let him know she didn't buy it. Nathan laughed, and she joined in. "So, what have you been up to while in Charleston? Are you glad you came?" she asked.

"Yes. I've fallen in love with the place," Nathan said sincerely.

"I'm really glad to hear you've enjoyed yourself here."

They talked for a while longer, unaware of the passing time. He didn't know how she felt about him. But he was sure of how he felt toward her, and he knew he wanted to see her again. He loved that she was obviously well read and able to talk in depth about a lot of things—this was a big deal in the world he came from. But there seemed to be so much more to her than an impressive intellect and incredible looks. She liked to joke and laugh, to enjoy the moment. What struck him the most about her, however, was that even though they hardly knew each other, she seemed to care about him as a person. What he had to say was important to her.

⊷⊷⊨◉ ◉⊨⊷⊷

Eight hundred miles up north, an angry John Berkley paced around his living room. As soon as Sandra had walked through the door a few days ago, she had known something was wrong. Ever since the TV interview, she had watched him withdraw more and more, and she was getting very worried.

"John, dear, you need to stop pacing and relax. This is not doing you any good. I'm getting really concerned about you." She knew her words wouldn't help but felt as if she had to say something.

After a long silence, he turned around and showed her a newspaper he was clenching in his right hand. "How dare they, Sandra! How dare they!" He was fuming mad.

"Dear, so what if they disagree with you? It just means they don't know what they're talking about. You've said it yourself a million times. They are a bunch of uneducated, backwoods people who would rather live stuck in the past than in the real world."

Her words seemed to fuel his anger even more. "Then who do they think they are—bunch of classless morons! If they knew what I know, they'd be begging for an apology! I'm not wrong. They are!"

"John, that's how religious people are, and you know that. They've always criticized you. They're afraid of you because millions of people see you on TV and read your books. You're opening people's eyes and drawing them away from their way of thinking. Their hoax has given them power and money they don't want to lose when someone like you challenges them."

John began pacing again, feeling energized by her words and becoming more irate. Without speaking another word, he stomped toward the front door.

"Where are you going, John?"

"To stop them." And with that, he stormed out.

Chapter 14

AT NATHAN'S REQUEST, Kate agreed to meet him the next day and give him a tour of the city. They spent most of the afternoon and the early hours of the evening walking, talking, and laughing through the streets of Charleston. As they walked by the historic landmarks, she told him about some of the more significant things that had happened there, sometimes making up stuff just to see if he would believe her. More often than not, he wouldn't. Whenever he believed one of her little stories, she would chuckle and look at him, her blue eyes glistening as the sun reflected on them. At times, he would get so caught up in the purity of her beauty that he didn't hear what she said anyway.

He loved how smart and fun she was, and the thought of not getting to spend time with her the next day was already depressing him. Everything felt so right with her. He couldn't recall a time when he had felt so at peace. Life in New Haven had always seemed so rushed, as if he was constantly running late or not doing something he should be doing. And being himself was never enough—most of the people he knew seemed more interested in his father's fame and influence than in Nathan. He didn't get the sense they really wanted to get to know him. They just wanted to be associated with him, to feel the importance of knowing John Berkley's son. Nathan felt as if he lived in somebody's shadow instead of casting his own.

Although he'd just met Kate, he knew she really cared about him as a person. He couldn't explain it, but he was sure of it. Something about her was so different from the people around whom he had grown up. It was also obvious she cared regardless of whether someone cared in return. She displayed a common-sense wisdom about life that he'd never seen before. Somehow, everything made more sense around Kate.

It was eight in the evening, and although they had been together for well over three hours, it felt as if it had been only minutes. Walking on Meeting Street, Nathan asked her if she would like to get a bite to eat. Kate jokingly accused him of trying to turn the tour into a date, which he denied.

"Do you eat something other than fried chicken?" she asked.

"Indeed I do. How about we find a place with spill-proof plates?" he responded, not wanting to be outdone.

"You got me with that one," she said, laughing. "There is a place close by that has fresh seafood. How's that sound?"

"Great. Let's do it."

The restaurant was having a slow night, and it didn't take them long to get their food. There were a few seconds of silence as the waiter made sure their table was all in order before he walked off to tend to someone else. Nathan looked around and took notice of the more classic, brick-and-wood look of the place. A young family was eating a couple of tables over, and one of the children spilled his drink, which got Nathan's attention. He turned toward Kate, ready to make a comment, but he saw that her eyes were closed and her head was bowed. He sat there for a moment, not knowing what to do while she prayed. He was not used to seeing someone pray in front of him before a meal, and it felt very awkward. He didn't know what the right thing to do was—bow his head too, just sit there? For a moment, he considered taking a bite of his food just to play it cool, but he figured that would be rude, so he just waited.

"This looks pretty good," Kate said as she looked back up, acting as if nothing out of the ordinary had just happened. She could tell, however, that he felt a little uncomfortable.

"Um, yes, it sure does," Nathan responded as he picked up a hush puppy.

Kate smiled, thinking that the whole nervous thing was kind of cute.

"I hope you don't mind me asking, Kate…"

"Not sure if I do yet, since I don't know what you're going to ask me." She loved to make him sweat.

"What were you saying…" He paused, wondering if he really should ask about something so personal, but he continued. "While you were praying, I mean."

"I said, 'Lord, I sure hope this fella pays for my supper!'"

He laughed, glad she didn't seem offended.

"Do you remember when you were little and you'd been playing outside all day with your friends?" Kate asked, smiling at him with an endearing look. He nodded.

She continued, "The weather had been perfect. You'd done all those weird things you boys do when you're smaller. But somehow you stayed in one piece!" Nathan smiled as some of his childhood memories came to mind.

"You had nice clothes on but got them all dirty, and they looked as if the only thing you could do with them was throw them away. Then when you got home, your mom gave you that 'what have you been doing' look, but she had a smile on her face and put you in the bathtub. As she dressed you in clean clothes, you realized she had cooked your favorite food for supper because you could smell it from the bathroom. How did that make you feel?"

Nathan thought for a moment before he responded. "I felt safe and taken care of. Thankful, I guess."

Kate smiled and nodded, confirming his response.

"That's how I feel, Nathan—thankful."

Some of Nathan's friends back home had warned him about all the Christians in the South. He wasn't going to ask her, but he was pretty sure Kate was a Christian. His mind was going into overdrive as the questions began to pour in. How exactly did that work, that people could thank a being they couldn't see? It seemed so bizarre—impossible, really.

Kate was definitely smart. There was no doubt in his mind about that. He couldn't believe someone like her could have been easily duped into believing in an unseen being. She had more common sense than most people he knew. His dad had always had an unshakable disdain for people of faith, especially Christians. He didn't know why he abhorred them so much, but it had clouded Nathan's own judgment. He found himself in an interesting conundrum—the most beautiful human being he'd ever met was probably a Christian, and the last thing he wanted to do was stop seeing her. *Oh boy, I would love to see the look on Dad's face if he could see me now.* The sudden thought brought him a defiant sense of satisfaction.

Nathan had never really formed his own opinion about faith. It simply had never mattered. He had no real belief system he could claim or live by. And as far as he knew, it was just a matter of preference whether a person had one or not. If someone wanted to believe in something and apply it to life, fine. If someone didn't, that was fine too. In a way, his thoughts mirrored his parents' because those were all he'd ever known. He was, by nature, inquisitive and more open minded than John, but he had never needed to probe into matters of faith.

But today his curiosity was getting the best of him, and he wanted to ask Kate about her faith. After all, she struck him as someone he could talk to. If anything, he figured it would make for an interesting discussion, and he could impress her with his intellect. But the more he thought about it, the more he talked himself out of it. *I may get the whole "you're going to hell" speech if I don't become a Jesus freak*, he thought. He didn't want to have that conversation with Kate and risk not seeing her again.

He had gotten that speech from other people in the past, and not only had it not made any sense to him, but the last thing he wanted to do was see that person again. It had only made him reject anything of faith because it felt more intrusive and threatening than real. He decided to drop it. Why take a chance at ruining a perfectly good evening with a gorgeous southern girl? Besides, what if she wasn't a Christian after all? How dumb would he look after assuming something like that?

Kate was the first to break the silence. "What's going on in that head of yours, Nathan? I can tell you're thinking about something. I might even see a little smoke coming out."

"Nothing. I'm just taking in the moment. I'm really having fun, Kate. It's been a great day."

She seemed glad to hear him say that. "I've had a good time with you too, Nathan. Thank you. I needed a few laughs. I'm glad we ran into each other again."

"I am glad we ran into each other too. Although I still think you were following me." She laughed, and Nathan continued. "This has been such an incredible trip so far. I've only been here four days, and already I feel more at home here than I ever did back in Connecticut."

"I'm glad too. What's so different between here and home?" Kate asked.

"Life feels different here. I've got that 'away from it all' feeling. It's like I've been able to think more clearly and put some things in perspective. Even though I chose to come to South Carolina for no other reason than I wanted to see what it was like down here, it's like I was supposed to come to this exact place." He looked down at the table, letting what he had just said sink in for himself. He looked at her, seeking confirmation that what he was saying made any sense. "You know what I mean?"

"Yes, I do. I know exactly what you mean. Sometimes it's good to go some-place new, where nobody knows you or has any expectations of you. You get to be yourself, and that's very freeing."

"Exactly!" Nathan exclaimed feeling a sense of freedom rise from within. "I think you're the only person I've ever talked to who gets that. Everybody has always expected so much of me. The bar was set very high for me from the moment I was born." He wondered if he should say what he wanted to say next, but something about her inspired trust, and at that moment, he felt as if he could tell her anything. "My dad has a world-savior complex, and the last thing I want is to pick up that baton. But that's what I think people expect from me at home."

Kate looked over at the young family sitting close to them as she thought about what Nathan had just said. The father was disciplining the little boy, apparently for picking on his baby sister. The restaurant had gotten much busier, and she couldn't hear what the father was saying. But from the body language, she could tell he was disciplining his son in a loving way.

She too had felt the type of pressure Nathan was talking about. Who hadn't? But she'd never let it bother her because she knew it was part of life. Seeing the young dad discipline his son reminded her of how her parents had always had clear expectations of her. They had made their share of mistakes, but she never had to doubt their love or their intentions. Their actions and their instruction had helped her understand life and people in a way that inspired trust rather than suspicion. And it was that ability to trust that had allowed her to believe life was worth the hassle and to refrain from giving up. She realized now more than ever how well her family had prepared her for life.

"Sorry, Kate. I probably shouldn't have said something like that. We just met, and I don't need to unload my issues on you. Let's change the subject," Nathan said, interrupting her thoughts.

"It's okay," Kate said. She wanted to know more about what he meant, but it was obvious that he didn't want to go into it, so she didn't pry. "Life is a very precious gift, though, Nathan. Things don't always have to feel right or make sense for us to keep trying to make the most of it. Keep trying your best, and you will see time and time again what a gift life really is."

Her words rang so true. He couldn't help but marvel at how simple but how true they were.

"You are really different. You know that?" Nathan said as he signaled the waiter for the bill.

"Jeez, thanks a lot, Mr. Berkley. Just how do you mean that?" she said playfully.

He looked at her, wanting to reach for her hand, but he held back. "I'm so glad I got to meet you, Kate. I feel like I've lived more in one afternoon with you than in several years of my life put together. Most people I know lack depth and understanding. They try to seem like they have their lives all under control, but it's obvious they don't. You seem to have it together more than anyone I've ever met. You know who you are, and that is so rare."

"I don't have it all together, Nathan. Trust me!"

"I think you're amazing. Anyway, if you're not doing anything tomorrow, or you're not following some other guy around..." She smiled and gasped. He continued. "Would you like to do something?"

"Let me check my stalking calendar so I can let you know," Kate began to respond as Nathan laughed. "Yes, I'd like to see you. What do you want to do?"

Nathan was ecstatic and didn't bother to hide it. "Well, this may sound corny, but I think it would be fun. We could take a picnic to the beach. You know, there's nothing like having some actual sand in your sandwich."

Kate laughed and nodded her approval of his plans. "Where are you staying? I'll come pick you up. I know just the place we can go."

"Sounds good. I'm staying at the Harbor Inn downtown."

"Okay, see you at five."

"Sounds great."

Her car was close by. They walked over to it together, and he opened her door after she unlocked it. "I'll see you tomorrow," he said as he closed the door. She smiled and drove off, looking forward to the next time she would see Nathan Berkley.

Chapter 15

WHEN KATE GOT home, she was pleasantly surprised to see that Edee had brought her sons Joshua and Caleb over for supper. Joshua was in first grade and Caleb in kindergarten. To them life was a party, and Kate loved it when they were around. After finding out how school was going, Kate started to tickle them—which quickly got turned on her, and they all ended up rolling around on the den floor as the two brothers ganged up on her.

"Well, I would help you, sis," Edee said as she looked over to Rachel, who was shaking her head. "But you always get yourself into the same mess."

"Hey. I don't need any help! I can take these two knuckleheads with my hands tied behind my back," Kate said. To the boys that sounded like a dare, and it incited them to fight a little harder.

After a few moments, Kate knew she was definitely on the receiving end of what they had termed tickle wrestling. "Wow! Okay, okay, I surrender. You have proven yourselves very worthy opponents." With this, she got up, as did Joshua and Caleb, who stood up straight, apparently feeling quite proud of their victory.

Warren was just getting home, and from the look on everyone's face, he knew exactly what had just happened. He walked over to Kate, kissed her on the forehead, and went to hug Joshua and Caleb. "You have one crazy aunt, boys."

After supper, Warren went to the couch, and the boys knew what that meant. They grabbed a book and went to sit on their grandpa's lap so he could read it to them. The TV was on one of the news channels with the sound turned down low. After tidying up a little, Kate, Edee, and Rachel came to the couch and talked as Warren read to the boys. They looked over at the television from time to time, not necessarily interested in what was on.

The girls found a moment of silence in their conversation and looked over at grandpa and the boys reading. The volume of the television seemed to suddenly go up as a news anchor announced the development of a story. The heading read, *Worldviews on a Collision Course.*

Everybody in the room but the boys directed their attention to the television when they saw pictures of the two men displayed. Warren turned up the volume and listened intently to the anchor.

"During an interview, Dr. John Berkley, a well-known expert in postmodern philosophy and evolution, challenged Dr. James Robertson, a widely read author and professor of Bible studies from the University of Southern California, to a debate."

Kate edged from her seat toward the television, listening more intently as the anchor continued.

"Dr. Berkley is a bestselling author and is often referred to as 'the Missing Link.' He has struck a chord with his work in modern philosophy and thought, and gained wild popularity. He appears often in talk shows, on cable news, and in conferences to offer explanations and practical advice regarding many areas of life. Dr. Berkley is an adamant defender of the theory of evolution who often uses its principles to back up his own theories. Many think this challenge stems from an editorial by Dr. James Robertson printed last week in the *New Haven Times*, titled 'How the Missing Link Has Missed the Truth about God.'"

Warren was familiar with the article. He put the book down to focus on the television. The anchor spoke louder and faster to build up excitement as the piece progressed. He gave the signal to start a video of Dr. Berkley during the interview.

"The article last week was a blatant attack, both on me and on the work I've done. And that's just one of several attacks directed at me lately." It was obvious from his tone that he was irritated, but he kept his composure. He continued, "There are many questions that perplex us, that drive us to look for answers. I have spent my life seeking those answers in a relentless pursuit to define truth for humanity, and I have found no need to create a god to give my work merit.

"That's why I am inviting Dr. Robertson to debate the existence of a god and whether or not there is such a thing as ultimate truth. I will argue that the notion of a god is nothing more than wishful fantasy created by people and that the only definable truth is what can be discovered and explained through science. He will argue for the existence of a god and offer a defense for ultimate truth from a Christian worldview. Let's have an honest dialogue about our origin, our existence, and the way we define what guides us so people can decide for themselves. By the end of our time, each of us should have presented arguments for whether our existence is the result of evolutionary processes, whether there is a god in the equation, and what should guide our lives."

"We contacted Dr. Robertson today," the news anchor reported when the camera returned to him. "He did not say if he would debate Dr. Berkley, but rest assured that Channel Eight will stay on this story and will be the first to report any new developments."

Kate sat back in her seat as the experts queued into position to offer their analysis of what might happen next. The excitement was obvious as they each offered their opinion. Warren looked at Rachel; this was a big deal.

As the dots connected in her mind, Kate was bewildered. *Could it be, really? Is Nathan Dr. Berkley's son?* Their looks favored each other, Nathan was from New Haven, and his last name was Berkley. She casually grabbed the laptop on the side table. Within a few clicks, her thoughts were confirmed. Dr. and Mrs. Berkley had a son named Nathan Berkley, who had just received a business management degree from Stanford University with a 4.0 GPA.

Chapter 16

KATE AVOIDED THE usual chatting with other nurses after her shift so she could go get Nathan. She arrived at the hotel lobby a couple of minutes early, but he was already waiting for her.

"How was work today?" he asked her.

"Great. Are you ready to go? I've brought a lot of food, so I hope you're hungry. And I'll take it personally if you don't like my cooking, even if it's just sandwiches."

Nathan loved the idea that she had gone through the trouble to prepare a meal for him. "I'm ready. Do you still want to drive? I'm not driving what anyone would consider a cool car, but it gets the job done and is quite roomy. There was a mix-up at the airport, and the rental company put me in a minivan." Kate laughed, shaking her head, and he shrugged.

She leaned toward him and put her hand on his shoulder. "Either way, I'm not about to let you get us lost. Y'ain't from around here, after all," she said.

Her exaggerated southern accent made Nathan laugh. "Believe it or not," he said as he realized this for the first time, "I haven't gone to the beach since I've been in Charleston."

"Well, you're in for a treat then!"

"Oh boy. Hearing you say that concerns me for some reason."

"Watch it, there, sir! I was planning on taking it easy on you today, but I may change my mind."

Nathan jokingly shrank down into his seat as if conceding the fight. Kate gave a look of approval, put the car in gear, and started down the road to Folly Beach.

Kate chose the scenic route on Riverland Drive. And once again, Nathan couldn't help but marvel at the beauty of the old oaks and the Spanish moss that hung from their branches. The place had a way of taking one back to a time before any of the things of modern life really mattered. The houses and cars almost seemed out of place in such natural beauty. He felt the same peace come over him that he had experienced a few days before while sitting in front of the fountain and watching the children play. He wanted time to linger, to capture it somehow so he could relive it later.

The sound of the wind rushing in the car through Kate's window caught his attention, and he looked over at her. A few strands of hair were blowing in front of her face, but she didn't seem bothered by them. He noticed she was smiling, and he thought about how different she was from anyone he'd ever met. She understood life and people in a way that inspired him to be better, and she was comfortable just being herself. Kate didn't display the selfishness he'd seen in so many people. She seemed perfectly happy to give and make others' lives better. Nathan was struck by her genuine personality and was baffled by the question of where it might come from. She was as beautiful inside as out. But what surprised him the most was that she truly cared about him, and he knew he could trust her. He felt as if Kate understood him like no one had before or ever would.

Just a few days ago, when he was planning this trip, he had expected to visit a few sites, take some pictures, eat some good food, and go back home. He never would have expected it to turn out as it had. But he knew this was more than a good trip becoming great; he knew life had taken a right turn, and Kate was the reason for it. The thought of leaving her behind in a few days was already unbearable.

"Here we are," Kate announced. "Welcome to Folly Beach."

Nathan looked around and gave an approving nod. Neither one of them was hungry yet, so they decided to take a walk on the beach. The breeze felt great after a hot day, and as they walked and talked, they busied themselves watching a band of seagulls flying low in hope of finding bread crumbs. Their conversation was light and fun, and they were both having a great time getting to know each other.

Nathan got quieter during their meal, and Kate could tell something was bothering him. They cleaned up quickly and decided they would walk to a nearby pier.

"Watch TV last night?" she asked, still wondering if she should bring up the subject.

"I did," he answered matter-of-factly. "Did you?"

"Yep," she said, and the two lapsed into a comfortable silence for several moments.

"So that was your dad on TV?" Kate asked.

Nathan bent down to pick up a seashell, and after a quick examination, he threw it toward the water. "I bet you were surprised," he said, his troubled gaze fixed toward the ocean. She ignored the trajectory of the shell and kept her eyes on him. "Well, I wasn't. It was just a matter of time before he pulled something like this. I read the article they mentioned on the news the day after it came out. I bet you a hundred people forwarded it to me the moment it was posted online. I talked to him a couple nights ago, and he was going nuts." He paused for a second, smiling as he shook his head. "Trust me," he continued. "The man's ego has no bounds."

"I'm sorry. I really didn't mean to upset you," she said, trying to give him a way out of the conversation.

"No, it's okay. It's kind of nice to talk about it. When he's pulled these stunts before, I've always been around people who tell me how great he is or want to know more about him. There's never been a shortage of them. I remember once during a swim meet in high school where I was blasting away the competition. I had just set a regional record and one of the officials approached me. He gave me a quick congratulations, but good ole Pops had been on TV the night before, and when the official saw my name, he couldn't wait to see if I was John Berkley's son. When I told him I was, he proceeded to tell me how great he thought my dad was. It seemed that no matter what I accomplished, it paled in comparison to my identity as Dr. Berkley's son."

"I think you're pretty brave."

"How's that?" he asked.

"Well, for one, you're trying to figure things out for yourself. Some people don't have the courage to do that."

"I appreciate you saying that, Kate. I really do. I was just hoping I could get away for a few days and just be Nathan, but my dad casts an enormous shadow, and I can't get away from my last name."

"Well, you're not just a Berkley," Kate said firmly. "You're Nathan Berkley, your own person. You don't have to live according to who you are related to or who you know. You have your own life to live, and you can't miss sight of that."

"You're right. It's just not that easy. Trust me. But thank you. Part of me is impressed by him. But there's another part of me that is afraid I will turn out to be like him."

They stopped walking and faced each other. She held his hands in hers and looked straight in his eyes. The glow from the early evening sun brought out the green in his hazel eyes, which made him look more like his dad. "And you don't have to, Nathan. Remember? Every day is a precious gift. It is ultimately up to you if you want to waste it or make something out of it."

"Kate, I've never known anybody like you. I feel like I came down here just so I could meet you. Our time together has changed my life for the better, and I can't tell you how much I hope I'll be seeing a lot more of you."

"I hope so too," she said with a reassuring smile. "Enough about the Berkleys. Tell me about Nathan."

Her tone was genuine and confident, and it gave him the freedom to let go of all the feelings of anxiety and anger he felt. Her words, her touch, the way she looked at him, had released him from the type of bondage he often found himself in. John Berkley seemed a thousand miles away again, unable to ruin his trip. He kissed her, and she gladly kissed him back. Without the need for words, they took each other's hand and walked toward a pier in the distance.

⊹⊱⊰⊹

Over the next few days, Nathan and Kate spent every minute they could together. Neither could wait to see the other, and the next day couldn't arrive fast enough. Nathan had grown to depend on her smile—which made him feel as if he could do anything. He was amazed at his ability to relax and enjoy each moment when he was with Kate—something he had always found hard to do.

Nathan loved history, and Kate cherished the time she spent walking with him through the streets of Charleston and being his personal guide. She knew the same streets she'd walked thousands of times before would never be the same without him at her side. She found herself looking at him often, taking pictures in her mind to recall when he wasn't there. Kate knew she was going to miss everything about him when he left.

There were a lot of qualities she admired about him, but mostly she respected his resolve to find himself. Although he came from a well-known family who had considerable influence, he had chosen to be himself and take control of his own identity—not just ride on the coattails of his last name.

Nathan had a rebellious way about him and a sophisticated flair that intrigued Kate. She could tell he was the kind of guy who would take any action necessary to do what he felt was right. But he didn't feel the need to walk around like a tough guy, which was a refreshing change from many guys she'd known. Even though they had only known each other a few days, Kate felt very drawn to him. They were having a great time together, and she hated the thought of him not being around.

Chapter 17

THEIR LAST DAY together sneaked up on them, and it was harder than anything either of them could have imagined. They met up early and decided to walk around and get some supper. From the moment they met at the lobby of his hotel, time went by at fast-forward speed. Supper was bittersweet, filled with laughs interrupted by long stares of sadness as the time to say good-bye quickly approached. Kate's eyes teared up a couple of times as they recalled some of the things they had said and done over the past few days. Nathan hated to see her upset, but there was nothing he could do. If there were a way to stop time so they could be together a few minutes longer, he would've done it.

Nathan was heartbroken—but also thankful that he'd had the opportunity to experience this kind of love. Because of Kate, feelings of love and belonging, which he'd never known were possible before, were now a reality. She seemed to understand him and to want the best for him without expecting anything in return. It was so hard to sort through the intense sorrow and the deep happiness he felt at the same time. Even though he couldn't understand why, he believed that meeting Kate had been his fate.

Neither of them finished their supper. They just wanted to be alone, away from people and noise. Nathan gestured for the check, and within minutes they were out the door. The streets were busy with tourists and activity, but they ignored everything except each other. Lost in thought about what their future might look like together, they walked with a tight grip on each other's hand without saying anything for a while.

The sun began to set with a breathtaking glow of orange, red, and purple hues that lit up the streets and accentuated the beauty of the buildings. A cool sea breeze picked up, and Nathan used it as an excuse to pull Kate close. She welcomed it gladly. The mix of emotions was overwhelming. They wanted to hold on to the moment for as long as possible, but at the same time, they needed to get their good-byes over with because they were emotionally drained. Nathan didn't know what to say to make them both feel better. He just held her, and this was fine with her. Even though they had only known each other a few days, he knew his love for her was real because he couldn't imagine being away from her for any extended period of time.

Kate represented a worldview his parents despised, but through it she had touched his soul and sparked a newfound curiosity. He'd always felt a tremendous void in his ability to understand life and himself. Like many people, he'd thought getting away from home and going to college would allow him to find himself, but all the partying, knowledge, and miles between him and his parents had done nothing to help him. The void had just grown deeper, and he'd felt more helpless. Her way of looking at life had captivated him, and the tenderness of her heart was filling the void in a way that money, recognition, friends, or a Stanford degree never could have.

Nathan contemplated all the what-ifs the future may bring. Would this be the last night they would be together? Had the chance to experience this kind of love been one of those rare, nice treats life allows, or was it the beginning of something? Uncertainty about their future together hurt, and contemplating this relationship as merely temporary tore him up inside.

The evening was coming to an end, and Kate could no longer hide how upset she was. As tears flowed from the blue eyes Nathan had fallen in love with, he reached for her and held her close.

"You're not going to be able to stay away from me. Are you?" Kate said with a faint smile as she wiped her tears.

"Shoot!" Nathan responded, glad to see her smile. "I was just thinking the same thing about you. I mean, how could you? I am the whole package, van and all."

"You could lose the van. The rest of the package I'm good with," Kate said, laughing. She waited a moment before speaking again as she took something from her pocket. "I don't want to go, but you need to get some rest before tomorrow. You have a long trip ahead of you."

Tears returned to her face, and Nathan did all he could to fight his own tears back.

"Well, Nathan Berkley," Kate said, looking intently into his eyes, "you sure have made an impression on me."

He felt the warm touch of her hand as she put a silver coin in his. He turned it over a couple of times and examined it. His expression came up empty. "What's this?" he asked.

Kate had expected the question, and she smiled. She turned the coin over in his hand and began to explain as she placed her other hand under his. "I had a good friend of our family design and make this coin for you. He was able to shift some work around and get it done before you left. The engraving on this side is a barley plant. There's something very special about barley grain. It doesn't make the best-tasting or the healthiest bread, but it can grow in tougher conditions than other grains. While other grains usually can't survive unless they have a certain amount of water and particular weather conditions, barley will. It's a good reminder that, no matter what is going on in our lives, no matter what's happening around us, we can prevail and be the better because of it. If we just hang on and wait on God with trust, the outcome of any situation can be better than anything we could've expected. No matter what!" She emphasized the last point to make sure it would stick in his mind.

She continued, "The world is going to tell you that you should be that more exotic grain; that you should have this and that or be like someone else to be good enough. But it's our responsibility to know who we were created to be and then to be the best us we can be."

Nathan turned the coin over to see what was on the other side, and what he saw made sense already. She lifted his hand to eye level so his face would reflect on the small mirror embedded in the coin.

"Know who you are, Nathan. You are wonderfully and perfectly made, and don't ever let anyone tell you any different."

He looked into her eyes, her words ringing of a truth and significance he didn't understand. What she said, and how she said it, however, gave him a sense of value he had never felt before.

"Kate, I don't even know how to begin to tell you what the last few days have meant to me." He paused and looked away as he tried to hold a rush of emotion from coming to the surface. "My whole life until meeting you...I feel like I didn't know how to love without selfish motives. You have modeled true love for me, and I am hooked. You see and experience life like most people never could, and you've helped me see how much I was missing. I've been changed in the last few days because of you, and I can't bear the thought of this being the last night we have together."

His words were honest and heartfelt, and he was taken aback by this new Nathan that was emerging. He liked the way it felt to love another person more than he loved himself. "Your gift means a lot to me, Kate. I will keep it with me always and remember what you said. I promise."

Kate, touched by his words, had tears in her eyes again. "Will you do me a favor, Nathan?" she asked, squeezing his hands.

"Sure. Get rid of the van?"

"Yes, by all means do!" she said, pretending to be serious. "But also, when you get back home, look for a chance to tell your mom and dad you love them."

Nathan was startled, and he thought for a moment. "Why?" he finally asked, but he continued before she could answer. "They'll think I've lost my mind. We don't really say that to each other. It's just assumed we do." He hoped this would be enough to waive her request. But she just smiled at him and conveyed a look that said, "No matter—you still need to do it."

This made him feel uncomfortable, but given the circumstances, he committed vaguely. "I'll try. Okay?"

For now, that was good enough for Kate.

"Nathan, I wish we could sit out here all night and talk, but it's probably best that you go pack and get some rest."

Nathan looked into her tear-filled eyes, taking in their beauty one last time, and pulled her into his arms. She rested her cheek on his shoulder, allowing herself to feel weak and get lost in the moment.

Chapter 18

KATE WAS WEAVING in and out of thoughts as she drove home from her last date with Nathan, trying to process everything and wondering what might come next. She had wondered what their last night together would be like. Would she be an emotional wreck? Could she really let him go? Should she be falling in love with someone who didn't share her faith? The only thing she knew at this moment, however, was that she had no regrets about seeing Nathan the last few days.

Warren saw the lights from Kate's car reflect on the driveway and into the living-room windows. He quickly got up from the couch and took off toward the refrigerator, pretending he was just looking for a quick snack. Kate was relieved to see he was up. She had known he would be because he always waited up. His pretending it was just a coincidence was not convincing. It never had been.

He knew she had met someone with whom she had spent a lot of time over the last few days. And this young man had, no doubt, made an impression on her. Warren knew this was his last night in Charleston and that Kate would come home sad.

Knowing that her dad would be up waiting for her, ready to help as he always had, was a source of strength for Kate that night. Warren had always made a real effort to know his kids, and when they were hurting, he knew it. Her pain was obvious as she walked through the door, and his heart naturally ached for her. She laid her keys on the table by the door, and in an unusual show of effort, Bully walked to the door to greet her. Kate got down on one knee and petted him with her right hand as she wiped a tear with her left. Before she walked through the door, she had decided not to cry, but the whirlwind of feelings and thoughts overwhelmed her.

"How are you, honey?" Warren asked. From the tone of his voice, she knew there was no point in hiding how upset she was.

"Not great, Daddy. Not great." With this, the tears started flowing, and Warren came to hug her. After a long hug, they sat on the couch and talked for almost an hour. He wanted to know more about this Nathan who had captured his little girl's heart. She told him about where he was from, what he was like, and what things they'd done over the past few days. She even mentioned the van when the mood lightened, and he got a good laugh out of it.

Warren hated to see his little girl hurting. He knew she was tired and that made things seem worse, so the best thing for her would be to get some rest. He offered a few words of comfort before they said good night.

"You have a big heart, Kate, and you've always felt things strongly. You get that from your mama. But you're also very tough, which you get from her as well."

Kate nudged into her daddy's arms, feeling a wave of encouragement from his words. This was something he always welcomed, and he gladly engulfed her in his arms.

"You'll be fine, honey. Just fine."

⋆⋅◉ ◉⋅⋆

To make his flight at eleven thirty the next morning, Nathan had to leave his hotel by seven. The van was all packed, and he quickly went over the directions to Columbia in his mind as he settled in the driver's seat. The early morning light was just right to bring out the beauty of Charleston so he could enjoy it one last time as he drove off. He felt a strong connection to the place, and he vowed to himself that this would not be his last time there.

Proud of himself for finding Interstate 26 without getting lost, Nathan joined the sparse morning traffic leaving Charleston. Zipping past the trees that lined the interstate, as three lanes turned into two, he thought about what the next few days might be like without Kate. Her words and expressions played over and over in his mind. He knew he had fallen in love, hard, and as the distance grew larger, so did the pain of not being with her. He liked who he was around her so much more than his usual self. When he was with her, he felt alive inside, and he wondered how he had ever made it without experiencing these feelings. How could he have been so blind before? Love, true love, had brought with it joy, life, and hope. In a very short period, Kate had inspired him to become his best.

He felt relaxed, despite the fact that this was a day he had really dreaded. He figured Kate had rubbed off on him. She was the only person he knew who lived the virtues many people only talked about. His mind went to their afternoon at Folly Beach and the delicate and thoughtful way she had handled the conversation about the TV interview with his dad. Having someone like her to talk to and process through his emotions had been so helpful. Kate had not tried to turn the conversation into a drama or a gossip session. Instead, she had found a way to validate and encourage him. Thanks to what he had seen modeled by her the last few days, he felt more liberty to be at ease. He realized that it was okay to enjoy the moment; he didn't need to overreact and sweat the small things.

With all traces of Charleston gone, I-26 became just an interstate. His departure felt final, and he knew he was leaving a part of himself behind. "You've made my life bearable, Kate Johnson," he said out loud. "In just a few days, you made it worth something. I'll be back. I promise."

Chapter 19

As Nathan settled in his seat on the plane, the weight of fatigue from the emotional roller coaster of the last day suddenly fell on him. Sleep rushed in, and before he knew it, he was weaving in and out of short, nonsensical dreams.

Nathan awoke to the voice of the captain announcing they were in their initial descent into Hartford. This made the distance between Kate and him seem far and real. He knew their separation wouldn't be easy, and although he wasn't sure how it might all turn out, he was determined to go back to Charleston soon—very soon. He remembered one of the last things Kate had said to him: "Tell your mom and dad you love them." *Why would she want me to do that?* he wondered again, still both perplexed and fascinated by the request.

Nathan ignored voice mails from Sandra and John offering to pick him up in Hartford, instead preferring to hire a cab to New Haven. He knew they would want to talk about the trip, and he wasn't really in the mood to speak with anyone, much less them. He just wanted a quiet cab ride and an hour or so to straighten all the thoughts and emotions buzzing around in his head before getting back to his world.

From the moment he entered the cab, the whole weight of the driver's frustrations descended upon Nathan. The man was wound up tight, and he seemed to have no choice but to unload on someone.

"My god! How can people be so stupid around here?" the cab driver demanded as he waved his right hand in all directions, making a plea for Nathan to agree with him. "They'll give a driver's license to any idiot out there, won't they? They don't use their blinkers. They cut you off, and they just don't give a rip. Is my car invisible? I mean…you saw my car. Didn't you?"

Nathan knew the quiet hour he'd hoped for wasn't going to happen. He wondered how Kate might react in this situation. She struck him as both caring toward others but firm when she needed to take a stance. The cab jerked to the right, interrupting his train of thought. He popped his head up for an investigative look through the rear and right side windows and figured the driver had been about to miss their exit and that's why he had swerved. In the process, he had cut off a minivan, the driver of which was apparently not so happy, judging by the hand gesture with which he responded.

The cab driver was sweating profusely as he barreled down the exit road, looking at Nathan through the rearview mirror. "Can you believe that guy?" He paused for an answer.

Nathan laughed and said nothing.

With the minivan out of sight, and as if the guy driving it could hear him, the cab driver said, "Why don't you go back to driver's ed.? You jerk! They shouldn't let people like you drive!"

Trying to avoid eye contact, Nathan looked out the window, hoping the guy would run out of ranting material and somehow get them to their destination alive.

After the worst hour-and-a-half cab ride of his life, Nathan paid the driver and sealed the cab number in his mind to make sure he never got in it again, especially if Kate ever came to visit him. When he got in the house, he put his suitcases down on the floor of the foyer. As he did so, his keys fell on the hardwood floors, making a loud enough noise to alert Sandra.

"Nathan, is that you? Are you home?"

"Hi, Mom. Yes, I'm home."

"Oh, good. I'm coming down."

Nathan walked to the study to say hi to John. He assumed his father was there because as soon as he'd walked through the front door, he had smelled the unmistakable aroma of a fresh pipe. John usually rewarded himself with a pipe when he took breaks from his work. This meant one of two things: either he was writing or he was preparing for something important. The pipe was still smoking, so he'd obviously just walked away for a couple of minutes.

As he glanced around the room, he was struck by how different things looked in his world. This time he paid closer attention to the decorations in the famous Dr. Berkley's office. They were busy, and they consisted of mostly Italian paintings and a prominently displayed picture of Charles Darwin. He'd seen that portrait in the same spot since he could remember, but for the first time ever, he noticed the expression in Darwin's eyes. He looked sad and empty, as if he was searching for something that couldn't be found.

He thought about the life in Kate's eyes, still so fresh in his mind. It was so irresistible and contagious. The contrast between the look in her eyes and the one in Darwin's was astonishing, and he wondered how such a difference was possible.

Lost in thought, Nathan felt a strong tap on the right shoulder. "Hi, Nathan," said a familiar voice. He felt both happiness and disdain as he turned around to greet his dad. They embraced quickly and awkwardly.

"Hi, Dad. How are you?"

John took a step back. "I'm fine," he responded.

Sandra entered the room, and both men turned around, glad someone else was coming into the scene.

Sandra's eyes opened wide and she increased her pace when she saw Nathan. "Give me a hug. It feels like you've been gone a month!"

"It wasn't that long, Mom."

"Well, it felt like a month to us." She looked at her husband. "Didn't it feel like a month, John?"

John shrugged and forced a quick reply. "Yes, it did." He looked at Nathan and rolled his eyes. Nathan shrugged too and forced a smile.

Nathan wondered when they were going to ask him why he hadn't responded to their calls saying they would pick him up, but it looked as if they'd decided to drop the matter.

"So how was your time in South Carolina? What did you think?" John asked.

A whirl of thoughts and emotions rushed through Nathan's mind. *Where to start? Maybe tell them about Kate, my Christian girlfriend? That would make for an interesting conversation.*

"I had an amazing couple of weeks. South Carolina is beautiful, and the people were for the most part warm and genuine. I couldn't have asked for a better time. I'd definitely like to go back sometime." *You just don't know how badly,* he thought.

He yawned, not trying to hide the fact that he was tired from his trip. Sandra realized this and said, "That's great, Nathan. We're going to want to hear a lot more about it, but it doesn't have to be today. I'm sure you'd like to get settled back in and get some rest."

Nathan smiled at her appreciatively. He looked over at the pipe, which was still smoking. "You must be working on something big!" he said to John, figuring his father was preparing for the debate to which he had challenged Dr. Robertson.

John tracked with him, sure he must have seen the challenge on TV, and nodded. "You heard, huh?"

"I sure did," responded Nathan, his face reflecting displeasure as he remembered the way his father had acted during the TV interview. He looked away and tried not to comment on it, but he could not hold his tongue. "Why do you have to have that debate?"

John extended his arms, gesturing to his office full of books and artifacts as evidence to make his point. "It's what I do, Nathan," he said in a frustrated tone, not trying to hide the fact he was annoyed by the question. "It's what I have dedicated my life to."

Nathan looked around the room, shifting his gaze from the hundreds of books on the shelves to the artifacts his father had collected during his travels. He was reminded, once again, of how much he resented all of it for being John's passion through the years, taking the place of his family.

"Nathan, people like Dr. Robertson..." John continued. "They are so gripped by the fear they've tried to instill into people for centuries that they have suspended thinking altogether. They think they believe in what they can't see, and they put all their blind faith on it. Their whole lives are based on beliefs that can't be proved by science." He paused for a moment, trying to suppress an angry rage surging from deep within. "It's simply not possible. What they believe can't be, and I am amazed that anyone falls for it. I want to expose them for what they are. I do...And I want so-called Christians to see it once and for all so they will wake up from this dream they're stuck in. I intend to argue during the debate, and for the rest of my life, that the only believable truth is what can be proved through science and that we don't have some imaginary friend in the skies to depend on or define truth for us. So that's why, Nathan. I'm surprised you'd even ask that question."

Nathan thought about Kate. John was actually talking about her. He'd heard his father talk this way all his life, and although he hadn't totally embraced his family's belief system, it was all he knew, and he accepted it on the surface. But how could someone, then, explain who Kate was? How could she have such understanding about life and people? He beliefs seemed like so much more than superstition and fear. There was no doubt in his heart that she could see things more clearly than anyone he knew.

He felt confused. What his dad said made sense, but he also knew what he had seen and experienced in Kate. Annoyed, and not wanting to talk further on the subject until he could sort things out for himself, Nathan decided to end the conversation.

"Whatever! I'm really tired. I'm going to go rest awhile."

John nodded, and Sandra shot him a look pleading that the conversation be dropped.

John walked to his desk and opened a book as he sat down. "Yes. Get some rest, Nathan." He paused and searched for something to say. "It's good to have you back. We'll catch up more later."

Nathan nodded as John began to busy himself with his work. He knew catching up more would never happen.

Chapter 20

THREE DAYS HAD passed since Nathan left. Kate had gotten back into her daily routine of going to the hospital, working crazy hours, and coming home wiped. Nothing felt the same to her now, though. Everything in her everyday life, even things that had nothing to do with Nathan, somehow reminded her of him. She had liked other guys before, but this was so different. Her feelings this time had a depth and a sense of urgency she'd never experienced before. They caused her both great joy and sadness at the same time, and there was always a persistent sense of melancholy in her heart.

As she arrived home from the hospital one afternoon, after a particularly long shift, she thought it odd that Warren was there at that time of day. He was in the kitchen fixing a sandwich, and he seemed startled when she came in.

"Hey, Dad. What are you doing home?" she asked.

"Oh, hey, honey. We've had a particularly busy couple of weeks at the church, and I told everyone to go on home and spend some time with their families. I took my own advice. Did you have a good day?"

"Yes, great."

Kate looked a little sad to Warren, and he gave her a small squeeze. "This fancy boy is not taking my place, is he?" he asked jokingly.

"Of course not, goofy!"

Warren followed Kate with his eyes as she walked toward the kitchen counter to lay down her keys and pocketbook. "Okay, then he's okay with me!" he responded, laughing.

"I thought it'd get easier, but it's getting harder."

Warren just looked at her, giving her a chance to speak, trying hard not to jump in and attempt to fix everything.

Kate sat on the stool and stared into the granite countertop. "A few days ago I didn't know him, and I was just fine. Now, everything feels so different."

"That's love, honey. You could liken falling in love to having a baby. Before you know you're going to have a baby, you're just excited that a new person will soon be in your life. But as soon as that baby is born, it's a part of you, and your life is never the same again."

"I understand. Just wish he wasn't from so far away," Kate said as she laid her chin on her forearms. "First, Austin leaves. Now Nathan..."

"Honey, there are things the Lord allows that we can't understand at the time they happen. They may be hard—maybe they even seem impossible to endure—but one thing I've learned is for sure: He does them for us, not to us. His plan is perfect and for our best. If we trust and obey Him, the outcome is better than anything we could have ever hoped for."

Kate teared up as Warren's words and her circumstances clashed in her mind. He wanted to go hug her, but instead he gave her a chance to gather her own strength.

"Do you believe me, Kate?"

"I do, and I know you're right. It's just hard."

"Must be some fellow, this Nathan," Warren said, and Kate nodded. "I hope I'll get to meet him soon."

He started to walk toward her, but suddenly the song *Born in the USA* filled the room. Warren checked his pockets and within seconds pulled out his cell phone, with the sound now louder than before. He looked at Kate with a shrug. She rolled her eyes and smiled, shaking her head.

"Nice ring tone, Dad," she said, laughing. "Please take it. I'm fine."

Warren laughed and listened for the caller. "Jimmy! Oh my goodness! Is it really you, old boy?" he exclaimed as he gestured for Kate to stay. He looked over at her and whispered, "It's James Robertson." Into the phone, he said, "How have you been, my friend? To what do I owe this honor?"

"I've been doing good, you old dawg," James said, trying to simulate a southern accent.

Warren laughed. "I see you're still a redneck wannabe."

"One can try. Right?"

They asked about each other's wives and kids and quickly caught up on the last couple of months. Kate listened intently to what Warren said, trying to piece together the conversation between them.

"I'm so glad you called me, brother. It really is good to hear from you. What else have you been up to lately, other than getting yourself in trouble? You just can't stay away from the cameras, can you?"

James started to answer, but an uncontrolled cough interrupted his words.

"Is everything okay?" Warren asked with a concerned look on his face. Kate listened even more intently.

"Well, I'll be fine. Just been having a few tests done here lately. My energy levels have dropped in the last few months, and my doctor is really trying to slow me down."

"Better get it together," Warren said with a tone meant to cheer him up. "You have that big debate coming up!"

James paused a few moments before he said anything else.

"Yes, the debate. I'm glad you mentioned that. That's why I'm calling you, by the way."

"Talk to me, James. What's going on?"

James sighed on the other side. "I'm not going to be able to do it. My health won't allow it. And certainly my doctor won't either. Any other time I would've ignored him, but I think he's right this time."

"I'm sorry to hear that, James. I was really looking forward to what this debate might do for people. Dr. Berkley is world renowned, and it'll probably get a lot of attention since these are things people want to hear about. I'm sure at least a couple networks will televise an event like this."

"It's just that, Warren. I can't do the debate, but I too feel very strongly that it is too great an opportunity to miss."

"Right!" Warren affirmed as James finished his sentence.

"I won't beat around the bush here, Warren." James paused, and Warren heard coughing in the background. "The debate needs to take place. That's why I'm calling you." James emphasized the "you," and Warren sank into one of the stools in front of the kitchen counter as the reason for the call became obvious.

He started to say something, but James quickly came back.

"Dr. Berkley is very smart and the top man in his field. We both know this. I can't ask just anyone to go toe to toe with him. And he won't accept just any replacement. He has a point to make, and without a big name on the other side, he won't waste his time."

"Oh, James...Wow." Warren paused as he looked around the room to collect his thoughts. "I appreciate the confidence. But there are so many others who could do so much better."

"Warren," James said, "Dr. Berkley wants this to be a philosophical debate based on facts. He wants to prove that his worldview applies to everyday life—that it explains why we are here and how we should live. You know as well as I do that people everywhere are hungry for these answers. They need to know if there's anything out there they can put their faith on. This is your forte, and that's why it must be you.

"Dr. Berkley challenged me. You know that neither he nor the public will accept just anyone as a substitute. You will draw the numbers. It has been a while since you were in the spotlight, but the ripples from your work in apologetics are still being felt." There was a heavy silence for a few seconds as Warren thought through all the implications. Not wanting to beat around the bush, James went in for the kill: "This is too important, Warren. I will cancel the debate altogether if it's not you."

Kate was staring intently at Warren. They heard the front door close, and within seconds Rachel walked into the kitchen. She quickly perceived something was going on, and the smile on her face turned to puzzlement and concern.

"What is it?" she asked, looking at Warren.

Kate whispered, "It's James Robertson."

Warren said a quick prayer in his mind and waited a few moments before saying anything.

Rachel was intrigued. Kate was too, but in a different way, as she started to figure out the reason for the call.

"Okay, James, I'll do it."

James let out a big sigh of relief. "Thanks, brother. I know this is a lot to ask of you, and I wouldn't do it if I didn't believe it was the right thing to do."

"I appreciate the confidence. What's the next step?" Warren asked.

"I'll take care of the next step," James said. "We will contact the media and set everything up. Can you be ready by July?"

"Sure. Of what year?" Warren joked.

"This year," James answered with a serious tone.

"Boy," Warren said as he looked at Rachel, wondering what she might be thinking. "I'm not sure I can handle too many calls from you. They come fully loaded."

James laughed and said, "You should've known better than to answer the phone. I have full confidence in you, brother. I'll be praying every day that God will use you to draw others to Him as you defend His truth. Please remember, Dr. Berkley is brilliant and very passionate about what he believes. He won't go down without putting on quite a fight."

"No pressure though, right?" Warren said.

"Lots of pressure, Warren, I know. I am forever indebted to you."

"No problem, James. Listen, it's great to hear from you. Please take care of yourself and let me know how you're doing."

"I will. I can't thank you enough for doing this."

They said good-bye and ended the call; Warren waited to say anything until he could collect his thoughts and emotions.

Rachel was the first to break the silence. "Is James okay?"

Warren didn't respond. He just looked at her.

"What's going on, Warren? Is everything okay?" Rachel asked with concern as several scenarios played in her mind.

Warren put the phone back in his pocket and sank into the stool. "He's having some health issues."

"I'm sorry to hear that. What's he going to do about the debate?" Rachel asked.

Kate looked intently at Warren, her heart beating a mile a minute.

"That's just it. He feels very strongly that Dr. Berkley's invitation must be accepted. And so do I." He had a stern look of resolve on his face.

"So what's he going to do?" Rachel asked again.

"He's not going to do anything. I am. He called to ask me if I would take his place in the debate."

Silence hung in the air for a few moments. Rachel sank into the stool next to his and took his hand in hers. "Oh, honey, are you sure?"

"I have to do it."

"Okay," she answered. "You have our full support. Doesn't he, Kate?"

Kate was speechless. She had a look of utter disbelief on her face.

Rachel looked at Warren, then back at Kate. "Honey, are you okay?"

Oh my gosh! Kate thought. *Oh my gosh! What in the world is going on here? How could this be happening?* She was trying to come back with something good, maybe try to play it off until she could figure something out, but her mind was spinning out of control.

"Daddy," Kate answered shifting her gaze between him and Rachel, "everything just changed! I can't believe this is actually happening. Nathan's last name is Berkley. He is John Berkley's son!"

Chapter 21

BULLY WALKED INTO the kitchen and looked up at Warren, obviously expecting to be petted, but Warren ignored him as the colossal significance of what Kate had just said took hold of him. He knew life had just taken a whole new direction he hadn't expected, in more ways than one.

"Nathan? The guy you told me about?" asked Rachel, surprised.

"Yes!" Kate replied. "Dr. Berkley is Nathan's father!"

"No way!" Rachel said in disbelief.

Nobody said anything for a few seconds as all the implications formed in their minds. Kate felt as if her relationship with Nathan might be in jeopardy. She wondered about what impact the debate may have on their families' future relationship.

How does something like this happen? she asked herself. Growing up, she'd believed that all things happened for a reason, but the magnitude and incredulity of the situation just didn't seem to apply to that belief. This had to be an exception to the rule. She wanted to run out of the room and find a place to scream, mainly at God for allowing this to happen. She was afraid to speak, to think. All she could do was look at her dad. She didn't know what he might be thinking about all of this, of her.

Warren was stunned. This certainly was a lot to take, but he had seen over and over that when something unimaginable happened in life, there was a reason for it. And instead of being a problem, it was an opportunity. He couldn't imagine how Kate might be feeling right now.

He went to her and put his arm around her. "Sweetie, Jeremiah 29:11 says, 'For I know the plans I have for you, declares the Lord, plans to prosper you and not to harm you, plans to give you hope and a future.'" He squeezed her closer. "Listen to me, Kate. I'll admit it. This is really something. Just a few minutes ago, we were talking about this man you had fallen in love with. Now, well, now I'm debating one of the most brilliant minds in academia. And he is this man's dad."

"Dad, I'm so sorry," Kate said, worried this would cause them to dislike Nathan.

Warren shrugged without a trace of concern. "Kate, I'll be honest with you. I don't understand it myself, but what I'm sure of is that this is a situation God has put all of us in. And I don't just mean us—I also mean the Berkleys and everyone who will be listening. Our job is to trust and obey God and do whatever he asks. I'm ready to do that. Okay?"

"Please don't think poorly of Nathan. He and his dad don't really see eye to eye, and I know this will probably be really hard on him."

"Of course not, honey," answered Rachel.

"But what's going to happen now?" Kate asked.

Warren didn't have to think about his answer. "I'm going to share God's truth with whoever will listen. I don't see this as a fight. I see it as an opportunity to let God use me to show his love to the world."

Rachel walked to Kate and hugged her. Kate was shaken and confused. She wanted to call Nathan, but first she needed time to think. The world was spinning around her, and she wondered how he would feel about her once he found out about this. The ringing of her phone startled her. She looked at the caller ID and her heart sank. It was Nathan.

Chapter 22

Ivy Java was Nathan's favorite coffee shop in New Haven. It was located right across from the Yale campus, and he had spent countless hours there reading and hanging out with friends. Despite all the student activity at nearby tables, he felt it was less busy than at home, and he preferred to be there anyway. During his time in Charleston, he had told Kate more than once that if she came to visit him, he'd have to take her there.

When Kate didn't answer the phone, he figured she must be busy. His friend Jake would be there at any moment, so he decided to try her again later. Nathan thought about how much he couldn't wait to see her again—he had fallen more in love with her every day they were apart. The loneliness he felt being away from her had been an ever-present companion. Ironically, however, it had also become a friend, a teacher, and a reminder that what he was feeling was beautiful, powerful, and real. This realization of the true meaning of love was transforming him from the inside out, and the unexpected wisdom was helping him gain new insights and perspective on life.

Nathan snapped out of it when he saw Jake come through the door; he had been looking forward to catching his friend up on the Charleston trip. Jake was a low-maintenance kind of friend and a good listener. He and Nathan could easily talk for hours and lose track of time.

They had talked a while, and Nathan was well into his third cup of coffee and second piece of tiramisu, when his cell phone went off. He searched for it frantically, hoping it was Kate, but the caller ID revealed otherwise. Disappointed that it wasn't her, he looked over at his friend and signaled with his hand for him to hang on a minute because he had to take the call.

"Hi, Mom. What's up?"

Sandra sounded out of breath and excited. "Nathan, can you come home?"

"Why? What's going on?"

"Have you watched TV?"

"No. I'm at a coffee shop…"

"Come home as soon as you can, please. We'd like you to be here."

"I'll try," Nathan said and hung up.

"What was that, man?" Jake asked as Nathan threw his phone on the table.

"John must be up to something he's happy with, and my poor mother is trying to make a big deal about it."

"Did she tell you what it was about? Are you sure it's not some kind of emergency? It sounded kind of serious."

Nathan picked up the bill from the table and got his wallet out. "No, no emergency. She would've told me first thing. I could tell from her voice they're excited about something."

"Do you think it's related to that debate?" Jake asked.

Nathan smiled and nodded. "I can pretty much guarantee that. John is in his element, and he's thoroughly enjoying basking in his glory. Let me just say that he is definitely enjoying the attention."

"Don't be so hard on him, man," Jake said, tapping Nathan on the arm. "You're going to have to try to meet him halfway somehow. Go see what they want. We'll meet up again soon."

"Ugh," Nathan responded, both kidding and being serious. "Okay, I've got lots more to tell you, so let's talk soon."

"About that southern belle you mentioned when you called me from Charleston?"

"Oh yeah!" Nathan responded with a big grin on his face.

"That sounds good. I can't wait to hear all about her."

"I appreciate you always being there for me," Nathan said. "See you soon."

"Be nice when you get home," Jake responded, smiling. "Talk to you soon."

"Ugh," Nathan said, and they both laughed.

The coffee shop was close to Nathan's house, and he made it home within a few minutes. As he unlocked the front door, the first thing he noticed was that the TV was blaring, which was very unusual. John was very sensitive to loud noises and didn't like it when the TV went above a certain volume level. Nathan followed the sound and came into the main living room of the house, a large party-hall-like room with sixteen-foot ceilings decorated with very expensive taste. He picked up the scent of scotch, which had been prohibited by John's doctor. But when something good happened, John ignored the orders.

"Wow. This is big," Nathan exclaimed as both John and Sandra turned around and pointed at the TV, which at the time was playing commercials. Now Nathan was even more annoyed about having to leave the coffee shop. "Okay, so, you tell me to come home because something big is happening, and I see you're watching diaper commercials."

They were both in a good mood, somewhat aided by the scotch, and they started laughing.

"Wait…wait," Sandra said.

"What is it? Just tell me!"

The announcer came back on, but it was just to tell the viewers that they would be back on the air in less than one minute. Sandra knew that would be too long to wait, so she broke the news to Nathan. "You dad's challenge to a debate has been accepted."

Nathan looked over at his dad, who had a notable look of excitement and satisfaction on his face. He didn't want to be rude, so he offered half-hearted congratulations. John nodded and quickly directed his attention back to the television as the announcer came back on.

Oh well, Nathan thought to himself. *So be it. Kate and I already decided that what he does for a living will not affect our relationship or our plans.* With that, he turned his attention to the TV and resolved to try to make an effort to be nice about it. He knew that was what Kate would want him to do.

The unexpected words flashing at the bottom of the screen to announce the breaking news popped from the screen and captured Nathan's attention instantly. "Breaking news: Dr. Warren Johnson accepts debate challenge by Dr. John Berkley." Nathan knew exactly who Warren Johnson was. *Why in the world is Kate's dad agreeing to the debate my father challenged James Robertson to?* Nathan asked himself in the surreal moment.

"Even better!" exclaimed John, excited. "I've wanted to debate him for a very long time. This just keeps getting better and better."

Nathan didn't know what to think as the reality of the moment sank in. "I thought you were going to debate a Dr. Robertson. What happened?" Nathan asked, playing dumb.

Sandra explained that John had been contacted by someone in Dr. Robertson's staff that day to present the possibility of debating Warren Johnson instead of James Robertson—something related to Dr. Robertson's health.

Nathan thought about the strange turn of events as the news program went through Warren's résumé in order to build up excitement for the debate.

"Dr. Warren Johnson's name was well known in many American households in the eighties," the man being interviewed explained. Nathan tuned in, his curiosity piqued to hear more about Kate's dad. "Through his books, speeches, and interviews on every media outlet, Dr. Johnson spoke the language of both the intellectual and the common person to communicate a message many in those times thought had run its course and was no longer relevant in the modern world." He paused, and the commentator waited for him to finish his point. "He was able to convince many not only that God created everything we see, including us, but that He is alive today and wants to be involved with us personally."

John looked at Sandra; his demeanor conveyed a passion that showed he couldn't wait for the day of the debate. Nathan recognized the look in his father's face and thought with an ironic sense of pleasure, *Yeah, just wait. If I have my way, you and he will be related one of these days.*

Chapter 23

ANOTHER COMMENTATOR HAD joined the news panel during the same program to inform the public about who Dr. John Berkley was. She spoke loudly and confidently. "There is nobody in the world who can match 'the Missing Link.' Come on! This guy in South Carolina may want to call in sick the day of the debate and save some face."

Kate and Warren were in their family room watching the same interview. It brought back similar memories from years ago, when Warren had been in the spotlight. She knew comments like that were part of it, but it was still annoying.

Warren looked at her. "I guess your future father-in-law and I won't get off to a good start. Will we?"

Kate laughed and slapped his knee. After such an unexpected turn of events, she really appreciated this kind of reaction from him. She decided to follow Warren's lead, to refuse to take it all too seriously and go with the flow.

The station began to play a collage of muted short clips of Dr. Berkley from previous interviews as his accomplishments were listed. She noticed he and Nathan had some of the same mannerisms, but they didn't look much alike. Dr. Berkley seemed a little taller and had a slightly lighter complexion. He had thinning light brown hair and an intentional look of determination in his pale green eyes.

Her cell phone seemed to erupt as a call came in and interrupted her thoughts. Warren noticed that Kate was looking at the caller ID. He figured it was Nathan trying to reach her. The story was on a prominent cable news channel; Nathan had to know.

Kate looked at her dad to see if he'd noticed who was calling. Warren was looking at her with a subtle smile—he knew who it was. Kate clicked the button to answer the call as she walked out of the room to talk.

"Hey, Nathan," she answered with a little angst, wondering what the first thing he'd say might be.

"Kate, hi! I'm so glad I got you," he said, sounding like his usual self.

"I'm so glad to be talking to you too. I wish you could be here right now," Kate said, realizing how much she needed him in her life.

"Yeah. Me too. So you've heard, huh?"

"I sure have."

"So I guess we are bitter enemies now, huh?" Nathan asked jokingly.

"Not necessarily—maybe more like Romeo and Juliet. When are you coming to rescue me, my Romeo?"

"I wish I was there right now. Man, I've missed you."

"I have too. Isn't this crazy?" Kate said as she walked back in the family room.

Nathan was watching the same channel. The pictures of their dads were side by side, and under each picture was information about where they lived and which schools they attended.

"You could say that. Mind boggling...Surely this is some kind of sick dream. I guess your dad must be furious that you're madly in love with me," Nathan said, recognizing Warren from the day he met Kate at Nawlin's.

"He's not. He has actually been very understanding."

Nathan was glad to hear that. "Really? I figured once he found out who my dad was, he might be ticked. They're not exactly on the same page about things, you know?" He paused as he looked over at his parents, making sure they couldn't hear him. "And now, they're debating each other? Man, this is just so wild. I feel like we are stuck in a movie or something."

"This is beyond insane, Nathan," she exclaimed. "I was with my dad when Dr. Robertson called him to see if he would do the debate. My dad knew about you, but he didn't know you were John Berkley's son until after he accepted the offer and got off the call. I didn't think he would be mad, but in a crazy circumstance like this, who knows how someone might react."

"Well, I'm very glad to hear that. It's going to get interesting over the next few days, though, and I don't want it to affect us," Nathan said.

Kate paced between the hall and her dad's study while they talked. She was playing the next few days and weeks in her mind and feeling a sense of irritation growing within. She wanted her relationship with Nathan to develop more conventionally. But as Nathan said, this would indeed make things interesting for them.

A photograph in Warren's study caught her attention. It was a picture of him in Africa shaking the hand of another man. The background revealed a congregation that had met to hear him preach. In the picture next to it, Warren and Rachel were handing out medical supplies to a woman.

Kate then glanced at a large painting depicting Jesus, who was lifting his hands over a basket of loaves and a basket of fish. He was praying to multiply the food so five thousand people who had come to hear him preach could eat. Under the picture, a small plaque read, "His commission. My Purpose." Kate was reminded of Warren's commitment to the great commission, in which Jesus had told his followers to go to the entire world and share his love with others, no matter the cost to themselves. She directed her gaze to her favorite part of the painting: the face of Jesus. The artist had done a remarkable job of reflecting a deep sense of love in his eyes. Kate believed the love depicted in the painting was real because she had experienced it, and thinking about that allowed her to let go of her irritation.

She took a deep breath and said, "There is more than meets the eye here, Nathan. We don't see it now, but I believe there is a reason for all this."

"I don't understand, Kate. What do you mean?"

"My dad wants to do this debate because he wants to share the love he feels from God with others. Our fathers' debate in front of a bunch of people is unexpected, and things may get interesting at times, but it'll all be worth it."

"Well, that sure isn't how my dad looks at this debate, Kate. He just wants to show the world he is right. And please don't take this personally, but I think it would bring him great pleasure to humiliate your dad in the process. He wants to win! He really isn't a bad person. He just looks at things from a completely different vantage point."

"I understand, Nathan."

"You do?"

"I do." She was walking through the foyer when she heard a barrage of small knocks on the front door. She knew what this meant: Edee and the boys were here. Joshua and Caleb would be excited to see everyone, and carrying out a conversation would be impossible.

Nathan heard the knocking through the phone. "What was that?" he asked. "Did a car run through your house?"

Kate laughed. "That means I need to get off the phone. The boys are here."

"Oh boy," Nathan exclaimed, pretending to be concerned for Kate. "It's about to be on like Donkey Kong, huh?"

"You know it. They keep getting bigger, though, and they are starting to win for real." Kate laughed.

"Well, play dirty if you need to."

"I don't need to do that yet. I can still take them," she said as she opened the door and bent down to kiss their heads.

"They're lucky to have an aunt who likes to have fun with them."

"I'm blessed to have them," Kate said as she hugged Edee.

"I better let you go so you can get beat up."

"Hey! Whose side are you on, anyway?" Kate asked. "I could probably take you too, so watch it!"

"You probably could. I will watch it."

The boys were calling for her to come to the den. It was time to play.

"Before you go, Nathan," she said more seriously, "do your parents know?"

"No, but they are around here somewhere if you want to introduce yourself and tell them. You would be much more gracious about it than me."

"I think I'll let you take care of that. I do want to meet your parents, though."

"You do?" Nathan asked, genuinely surprised.

"Of course I do."

"Then don't worry. You will the day of the debate."

As soon as they hung up, Nathan went back to the living room, where John and Sandra were. Something on the news telecast seemed to pique John's curiosity, so he went to his computer and began to try to look it up. Right away, it was obvious by the look on his face that the computer was irritating him. Nathan took over the keyboard, and within seconds he returned the search results his father was looking for.

John never could have expected what he saw. There were thousands of returns for the search on Warren Johnson. He browsed through the findings for a few minutes as he sized up the competition. "Hmm, this is going to be harder than I thought," he said as he looked up at Nathan and Sandra.

Chapter 24

THE DATE AND location of the debate were set within two days of the announcements on the news. There was widespread interest in the debate, so some of the major networks had committed to provide updates on the developments leading up to it. Relativist and humanist ideas were deeply ingrained into the fabric of Western society, and many people had stopped looking for answers from traditional religion and were instead looking to popular, postmodern thinkers. This opened the door for people like John to become more than philosophical thinkers. They were life gurus who offered relief through their answers to key existential questions, and their explanations were not as binding as the strings people felt were attached to a religious life.

It wasn't often two men like Dr. Berkley and Dr. Johnson agreed to debate each other, so when the news broke, powerful individuals with agendas had committed serious money to make sure the debate got as much coverage as possible. Money was no object.

The end of May was nearing, and July 29 was the official date Dr. Berkley and Dr. Johnson would travel to Salt Lake City and give the world a once-in-a-lifetime chance to hear a debate that had started more than two thousand years ago. The Salt Lake Convention Center was the chosen venue. It could hold up to two thousand people, and TV commentators predicted the place would be full, but the real money that night would be in advertising.

John and Warren got to work right away. Their wives and families had given the go-ahead to bury themselves in their work, and they were wasting no time. The church staff took on some of Warren's responsibilities so he could focus on the debate, and Yale had given John all the time and resources necessary to prepare. It didn't get any better than this for a university. They couldn't buy this kind of exposure, and the president of the university himself had told John he would bring him meals at home if that's what he needed.

Each of them worked an average of eight hours a day. John did research for about four hours a day, formulated answers to every possible question for another two hours, and spent the rest of the time rehearsing in front of a mirror, Sandra, or colleagues. His discipline and tenacity were equal to none, his attention to detail impeccable. He would be ready.

Warren spent a few hours a day doing research and practicing delivery. Most of his time, however, he spent in prayer. He wanted to be invisible during the debate so he could allow God to show Himself through him.

Kate and Nathan talked every day. They didn't know what to expect in the days leading to the debate or in the aftermath that would ensue, but in a strange and unexpected way, this was bringing them even closer together. Many so-called experts on television were saying things about her dad that were untrue, trying desperately to dwarf his persona as compared to John's. Although she never mentioned it, Nathan knew this hurt her. He appreciated how Kate was handling things. She wasn't defensive—her main concern was for him and his family.

Through this, Kate learned something about Nathan she appreciated: he wasn't the kind of person who had to be everything to everybody. Despite the strong stances and depth of his dad's beliefs, Nathan didn't automatically sign up to them. He didn't seem to be the kind of person who was willing to change to fit the environment and people around him. He thought for himself. Unlike a lot of people she had met, Nathan wasn't dead set on coming to a discussion with his mind already made up, unwilling to listen. This gave her a lot of hope.

One afternoon, Nathan went out for a stroll to clear his head and think about what came next for him. His feelings for Kate were not going away, and he wanted to be with her and see where their budding relationship might go.

He was walking in front of the Yale campus, and he thought about how different the streets in New Haven looked from Charleston's. New Haven definitely had its own charm. The stone-walled buildings of Yale University were majestic and historic. It was easy to be captivated, set back in time by the beauty of the campus and its surroundings. He thought about the walls inside, the knowledge and advance in thought. The school had produced titans of human advancement who went on to change the world and affect every walk of life—from teachers to scientists and even presidents of the United States.

Nathan noticed a homeless man nearby. He was dirty from head to toe, and he had an empty expression on his face. His eyes, however, revealed much pain and struggle inside. As Nathan walked by the man, he caught a reflection of himself on a storefront window. Right away, he felt guilty. His clothes and shoes alone had to cost over three hundred bucks, and this man had barely anything to eat for the day. He also noticed how other people walked by the man, pretending he wasn't there, just as he had this and every other time in the past.

It had never bothered him before, but as he walked by the man that day, Nathan felt compelled to look at him and smile. The man smiled back with appreciation. He was holding a cardboard sign that read, "I need your help. God bless you." Nathan stopped and searched his pockets for something to offer him. Within seconds he produced a five-dollar bill and gave it to the man, who took the bill and murmured something with his eyes closed.

The man then looked up at Nathan and said, "Thank you, son, for helping an old man." Nathan nodded and started walking away from him. "Son," the old man called out. Nathan turned around to see what he wanted. "We are all in need." Nathan nodded with a forced smile and continued to walk away.

He noticed the man had emphasized the word "all"—at least it seemed like he had. The words replayed in his mind as he kept walking. Something about the way the man had said them made the point in his mind that indeed nobody had it all together. He realized the man was right. Nathan knew so many people who had perfect lives on the surface but were total wrecks inside. Seeing his reflection on another storefront window reminded him that this applied to him too, and he wondered how obvious it was to people around him. He was amazed at how many times he had recognized this but ignored it as if he were helpless to change it.

An Indian restaurant sign caught his attention, and the smell of curry coming out of the front door instantly awoke his hunger and a desire for Indian food.

He walked in to get a table, but as he waited he remembered it was John's favorite cuisine. Kate's words from their last night together came to his mind: "Tell your mom and dad you love them." He hadn't yet, nor was he really planning to, but he figured he could show them by taking dinner home. It was one way to comply with Kate's wishes, he figured.

He pulled out his cell phone and made a call. "Hi, Mom. Have you guys eaten yet?"

"Not yet. We were waiting on you to decide what to do. Your dad is taking a break tonight, so we're up for whatever."

"Okay, great!" Nathan replied. "Don't cook. I'm bringing Indian food."

He ordered some of their favorite dishes and left the restaurant. On his way home, he stopped where the homeless man was still sitting and gave him enough food for two meals. The man's face conveyed utter thankfulness.

The warm aromas drifting from the bags were a treat in themselves. It would no doubt be a great dinner. Nathan found himself actually looking forward to a night with his parents and a good meal.

He knew he had waited long enough to tell them, and he hoped the night would not turn into conflict because of the news. But it was time. He needed to tell them about Kate—everything about Kate.

Chapter 25

By the time Nathan got home, Sandra had already set the table. Within minutes, they were all sitting down, ready to dig in. This was something they hadn't done together in a while. It had been a long day for everyone, and there was a collective sigh of relief at the chance to sit down and take a breath. Nathan got the sense that his parents were excited about the evening.

"This is very good, Nathan." Sandra was the first to break the silence once plates were filled and they started eating. "And such a nice thing for you to do," she added before taking her next bite.

"It's no problem, Mom."

"Yes, Nathan, very nice," replied John. "Are we celebrating something?"

"No, not really. The last few days have been pretty busy. I just figured I'd make it easy on Mom tonight. Plus, I know you like Indian food." John and Sandra looked at each other, saying nothing but looking pleased.

"Very nice. You definitely get brownie points for this," John replied, smiling at Sandra. He knew she wanted harmony in the house, and this was an easy boost for her. "I needed the extra fuel for the last stretch. This guy in Charleston has no idea what's coming at him."

Sandra put her fork down and gave John a look, making it clear he wasn't to talk about the debate over dinner.

John understood what the look meant but ignored it. "He'll need counseling after we finish the debate." As he said this, he lifted his hands up toward Sandra. With a look of innocence, he said, "And I won't say anything else about it." Sandra rolled her eyes and smiled indulgently.

Nathan put his fork down and stared at his food for a moment. *Man! What a terrible night to do this*, he thought regrettably. *Just when we're all getting along so well…*

He considered waiting until the next day to tell them, but either way they were going to find out. Tonight was as good a time as any.

"There's something you both need to know about this debate," Nathan said, with his gaze fixed on his plate. "I shouldn't have waited so long to tell you this. But anyway, you need to know." John and Sandra stopped eating. Nathan took a deep breath and looked at them, feeling five years old all over again.

"When I went to Charleston, I met someone who...well, I took a real liking to, if you know what I mean." Sandra smiled. "She's a beautiful southern girl in every way, especially on the inside." The thought of Kate made him pause and smile.

He looked intently at Sandra. "Her way of looking at life blew me away. I have never met anyone like her. And, well, you could say we fell in love."

"That's great, Nathan. But why wouldn't you tell us about her before now? She sounds wonderful," Sandra asked.

"I wanted to tell you about her before now. But the first few days, I just didn't feel like talking about it, and then everything going on with the debate just complicated things."

As he listened to Nathan, John tilted his chair backward without realizing it—his mind was consumed with trying to figure out what Nathan was trying to say.

"I know we've all been thinking a lot about this debate, Nathan, but you could've still told us about something like this," Sandra said. John nodded, rocking his chair back and forth on its two back legs.

Nathan looked intently at her, wishing it were as simple as that. But it was time to tell them, and Sandra made it easier for him.

"What's her name?"

"Her name is Kate—Kate Johnson."

Sandra crinkled her forehead. John kept rocking.

"Kate *Johnson* who lives in *Charleston*." He looked over at John, who was staring at him with an intensifying look of suspicion on his face.

"Kate's dad is a Baptist pastor in Charleston." With an iron expression on his face, he delivered the killing blow: "Kate's dad is Dr. Warren Johnson, whom we'll all be meeting very soon!"

A very large thump broke the short silence that followed Nathan's revelation. Both Nathan and Sandra shot up from their chairs at the same time and rushed around the table to find John laid flat on the floor. In his attempt not to fall, he had grabbed on to the tablecloth and taken it with him to the floor, causing a big mess.

"John! Are you okay?" Sandra shouted as she and Nathan bent down to help him.

"I'm fine!" he yelled, too mad already to care whether or not he was hurt.

Within seconds, they had John back up and sitting on his chair again. There was an awkward silence for a minute that felt like an hour. Sandra was already a nervous wreck, and she busied herself cleaning up John's side of the table and the floor around him.

Sandra wasn't going to be the first to say anything, and she intended to appear busy for as long as it took for either John or Nathan to speak next. John skipped being embarrassed from falling; he was fuming.

The tension in the room could be cut with a knife. In a way Nathan felt bad that he was causing them additional stress, but at the same time, there was more at stake this time than just hurting their feelings or being an inconvenience. He wanted Kate to be a big part of his life, and he wasn't going to let John intimidate him and get in the way of their relationship.

He knew how uncomfortable the situation might be for John and Sandra, though, so he was the first to say something. "Are you okay, Dad?"

John just tapped the table with his fork as if trying to measure his reaction. He looked over at Sandra, but she avoided eye contact.

"Nathan..." John started speaking but stopped himself to gain control of a rush of emotions bubbling to the surface. "I'll be honest with you. This is not good."

"Do you think I did this on purpose?" Nathan asked in a defiant tone. "I know how crazy it all is, but I didn't do this!"

John shook his head from side to side. "That's not what I meant. I know you couldn't help that. It's just that—well, I'll just come out and say it—you know how I feel about these people. And now it sounds like they're sucking you in." His voice rose as the thought brought with it a new wave of anger from convictions deep within.

Nathan slammed his fists on the table and leaned toward John, his gaze fixed intently on him. "I am old enough to decide what I believe in. Don't worry about it!"

As Nathan's words hung in the air, John composed himself and started to say something, but Nathan beat him to it.

"I know how you feel about Christians. I know! I've heard it all my life!" Nathan's voice rose. "I'll be honest with you; I wasn't too crazy about them either. But meeting Kate has been so eye opening. She sees life like you and I can't."

Nathan paused for a moment to temper his anger, and he looked at Sandra. "This may sound really crazy—it sure does to me—but there's something about her that is so real. I don't believe as they do. I don't think I ever will. But, even if they're completely crazy and they imagine everything they believe, it sure beats my reality."

"Are you kidding me, Nathan? Are those nut jobs really converting you?" John said, clasping a napkin so hard his knuckles turned white.

John's stinging question caused instant anger and disdain in Nathan. Staring at John with anger in his eyes, Nathan asked, "What do you have against them, anyway? What have they ever done to you?"

John rose to his feet; he was furious. But then something happened that took Nathan by surprise. John looked at Sandra with a trace of fear in his face for a split second, but then he turned back to Nathan with pure anger in his eyes. Nathan looked at Sandra, wondering what had just happened and looking for an explanation. Sandra's eyes were sad, as if suffering from an old wound.

"What is it?" Nathan asked, but neither would answer.

Nathan was taken aback by and very curious about what he'd just witnessed, but it was obvious they didn't want to talk about it, so he didn't ask again. He realized that yelling would only make a bad situation worse, so he tried to collect himself.

John and Sandra didn't expect the poised look on Nathan's face as he spoke.

"No! She didn't do anything to me. She didn't try to push anything on me. It's who she is. I never expected to meet someone like her." Nathan felt a rush of emotion from deep within. A chill came over his entire body, and he felt overcome by a kind of emotion that made him want to cry. "She is so alive!"

Sandra was listening to him intently.

"Regardless of what happens on July twenty-ninth and the weeks and months after that," Nathan said, "I would never do anything to purposefully hurt you. You're my parents, and I do love you. And that will never change."

Nathan felt Sandra's hand grip his tightly. She was obviously touched by his conviction; her whole countenance had changed.

"We love you too, Nathan," she said. "We do."

"I want you both to do something for me," Nathan said.

"What's that, Nathan?" she asked.

"Will you meet Kate the day of the debate and really give her a chance?"

"Yes, of course we will!" Sandra said as she looked to John for agreement. But John didn't nod or say anything in response. He just glared at Nathan with a deep-seated look of disappointment and anger on his face.

Chapter 26

THERE HAD BEEN no news from Austin for almost three weeks. That was unusual; ever since he left, the Johnsons had been able to talk to him at least once a week. When he wasn't going to be able to talk to them for a while, Austin would let Warren and Rachel know in advance so they wouldn't worry. The last time they talked had been on July 4.

Despite having been so far away from home, Austin told them it had been the most fulfilling Independence Day ever. His perspective on what the day meant was so much richer while defending the very freedom it represented. Austin's absence had been hard on the family, but he sounded happy and seemed to be doing well. Seeing how he was growing through the experience gave them peace and renewed their belief he was where he needed to be. But they couldn't wait to see him, and they yearned for the day of his return.

The American flag displayed at the entrance of the Salt Lake Convention Center in Salt Lake City brought out the anxiety in Warren's stomach as he recalled his last conversation with Austin. Twenty-four days had passed since their last call, and Warren missed talking to his best friend. The flag meant more now because it represented in a very vivid way the sacrifice so many had given to protect his right to even come to this debate. He said a quick prayer asking for Austin's safety and for his own ability to focus on the debate.

Rachel had a strong grip on his hand and a ready smile for encouragement every time he looked at her. Kate and Edee were walking behind them, talking and catching up on the last couple of weeks. Joshua and Caleb had stayed at home with their dad.

The debate was set to start in an hour.

They were led to the green room where they would wait until it was time to go on stage. Warren felt unusually calm about the debate, although the knots in everyone's stomachs tightened as the door to their room closed. At Warren's request, both men had agreed they wouldn't give any interviews before the debate. They wanted to avoid swaying any opinions and to minimize the material the media would have to comment on and twist before the debate even started.

Rachel looked over at Kate and Edee, whose chatter had completely stopped. She knew they had not run out of things to talk about because that never happened; they were nervous and worried about their daddy.

"So, do you want us to go over your study sheet with you?" Rachel asked Warren jokingly. They laughed, remembering their elementary- and middle-school days.

"We're very proud of you, honey. Are you ready?" said Rachel.

"Yes, I'm ready," Warren confidently replied.

Kate couldn't help but admire him. In less than an hour, he would face a giant in academia, a world-renowned expert in his field. He would also be battling the thoughts and feelings of the estimated millions of people who would be watching. Many wanted him to succeed, but many more wanted him to look like a fool in comparison to John.

Over the next days, the so-called experts would break down their arguments and write articles to explain what they were *really* saying. For some, their goal would be to craftily turn any one of the things Warren said into a badge of shame for him, hoping, in the process, to establish themselves further and to be invited to offer more of their opinions. Warren knew this. He had taken a lot of criticism before, and agreeing to participate in this debate would bring all of that back.

Warren had been watching Edee's and Kate's expressions. He knew they were nervous and concerned for him. As he made eye contact with them to draw their attention, he said, "If one person hears God through me tonight, this will all be worth it. That's what tonight is all about. It's not about me, okay?"

Edee and Kate nodded and smiled. Kate's cell phone went off with a Euro dance beat. Warren smirked and shook his head.

She returned the look and said, "Excuse me, Mr. Born in the USA."

Edee and Rachel looked at each other, wondering what that meant. Warren laughed and didn't offer an explanation.

"Hello," Kate answered while the attention of everyone in the room was directed toward her. A moment later, someone knocked on the door, and Warren went to open it. His face lit up as he saw Dr. James Robertson enter the room.

"Nathan, is that you?" Kate said over the new commotion.

"Yes!" came Nathan's excited response. "It's so good to hear you. Where are you?"

"We're at the convention center in a green room. Where are you? I can't wait to see you." As she said this, Warren embraced his longtime friend, neither one saying anything so as not to interrupt Kate's conversation.

"Me too!" exclaimed Nathan. "Sorry it didn't work out to see you before the debate, but we barely made it here with the traffic."

Kate smiled. "It's okay. I will see you afterward. This is crazy. Isn't it?"

"Bizarro world, more like," he responded.

When she hung up the phone, she could tell everybody in the room was pretending not to listen to her conversation. But they were not convincing.

Rachel looked at her and asked, "How's Nathan?"

"He sounded okay, but it was hard to tell because there was so much background noise where he was. It sounded like they were walking in the hall."

Dr. Robertson directed his attention toward Kate and gave her a reassuring look. "Sweet child," he said to her. "Your dad has told me about Dr. Berkley's son and you. I'm sorry to have put you in this situation. But you know this is important, and there's no one else I could've asked to do this but your old man."

"Hey, old fogey! Who are you calling old?" Warren exclaimed.

"You, old man! Who else?" Dr. Robertson responded as everyone laughed.

"Anyway," Dr. Robertson continued, "before I was interrupted, I was saying I know this has to be so hard, but if anyone can handle it, it is you. Things don't always work out in ways we understand at the time, but that doesn't mean something really good won't come out of it. I'm so proud of all of you. And don't worry about this guy," he said as he put his arm around Warren. "He knows how to take care of himself. And he won't be alone."

Warren patted his friend on the back, appreciating the vote of confidence and encouragement.

"Thank you, brother, for doing this," said Dr. Robertson. "I know this is not easy or comfortable for any of you. But thank you from the bottom of my heart. I love you. May I pray for you?" As he said this, they all bowed their heads, and they prayed for the next few minutes.

The knock on the door sounded like a sledgehammer trying to beat it down. They all knew it was time and directed their gaze at Warren. He was ready.

Chapter 27

"WE'RE READY FOR you, Dr. Berkley," said a stout voice as the door opened not far from where the Johnsons were. Nathan felt his stomach drop—the whole scene was somewhat overwhelming. But more than anything, he was anxious to see Kate in just a few moments. He needed to see her more than he needed air to breathe.

"This way, Dr. Berkley." The man beckoned to John, Sandra, and Nathan respectfully. They walked out of the room and followed the suited security guard, who had an impressive athletic build, through a set of halls. Within moments, they entered a massive room with stadium seating on one side and a theater-like drop on the other side. On the stage, two lecterns had been set up so the debaters could stand facing each other at a forty-five-degree angle and see both each other and the crowd. Fifteen feet in front of the lecterns was a desk for the moderator.

The crowd noticed right away when the famed Dr. Berkley entered the room; the man so many of them had read about and seen on television was right there in front of them. Most of the crowd suddenly rose to their feet in unison, breaking into an energetic applause to welcome him. A few people sitting in the front row greeted him and exchanged a few words. He was then led to his lectern, where he busied himself arranging his papers. Sandra and Nathan were taken to their reserved seats in the front row.

As the applause for John subsided, the crowd almost unanimously turned their eyes to another door in the cavernous room, through which Dr. Johnson was coming. Another big applause ensued as the momentum and magnitude of the event suddenly climbed to a whole new level. The air was charged with almost palpable excitement. Audiences everywhere couldn't wait to hear the two renowned intellectuals debate.

The flashes from the media's cameras rapidly fired at Warren, as if not to miss a millisecond of his entrance, and they lit up the room like the grand finale of a Fourth of July fireworks show.

Kate felt overwhelmed by the magnitude of the moment. She had known it would be a big deal, but being there had an incredible feel to it. She was amazed by both her dad and Dr. Berkley for willingly putting themselves in a situation like this.

A venue employee led Kate, Edee and Rachel through the crowd to their seats.

Nathan tried to get a peek at Kate, but with so many people standing, he could only see Warren because of his height. Kate also tried to spot Nathan but wasn't able to with all the commotion. She, Rachel, and Edee were shown their seats, and Warren was led to the lectern. As Kate watched him walk up the steps, in her mind he might as well have been climbing Mount Everest.

Nathan followed Warren to the lectern with his eyes, and right away he picked up on some of the similarities between the pastor and Kate. *Man, he looks so much like her!* he thought. They had the same hair and eye color and even similar facial features.

Warren laid a couple of sheets of paper on the lectern and walked over to greet John. As the two men walked toward each other, a sea of cameras followed their steps.

"Thank you for coming, Dr. Berkley," Warren said, extending his hand.

"Thank you for being here tonight, Dr. Johnson. I look forward to our discussion," John replied.

The two then walked back to their lecterns, and Warren arranged his papers as he took a sip of water. The commotion in the front row calmed down as people settled in their seats, anxious for the debate to begin.

Nathan looked over to his right, knowing Kate and her family would be sitting in the same row. As soon as he poked his head forward, he saw Kate doing the same.

Seeing her again felt so good. She looked beautiful, and it was all he could do to stay in his seat and not go to her. The debate was about to start, and he didn't want to get up and cause a distraction, so instead he just waved and smiled.

Kate waved back, smiling and thinking he was even handsomer than she remembered. At that moment, they fell in love with each other all over again.

As Nathan slipped back in his chair and looked toward the stage, he noticed that Warren was looking at him and smiling. He suddenly felt a lump in his throat and smiled back nervously. Warren nodded his head at him, looked over to Kate, and put on his glasses. There was something about Warren's smile that reminded Nathan of Kate. It wasn't really the smile but what came through the smile. There it was—that same sense of peace and joy.

People were sifting in their seats, waiting for the moderator to turn on his microphone and start the debate. Within moments, the moderator signaled the producer that he was ready to begin.

"Ladies and gentlemen," said a stern voice that commanded respect, "good evening. My name is Chris Turner, and I'm from Channel Twelve News in Salt Lake City. I'll be your moderator this evening. It is truly a privilege to welcome you tonight to what will no doubt be a powerful debate between these two titans of thought and knowledge."

Warren looked over at Rachel and smiled at her with a look that conveyed, *Oh boy! Here we go!*

"It's not often," the moderator continued, "that two experts of such caliber in their respective fields are in the same room to debate and share with us their passions and beliefs. Ladies and gentlemen, you are in for a treat, as I have no doubt tonight will be a history-making event. Dr. Johnson, Dr. Berkley, welcome to Salt Lake City. We are honored, and we thank you for being here tonight." The crowd came to their feet and clapped until the moderator waved his hands down, asking them to sit.

"Before we begin the debate, I would like to acknowledge Dr. James Robertson, who has been able to attend." There was no need to explain further why he was being honored in this way. Most people knew the chain of events that had led to Dr. Johnson's presence at the lectern instead of Dr. Robertson's. The crowd stayed on their feet and clapped as they watched a lethargic Dr. Robertson get up slowly and turn around to acknowledge them.

The moderator took the next couple of minutes to highlight the accomplishments and credentials of each man. As soon as he was done, he raised his voice with a burst of enthusiasm. "Let's get started, gentlemen!"

Warren slowly took off his glasses and looked at the moderator. Kate, Edee, and Rachel nervously grabbed on to each other's hands and said a quick prayer to themselves.

John laid a piece of paper on the lectern and stood straight up as he looked at the moderator with stone-faced determination. He had been waiting a very long time for this moment.

Chapter 28

THE LIGHTS OVER the stage glared over John and Warren as the moderator got down to business. "The rules for the debate are simple, gentlemen. There is no time limit for your answers, but I do ask that you be concise so we can get to as many questions as possible. If you so choose, the first person will have a chance after the second person answers to offer additional thoughts. Only the first to answer a question will have a chance for rebuttal.

"The questions come from everyday people, like you and me." Chris said this while looking directly at the camera, wanting people to know he was talking to them. "We received hundreds of questions from people all over the world. The questions we'll be asking tonight are representative of what you wanted us to ask these gentlemen. They represent the areas of life you struggle to understand, the things for which you need answers. This is a philosophical debate in which these gentlemen will argue the existence, or nonexistence, of God and of ultimate truth. They will do so by providing answers to some of life's toughest questions. Their responses can contain logical conclusions, thoughts, feelings, research findings, evidence, et cetera. However they choose to answer is up to their discretion. Dr. Berkley will represent a worldview that seeks to disprove the existence of God and the notion of truth using a solely humanistic and scientific standpoint. Dr. Johnson will make a case for the existence of God and truth from a Christian worldview and will defend the theory of intelligent design.

"Please keep in mind that we have a limited amount of time and a lot of ground to cover. Dr. Johnson and Dr. Berkley are vastly knowledgeable in their fields and could undoubtedly speak in detail to support their views, but I will reiterate the need for them to formulate their answers in a concise manner. There are a number of books that can be purchased to get into the minutest detail to try to support each side, but for the purpose of this debate, we want to know how they each reached their beliefs and how they support their very different worldviews."

Kate felt her heart drop again as the moderator said, "Gentlemen, are you ready?" She could see from the corner of her eye that Nathan had leaned forward slightly to check on her. She smiled at him, letting him know she was fine. Seeing her dad and Nathan's dad on stage, about to debate each other, seemed like such a bizarre dream.

She had to admit Dr. Berkley had an impressive persona. He had a polished and distinguished look that conveyed knowledge and wisdom. It was as if he had been groomed to be the very representation of Ivy League academia. Kate could match some of his features to Nathan's, but it was his mom that Nathan looked like the most. He had her olive complexion and high cheekbones. John had an intense and focused look in his eyes. He appeared to be the kind of person who might know what you're thinking before you do.

"Yes, sir," replied Warren.

"Certainly," agreed John.

"Very well, gentlemen," said the moderator, ready to begin with the question that would start the debate at the crux of their opposite worldviews. If anything would jump-start the audience's emotions, this would be it. "Let's get started then. At the center of your views and beliefs are two key questions. The first one is whether God exists. The second, why we exist. So the question is, were we created by an intelligent designer with a purpose, or are we here by mere chance? Are we just the result of random, unguided evolutionary events that ultimately resulted in the human race? Dr. Berkley, the question goes to you first."

John nodded at the moderator in acknowledgment. He had his game face on; he was in the zone. Nathan had seen this look many times before, and he knew what it meant. John was focused, ready, and confident. He didn't lose when he was in the zone.

"Is there a God, Dr. Berkley?" Chris asked again, as if to stress the importance of the question.

John straightened up and took a deep breath before he answered. "First, I want to thank you for having me here and allowing us to have this debate.

And thank you, Dr. Johnson, for accepting the debate." Warren nodded as John started to speak again.

"God does not exist," came his emphatic response, with a conviction that came from deep within. The crowd took a collective breath, and the impact of what he said hit Kate like a ton of bricks. She knew this was what he believed. But God was the most genuine person in her life, and hearing someone deny His existence so blatantly had an impact on her.

"I have seen no proof to the contrary," John continued. "I live in a material world, where I can see things, touch and smell them. That tells me, unequivocally, that they exist. I can interact with you, Chris, so I know you're here. You're physically and materially speaking to me, which tells me you and your voice are real. If I were to respond to you without really having heard your voice, I'm afraid it would mean I had gone mad. You can hear my voice and see my person, so there can be no doubt in your mind that I am here. There are people who unfortunately suffer from mental conditions who are convinced they can see, touch, and feel things that aren't real, but for the sake of this argument, I'm not referring to them. My point is directed to people of faith, without mental disabilities, who believe in the existence of the supernatural.

"I have not seen God. Have you?"

Chris squinted his eyes but offered no response.

"I've not heard him speak. You? My so-called faith can only go as far as what I can see, touch, hear, and smell. Even if I were blind, I could still believe a dog exists because I could touch and feel him, even though I wouldn't know what the dog looks like. I can't blindly put my faith and turn over my life to someone, or something, that I can't experience through the senses. I find that, and I say so respectfully," he said, looking toward Warren, "to be wishful thinking, paranoiac, and misguided. Life is hard, but I believe we have to face it head on with the tools we have. We can't wait on some mystic magic to fix our problems. We have to take control. If you were going to build a house, Chris, all you would have to do so is you, your tools, and the materials you purchased." John raised his voice slightly for effect. "No tools, no labor, no materials would appear on their own. In that case, you would not be able to build a house.

"Science has been able to explore and explain the natural processes that led to the beginning and development of life. Only the theory of evolution can account for the stages of development between species. And yes, there are gaps in knowledge, but that doesn't mean the evidence doesn't exist. I believe that in time—and using rational sense, science, new technology, and people who have committed themselves to discover the truth—we will gain ground in explaining away what others attribute to a god.

"The idea that an invisible god created everything you and I can see is naive. That is simply impossible. You can think it, hope it, and imagine it. You can even tell yourself you believe it. But at the end of the day, if we're honest with ourselves, the dots just don't connect. Because we can't see God. Because we can't hear God. Because we can't feel God."

John nodded at the moderator to indicate he was done as he picked up his glass of water to take a sip. Many in the crowd clapped enthusiastically, satisfied by what they'd just heard. Chris nodded, the impressed look on his face conveying that John had made a robust argument.

"The same question goes to you, Dr. Johnson."

Chapter 29

WARREN CALMLY LIFTED his gaze from the papers on the lectern and glanced at the crowd then Chris. "I too would like to thank those who put this event together and the audience both here and watching on TV, Chris." He looked at John as he laid his glasses on the lectern. "Dr. Berkley, it is truly an honor to be here discussing these issues with you." John stopped shuffling papers to acknowledge Warren. Knowing this event was also very trying for their families, Warren looked over at Nathan and Sandra to convey a silent thanks to them for being there. He then looked over at Rachel, Kate, and Edee, wanting them to know how much he appreciated their sacrifice and support over the last few weeks.

Warren was focused and on queue. "Chris, this is a question that, no matter who we are or where we're from, we inevitably all ask ourselves. It is also a question we all must have an answer for because there is no quieting the demanding voice inside each of us that is desperate for it. Throughout the centuries, thousands upon thousands of books have been written and many religions have been created to try to answer this question. Humankind, with all of our science, technological advances, and complex thought, has worked tirelessly to arrive to an acceptable answer. Our philosophers throughout the centuries have tried to explain away God using their intellect and rationale. Many scientists have worked tirelessly to explain the beginning and development of the world without a creator.

"But after thousands of years, Chris…" He paused as he looked at the moderator. "Here we are tonight, most people dissatisfied with all the answers we've come up with, hoping to hear something real that will quiet their spirit. That demanding voice in each of us knows that, somehow, there's a better answer. It beckons us to keep searching until it's satisfied. At the end of the day, Chris, nothing humankind has done to come up with an answer has worked. And do you know why that is? It's because the answer was not ours to find or invent. It has always been meant to be revealed and, consequently, to be accepted or rejected.

"I agree most people can't see God. But I believe we can see Him clearly through His creation. It's impossible to look at the way everything works in and around us and believe mere chance and coincidence brought it into being with such balance and precision. If you study and look at this honestly, the evidence is overwhelming that an intelligent designer had to be behind it. Just because we can't see Him, it doesn't mean He's not there. The Bible says God is spirit. He is not subject to the laws of time, space, and matter He Himself created. He can be invisible while at the same time existing. He's above it all and beyond it all. We want things to be explained and to be understandable at our level, but God can do whatever He wants because He created it all. He's in control. We want to think we are the ones in control, but nothing can be further from the truth. God is in control, but we don't like that. So we philosophize, write books, and create religions to suit our fancy. Or we deny Him altogether."

The moderator lifted his hand slightly and interrupted Warren. "You said there is overwhelming evidence that points to an intelligent designer. And by that you are implying, in opposition to what Dr. Berkley just argued, that there is evidence that a god, which we cannot see, hear, or touch, exists. Please explain and help us see God as you do."

Warren took a couple of steps back from the lectern. From the corner of his eye, he noticed John's focus fixed on him. "Certainly, Chris. Think about what it takes to support life in our planet. The location of the sun, and its distance from the Earth, is close enough to provide just the right amount of light and warmth so humans, animals, and plants can thrive and survive on Earth. Were it slightly closer, life couldn't be sustained on Earth due to what its heat would do to living organisms. Were it farther away, we would all freeze. Were it not for sunlight, plant forms would not be able to go through the photosynthesis process that keeps them alive. Were it not for plant forms creating our oxygen, you and I would not be able to breathe.

"Now, our planet has orbited around the sun for thousands of years and hasn't missed a bit. Incredibly enough, it hasn't gotten off course, which has meant the uninterrupted continuance of life on Earth. And it wouldn't take much for the continuance of life to be interrupted, because as you quickly find out, when you study the way things work, there is an extraordinary level of calibration in the delicate balance that must be kept for life to be possible on this planet. Another amazing example of this is the moon that orbits around the Earth. Our moon's gravitational forces help stabilize the Earth's rotation, tilt and climate so life can survive on the planet. Like the sun, Chris, our moon has continued to do the same thing for thousands of years, and life has thrived.

"And let's briefly mention gravity. How convenient is it that we have gravity to keep us firmly grounded on Earth? Notice we are not all floating around this room. Now that would be something, wouldn't it?" The crowd laughed at the thought, which gave Warren a chance to take a sip of water before continuing. "Because of gravity and its perfect calibration, not only are we grounded but we're also able to move around and do the things we do from day to day. And gravity hasn't missed a bit."

He waited a moment for the crowd to process the thought. "The oxygen levels, which support human and animal life, are also perfectly calibrated. A fractional variation in the oxygen levels, and life could no longer be supported. The oxygen levels, ladies and gentlemen, have not missed a bit. And what about water, which is absolutely essential to the sustainment of life for all living organisms? Just the fact that it exists, and in the abundance that it exists, is mind boggling. And when it needs to be distributed, we have rainfall. Don't want all that water to stay on the ground forever? No problem; it has a property whereby it can evaporate with the help of the sun. We can quickly see how water, the sun, our moon, and gravity work together to sustain life and the order of things we take for granted. And these are just a few of the things we depend on for life to survive.

"Like falling dominos, if you really pay attention to what is happening around you, you will quickly see that there is an established order and a set of must-have dependencies in creation for life to happen. Believing it all to be coincidental takes a lot more faith than it would to believe it just happened. Think about it like the components and dependencies at play in a musical orchestra. When an orchestra is playing, each instrument can't just do what it wants and expect a coherent melody as the result. There has to be a maestro guiding all the instruments. Then, and only then, the result can be a masterpiece.

"I will give you one more example and finish. Have you thought about how incredible it is for a new life to be conceived by the union of two people, and how incredible it is that a woman's body can nurture that new life until the child is born? And when it is time for the birth, her body will automatically start doing all the right things, right on cue, so the child can be born? Her body knows to dilate and push the baby out without her brain telling it what to do. I find that incredible. And I can't possibly fathom all these intricacies, this complex and ordered chain of events, to just happen by coincidence and continue to happen the same way over thousands of years. Wouldn't something in the process, in that complex order, change over time if it wasn't designed and meant to be as is?

"Natural selection can't explain this. The only explanation to life and what supports it is a loving, intelligent designer." Warren was getting increasingly animated and passionate in his argument as the audience tracked with him and hung on every word.

"Think about it. There is absolutely no way all of this is by coincidence. It's incomprehensible that everything developed unguided. And we've not even scratched the surface in the examples I've given. So while God has not chosen to be seen in person by you and me today, we can see Him clearly through His creation. His fingerprints are everywhere.

"You can take just about anything you see, using our scientific discoveries, and follow the thread to find the creator. Let's take the conception and birth example a little further and back it up with science. Think about how, once the baby is born, the new mother's body creates natural milk with the very best nutrients her baby needs. Her body only does this when she has a baby. Go further, even. As her child grows and needs to start eating the solid foods his body needs, he grows teeth. But these teeth are small enough to fit the size of his head at the time. As his head grows, his baby teeth automatically fall out so new, bigger teeth that will be more appropriate for his growing head just happen to come in. Can we really believe this is all coincidental? Does science not back me up on all of this? Through science, we can uncover evidence that leads us to a logical conclusion that there had to be an intelligent creator behind life.

"Let me also remind you that many of the explanations for the evolutionary development of life, previously espoused and counted as truth, have been disproved thanks to advancements in technology. Supermicroscopes today allow us to see inside a cell and discover very intricate and super advanced working and regenerating processes that can't be explained by mere chance. That is intelligent design, from a creator who made everything with a purpose. That is God. So no, today we may not be able to see Him, talk to Him in person, or hear Him audibly, but we can take an honest look around us and see Him, hear Him, and feel what He has created and how much He loves us. I challenge you, ladies and gentlemen, to follow the thread with an open mind and be willing to go wherever it may take you. As you see the puzzle come together, you will see that there is so much more than meets the eye. The intricacies and reality of a perfect design will astonish you. And then, if you allow yourself...you too will see God."

Warren concluded his argument, and the crowd sat motionless for a few seconds. Suddenly, almost on cue, most started to clap with increasing enthusiasm as the dots connected in their minds.

"Dr. Berkley, would you like to offer any comments following Dr. Johnson's before we move on to the next question?" said the moderator after a few seconds of clapping.

"Yes, I would," John answered right away, his elbows firmly planted on his lectern as he leaned forward in Warren's direction.

"Please proceed, Dr. Berkley."

"I have a question for Dr. Johnson, Chris. If I set it up quickly and he is willing to, can he use my rebuttal time to respond to it?"

The moderator waited to answer as he consulted with himself regarding protocol.

"Um, sure, Dr. Berkley. Go ahead. Dr. Johnson?"

Warren nodded in agreement, and John leaned forward again. "Those are certainly interesting observations, Dr. Johnson. But at best, I consider them to be an established order guided by the summation of millions of years of unguided evolutionary processes in which the stronger organisms have won over the weaker. Over time, they have fallen into place as you described today. Science backs you up in that what you're saying is scientifically accurate, but it can't prove that there's a creator behind any of it. We each, therefore, choose to believe whether there's a creator behind what we see or whether it's just the manifestation of millions of years' worth of random changes. If it were so obvious, Dr. Johnson, that there is a creator behind our physical world, why is it that so many around the world don't necessarily attribute the world around us to a god? Could wishful thinking not be the catalyst here?"

Taking a step from his lectern, Warren began to answer John's question. "It's because the world as a whole has adopted a naturalist mentality by which we want to explain things based on our intellect and what we want to be true. And the only evidence we're willing to trust is what we can see, touch, smell, or feel. This has led to a society who accepts what academia says and seldom questions things from God's perspective. Unfortunately, we're missing God in the process. We create a blindfold for our mind's eye by looking at life selfishly, and in the process, we miss the best life can offer.

"As far as unguided and coincidental processes, and voilà we have complex organisms, could a group of brainless scientists, who were given all the necessary materials, build a functioning NASA space shuttle over millions of years? No! Neither could unintelligent organisms organize themselves in a way to compose highly complex beings such as humans or animals. Only intelligent scientists could put together such a machine through creative and purposed processes. Whether you believe all this just happens by a series of astonishing coincidences, the odds of which defy all logic, or you believe they are a product of intelligent design, it still takes faith. But how much more faith does it take to believe such an intricate sequence of events is coincidental as opposed to guided by a creator? And how much faith does it take to believe that the initial matter that started it all wasn't created, that it magically appeared?

"Let me summarize. Evolution tries to explain all of life as a fluke and gives credit to an unguided natural selection. In Genesis, the Bible says God created the world and everything in it. I think this puts the two theories at odds. Could God have created some organisms with a design to adapt to its environment?

Sure! But the design we discover through science can't be explained by random natural selection."

John started to say something else as an increasingly enthused crowd clapped, but the moderator decided to move on. "Thank you both, gentlemen, for such insights. Dr. Johnson, the next question will go to you first, and then to Dr. Berkley."

As the moderator paused to let the room discharge, John decided it was time to take the gloves off and pull no punches.

Chapter 30

THE MODERATOR FELT the energy in the room after just one question and was ready to fire the next. "Dr. Johnson," he began, "in your response to the last question, you made a distinction between believing both in what we can see and what we can't see. Your position is not only that we can believe in something unseen, through faith, but that we can believe it so fervently as to give our life to it. Of course, I'm referring to your belief in God. Help us understand how this type of faith is possible and real for you."

Warren assumed his position behind the lectern, and as he did so, he glanced over at Sandra and Nathan. Sandra was looking at John, but Nathan was looking at him with intent and focus.

"Everyone has faith, Chris, whether they know it or not. As a society, we tend to talk about faith as if it only applies to religion, but in reality it applies to all of life. Let me give you a couple examples. Let's say you have the opportunity to go to the moon one day. You get into a space shuttle and right away are overwhelmed by all the buttons and computer systems that are going to get you to the moon. You have no idea how it all works but believe nonetheless it will get you to the moon and back. That's faith. Let's crank it up a notch," continued Warren. "Are you married, Chris?"

Chris nodded.

"Okay," Warren continued, smiling at him as a thank-you for humoring him. "When your wife looks at you and says, 'I love you,' do you believe she loves you?"

"Of course I do," Chris answered.

"Can you quantify that love in a material sense? Can you hold that love in your hands, see it, measure it, touch it, hear it?"

"Of course not," Chris said.

Warren pressed on. "But you just said that love is real. Can you or can you not prove to me she loves you?"

Chris thought for a moment, trying to figure out if this was a trick question before he answered. "I can't materially show you her love for me, but I know from her actions and her words that she does."

"Exactly!" Warren exclaimed. "Because of other material factors, like what you see, hear, and feel, you're able to believe in something unseen that in your innermost being feels more real than anything you can detect with your senses."

"I understand," Chris said with a smile.

"You see?" Warren said. "Faith is a real thing, and the objects of our faith can be as well. Faith allows us to take the leap to see and experience the reality of the unseen. We can't see, touch, or smell love and hate, but we all know just how real they are. We can't see data like songs and videos that come through the airwaves into electronic devices, but they are very much real when we receive them." He scanned the crowd before continuing. "The real question is: what do we put our faith on? God is one of the things we can choose to put our faith on, and we can only experience and get to know Him if we give Him a chance. He gives each of us that choice.

"And how is it possible and real for me? Simple, Chris. I've experienced it."

"What have you experienced, and how is your experience any more credible than any other person's?" Chris asked incredulously.

"Let me start by saying we are all born with a God-sized hole in our spirit that yearns to be filled." Warren looked at Chris as if talking only to him. "It's like an insatiable vacuum that, through the years, grows and becomes more and more unbearable. You have it, I have it, and everyone in the entire world has it. And we can no more turn it off than we can fly. But how we choose to go about filling it greatly influences how we experience life.

"We try to fill it with the things of this world: food, sex, material possessions, pride, good intentions, other people, millions of things. But because it is God sized, it can only be filled with God. And the more of the other things you put in it, the more desperate and hopeless you become. I, along with millions of other people throughout history, after fighting a losing battle and being exhausted, chose to give God a shot. And while life is not always a bed of roses, the desperation and hopelessness that used to cause me so much restlessness have lost their sting in my life.

"When you put your faith in God, your spiritual sight is awakened, and you can see Him through nature, other people, circumstances, et cetera. He interacts with you in a very personal way through a relationship that at times seems more real than any physical relationship you have. I have seen things happen in my life, and in the lives of others, that could only be explained by attributing them to God's intervention. But the most amazing thing I have ever seen is how He remade me from the inside out when I chose to follow Him—a work He continues every day.

"Our world today tells us that we must see to believe. But there are things you can't see until you have first believed. Jesus said, 'Come to me as a little child.' Why? Because a child doesn't have all the overly complicated preconceived notions we adults have as a filter between us and our ability to believe in something amazing. Children keep things simple, unlike us. So sometimes, as is the case with faith in God, you have to let go of things you believe to be true in order to give yourself a chance to believe in what really is true."

Warren nodded at Chris, signaling he was done, and the crowd began to clap. Kate looked behind her at the crowd and saw that numerous people were nodding enthusiastically at each other. She looked at her dad to give him a reaffirming smile, which he more than appreciated. She then turned toward Nathan, who noticed her and nodded. He was clapping with the crowd.

"Thank you, Dr. Johnson, for that response. Dr. Berkley, what are your thoughts on faith?" Chris asked without waiting for the applause to end.

Although frustrated under the surface, John looked calm. As an experienced debater, he knew it was essential to come across as likable. Fiery passion had to be used very strategically. "Dr. Johnson earlier said that for thousands of years we have created religions and philosophies to try to explain what we don't understand. I agree with him on that. And I think he would agree with me that many of them are based on emotion and manipulation. These philosophies have often been nothing more than ways to overpower people of less intellect and education for power, money, and fame. In other words, they were made up for the personal gain of the people promoting them.

"After thousands of years and probably as many religions and philosophies, what do their founders and followers have to show for it? I would say nothing tangible, really." John put significant emphasis on the word "nothing" and noticed that many in the crowd became more engaged, beckoning him to bring on the sting.

"Through the scientific method and common sense, however, we can actually prove tangible truths and realities that often correct previous errors in thought and beliefs that may have been accepted as fact for many years. So does faith exist? Sure, but it has to be based on something tangible! Otherwise we may very well be fooling ourselves and living in a world that is just not real. An intangible illusion is just that: an illusion. We can create a world we want to be real because it is easier to live in, because it is more tolerable than our actual lives. But in doing so we're really just living a lie, concocted either by ourselves or by someone else.

"Let me be very clear. No matter how wishful your thinking might be, there is no awakening yourself into an unproven dimension of your existence where you can see and experience things differently. No matter how badly you don't want to face reality, inventing a happy place with an imaginary friend is wishful thinking and deceitful. And promoting it is shameful."

Sting delivered.

Chapter 31

NATHAN FELT A knot in the pit of his stomach as he listened to his father's words. He knew this side of him too well—the side in which losing was not an option. He looked over at Kate, wondering if she might ever talk to him again. To his surprise, she was looking back at him—unaffected.

"Look, Chris," John continued with restraint. "I know life can be extremely tough. But here's the way I see it: our minds are capable of constructing new realities as a defense mechanism when life becomes unbearable. We don't know how this works, but we know it happens. In time, I believe we will be able to explain it. But we can't honestly, or wishfully, call this reality. And we certainly can't attribute it to a spiritual world where God lives. We can call it what it is. It's just something we do in our minds, and I would submit to you that putting our faith in an imaginary reality could be very dangerous to a person and those around that person. Our emotions can and will deceive us. If we go to our happy place enough, we will actually start to believe it's real." He nodded at Chris to indicate he was done, and a number of people got on their feet clapping, many of them laughing.

The crowd was enjoying the show and was obviously pleased with the answers coming from both John and Warren.

"Dr. Johnson, would you like to add something?" Chris asked, wondering how Warren would respond after the crowd-pleasing argument from John.

"Sure, Chris. I agree with Dr. Berkley that we've made amazing discoveries through science. And I certainly agree that scientific findings prove what is and isn't real in very tangible ways. But before the reality of something is proven, it is no less real. Let me explain. Living organic processes, such as the ones I mentioned earlier, are so complex that we sometimes have to go through years of research to figure out how they work. The underlying unequivocal truth of how it works still is what it is while we're trying to get to it. We follow the clues with a degree of faith, believing there's something there for us to discover. That undiscovered reality was as real before we knew what it was as when we knew.

"So to say God isn't real because we have not seen him is as invalid an assumption as saying a baby suddenly appears in the mother's womb. The big difference between these two examples is that the latter can be proven in a material sense, while the former is proven in a spiritual sense. Every single one of us can know that God is real. Jesus was very clear about this. In John 8:32, he said, 'Then you will know the truth, and the truth will set you free.' He asked that we exercise a little trust, a small portion of faith, to give ourselves a chance to believe in God. And when we do, we can see just how real God is."

Chris looked over at John as the crowd clapped, and noticed he was shaking his head. He then looked over at two of the debate sponsors standing to the side of the stage, who appeared very pleased with how it was going. Not wanting to lose momentum, Chris fired the next question.

"Dr. Berkley, the question of the existence of ultimate truth has been the subject of debates for centuries. Some adamantly believe there is such a thing as truth. And others, just as adamantly, say there isn't. What do you believe? Is there or isn't there an ultimate truth?"

John picked up a pen and held it up for everyone to see as he stepped away from his lectern. "What do you see here, Chris?"

Chris smiled and said, "Sure. I'll play again, gentlemen. Both of you have sure taken a liking to asking me questions to make your points."

John and Warren laughed, and the crowd joined.

"It's a pen, Dr. Berkley," Chris responded.

"Very well, Chris. And by the way, thank you for helping us out."

"It's no problem. I'm kind of enjoying it."

"Okay, good. What color is the pen?"

"It's blue."

"How did you arrive at that conclusion, Chris?"

"Very simple: it looks like a pen, and its color is blue."

"Are you sure?" John asked.

"I am."

"How did you come to those conclusions?"

"I was taught that it is a pen and that the color is blue."

"Very well. That's fair," John answered, nodding. "You were taught that this is a pen and that this is the color blue. Please humor me with the bad example, but you will get the point. What about if someone was taught that this is green and not blue? That would be true for that person regarding the color of this object, while your truth would still be that it is blue. Same object, two different truths. You see? Our upbringing, the culture we're raised in, what we're taught and what we experience, all factor in to construct our version of truth. So what may be true for me about an object or any other thing could very easily be different from your truth. If we're both being sincere about our individual beliefs, and especially when it comes to the belief in something we can't see, why would either of us need to claim we are more correct than the other?

"Here's the bottom line: the term 'ultimate truth' backs us into a corner and demands someone be right and everyone else be wrong. When, as you can see, there could be multiple equally credible truths about one thing. So having to choose one truth every time seems very closed minded to me, an impossibility if you will. In my opinion, pushing the belief of ultimate truth has been used by many throughout history to limit what a person can and can't believe—what they can and can't do or think. A religion, a regime, a government will manipulate people into thinking there can only be one way—their way. Requiring that there be a black and a white for everything, without allowing for the possibility of a gray in between, without allowing for a person's interpretation, is arrogant and closed minded."

Chris nodded at John and looked at Warren.

"Dr. Johnson. What say you on this subject?"

"You have been a great sport indeed, Chris, and we certainly appreciate it. I may not be done with you yet. Okay?"

Chris smiled and nodded.

"The object Dr. Berkley held up possesses very specific and absolute physical qualities. When you look at it, your brain interprets the image that comes through your eyes the exact same way mine or anybody else's would. The object is the same whether you, I, or someone in a remote jungle who's never seen a pen before looks at it. That's because the mechanisms you use to view and interpret images are the same as mine and the person's in the remote jungle. I know it's a pen. I also know it's blue. Chris, you do too because we grew up in the same culture and this is what we were taught. The person in the jungle has absolutely no idea it's a pen or that it's blue. He will interpret it as something different. But here's what can't be denied: the object of his interpretation is the exact same, with the exact same qualities, as the object of our interpretation—regardless of what he understands or calls it. That is an absolute truth none of us can deny."

Warren looked at John as he continued. "I agree with Dr. Berkley that the term 'absolute truth' has been abused my many, especially in religion. But that still doesn't negate the fact that things are what they are regardless of what we've been taught they are—regardless of what they seem to us or what we may want them to be."

Chris didn't seem completely satisfied with their answers, and he jumped in with a refining question. "There's something I'd like each of you to answer related to this same topic. Dr. Berkley, you started with the question on truth, so I will ask you first. Why is it or isn't it important that there be ultimate truth?"

"I don't think it is important," John answered without hesitation as he lifted up his pen. "Dr. Johnson's argument holds water from a physical standpoint. Of course we can't deny that the physical properties of this pen don't change based on how each of us sees it. But the truth we're really talking about here goes beyond the physical. We're talking about ultimate truth for things without physical matter. Our ideas, our beliefs, our emotions are invisible but are still very much real to us. It's in this realm, if we want to call it that, where each of our interpretations can be very different—and just as real to us regardless of the culture we grew up in.

"So we may hold on to very different truths when it comes to, for example, a belief in the existence of a god. And since we really can't prove this existence, how can any of us claim our view is the right one? We can simply choose to believe or not. So no, I don't really see how it is important since no two of us believe in the same things. I trust people to make their own decisions. And I'm not arrogant enough to think everyone should think or believe as I do."

Chris didn't try to hide how impressed he was by John's response. Judging by the size of the applause, the crowd was equally impressed.

"Dr. Johnson?" Chris asked.

Warren began his response without waiting for the applause to end. "If we each have free license to walk around and not only believe what we want but also determine what is right and wrong for us and others, based on what we think and believe, we are potentially getting into an area that has serious implications to our well-being and that of others. The truth of the matter is that as human beings we can be very selfish. We can construct a believable reality in our minds so the outcome of any situation is to our benefit.

"There has to be an ultimate truth to measure everything else against. Otherwise, no one can be held accountable for his or her actions. There has to be one set of laws and guidelines for all of us to follow so we don't selfishly choose what is right and what is wrong. That will get us in trouble sooner or later. History has proven over and over that some things are always right and other things are always wrong.

"For example, the hate of an entire race by Nazi Germany turned disastrous. That was wrong. We've seen the same results when something similar has taken place in other countries. In sharp contrast, we have seen where a culture that believes in equality for all people, as has been the case for the United States, has had very positive results. So we can, therefore, conclude that loving and respecting all people is good and right and that the opposite is wrong, even though this belief is not something we can quantify physically.

"Sure, we can each believe and do what we want to. But God is the ultimate truth, and being left to our own devices to define what He has created can get us in pretty big trouble. Even with the best intentions! Turn on the television to see what company executives do for money, what politicians do for power, what entertainers do for fame. Look and see what preachers who take their eyes off of God do to themselves and those around them. This is why it is so important that there be one ultimate truth for all of us to follow. There can only be one right way. Having more than one right way is a contradiction in itself anyway.

"Jesus spoke of one truth, and it was the truth that sets us free from all the conflicting ones out there. His truth can save us from the wasted time and pain we may experience as a consequence of the choices we make. If we're not careful, we build false kingdoms on foundations of sand, not of rock, and those kingdoms will inevitably crumble under our feet one day."

Chris smiled and nodded, satisfied with Warren's response.

Chapter 32

QUESTION AFTER QUESTION, the result of John's and Warren's responses was a palpable energy that permeated throughout the debate hall, television, radio, and the internet. After an hour and half, Chris unsuccessfully tried to hide a look of disappointment as he realized he needed to wrap up the debate.

"Gentlemen," he said, addressing Warren and John, "unfortunately for all of us, we must bring this debate to a close. We had additional questions we would've loved to get your thoughts on, but our time is almost over. I'd like to give you each the opportunity to present some final thoughts before we conclude the evening. There's no specific question to answer, just whatever you would like our audience to hear from you. Dr. Berkley, would you like to start?"

John nodded.

"Ladies and gentlemen in the audience and those of you watching through other media, Chris, Dr. Johnson, and I would like to thank you for your time tonight. I think we can all agree that there is a clear difference between what we feel, what we believe, and what we know to be fact. Yes, it's great fun to dream up something that may temporarily take us away from the reality we live in and turn it into something more pleasant in our minds. Our brains possess the incredible ability to build the appearance of reality out of something fictitious. So it is indeed tempting to live in that frame of mind. But is doing so responsible? No! As children it was okay. As adults who have spheres of influence that affect other people's lives, it is irresponsible and unacceptable. It will only lead to disappointment and pain. We must keep our feet planted in reality so we're not deceived.

"I have always used science and fact-based rationale in my research to ensure I arrive at realities that are quantifiable and qualitative. Yes, there's still much to discover and prove. But I believe that, given enough time, we will know and be able to explain a lot more. Until then, I won't live by assumptions based on a blind faith that makes me happy. Thank you, ladies and gentlemen, once again, for your time tonight."

"Thank you, Dr. Berkley. Dr. Johnson?"

"I too would like to thank all of you here and at home. Chris, what a great sport you've been. And Dr. Berkley, it has truly been an honor to discuss these important issues with you tonight." John nodded at Warren and offered a courteous smile.

"Dr. Berkley makes an excellent point. The proper and responsible use of science has led to amazing discoveries, and I believe he has been a great contributor to the advancement of knowledge. We've been able to learn the makeup of so many different types of organisms, and we know so much more about how things work. We have enormous amounts of information. But still to date, the theory of natural selection proposed by Darwin can't connect species to each other. Natural selection claims that because of the successful traits of stronger species, they remained in existence, and weaker species became extinct. Species evolved from one another and became stronger over time. But without a fossil record, it is nothing more than a theory that has to be proven. All the missing links have to be assumed to have existed because there's no fossil record to be found in order to prove it. The shame is how well known this is in the world of academia and that our schools and universities continue to teach assumptions as facts.

"Because of the technology available to us today, and the findings of many brilliant minds, we often arrive at what is called irreducible complexity. This means we are now able to study microorganisms using supermicroscopes and advanced scientific methods, whereby we discover a degree of complexity that could not have just happened or evolved from simpler organisms. If we dismiss our preconceived prejudices and give the discovery method an honest chance, we will see that believing complex organisms happened on their own is impossible. Our findings point us to an intricate, designed, and perfectly executed creation. That laptop in front of you, Chris. If we start to take it apart and begin to discover its complexity, we can only arrive at the conclusion that it was designed by an intelligent being with a purpose.

"God gave us a magnificent gift no scientific method or philosophy can explain: our consciousness. We have the ability to think, feel, and create. God created us in his image so we can do right by other people and his creation—but most importantly, so we can find him and have a relationship with him."

Warren paused and looked down briefly. He planted his hands firmly on the lectern and looked up at the crowd. Slowly raising his voice, he said, "Ladies and gentlemen, I didn't come here today to win a debate. I came here to tell you that God created me and you, and He loves us more than we could ever love ourselves. His creation is there so you can discover who He is and come to know him personally through a relationship with his son, Jesus Christ. But you have to take an honest look at Him before you can come to this conclusion. Do you want to get to know the real you? Then you have to get to know Him first. Thank you for your time tonight. It has been an honor to be here with you."

As he finished, most in the crowd stood up and exploded into a thunderous applause for Warren and John. Warren looked over at Rachel, who had tears in her eyes and was nodding at him. He knew the look, one of pride and confirmation of a job well done. Chris joined the crowd in their applause and rose to his feet.

After a minute or so, everyone sat down, and Chris leaned toward the microphone. "My goodness, Dr. Johnson, Dr. Berkley. What an incredible evening you have treated us to, gentlemen. I must admit that your thoughts and the way you articulated them has truly increased my understanding. Tonight you have equipped us with new tools to open our minds and help us gain more informed perspectives. Personally, I thank you."

"Ladies and gentlemen!" Chris said to the crowd. "All of you here and those watching at home, this concludes our debate. I thank you for your time and hope you got as much from this evening as I did. Won't you join me one more time in giving Dr. Berkley and Dr. Johnson another round of applause?"

Everyone complied enthusiastically. John and Warren stepped away from their lecterns and waved at the crowd as they walked toward each other.

"Great debate, Dr. Johnson. Thank you," said John.

Warren patted John's right arm with his left hand as they shook hands. "It was my pleasure, Dr. Berkley. It's been an honor to meet you."

As the crowd continued to clap, John walked over to Sandra and Nathan. Sandra hugged him and whispered in his ear, "You did so good, babe." Nathan shook his hand and congratulated him.

Warren walked to where his family was standing. Rachel took him in her arms and held him close. "You did your job tonight, hon. You really did. We're so proud of you."

Edee and Kate hugged him at the same time. "Great job, Daddy," Edee said.

"You showed up ready, Pops. Not bad at all," Kate said as she kissed him on the cheek.

"Thank you, guys," Warren responded. "Your boyfriend's dad certainly puts up a good fight." Kate smiled as she looked around trying to spot Nathan; it was practically impossible because there were so many people.

After a few seconds, she felt a poke on her side. She turned around, and there was Nathan, standing in front of her. They hugged and turned to her family so Kate could make the introductions.

Warren was the first to speak to him. "So you're the young man Kate's been moping around the house about, huh?"

Nathan was nervous about meeting her family, especially Warren, but he played it cool and laughed. "Yes, sir, Dr. Johnson."

"Oh, please, call me Warren. The title is just for pleasantries." He nodded in the direction of the lecterns.

"Yes, sir. You did a great job up there tonight. I'll have to admit that you gave people a lot to think about."

As Nathan spoke, Kate looked over at Edee to get her initial reaction to him. With a quick look, she understood Edee was saying, *He's gorgeous!*

"Thank you, Nathan. Your dad did a great job. He had me sweating a few times."

"Thanks, sir. Can I ask them to come over so you can meet them?"

"Of course, Nathan. Please have them come over," Rachel answered, patting him on the back.

"Great. I'll be right back."

John saw Nathan walking toward him and Sandra, hoping he was not about to ask them to go meet the Johnsons.

Chapter 33

NATHAN HAD A hard time getting through all the people waiting to speak with John. But he was determined, and he eventually made his way to them. John's fear came true as an enthusiastic Nathan said, "Dad, Mom, that's Kate over there. I want you to come meet her."

John did so less than enthusiastically, but he complied, and they started walking toward the Johnsons.

Suddenly, a man dressed in a suit approached John nervously and said, "Dr. Berkley, your flight leaves in an hour. The car is outside. We need to go."

The perfect out, John thought.

"We'll just be a few more minutes." Nathan intervened quickly.

"Okay. I'll wait right here," answered the driver. "Please hurry. There are no other flights to New Haven tonight."

Fighting their way through all the well-wishers, they got to where the Johnsons were standing.

"Mom, Dad, this is Rachel, Dr. Johnson's wife. Edee, Kate's sister. Dr. Johnson, of course. And…" Nathan paused with a big grin on his face. "This is Kate."

Sandra started to shake their hands, but except for Warren, who shook her hand, they all gave her a hug. She was surprised, if not shocked, but she understood things were done differently in the South, so she complied. "It's very nice to meet you all," she said, looking at Kate with a smile. "We've heard so much about you, Kate."

"Thank you, ma'am. I trust it was all pleasant?" Kate cut her eyes to Nathan as she responded to Sandra.

"Yes, you could certainly say that," Sandra responded, smiling at Nathan and then directing her attention to Warren. "Thank you for coming tonight, Dr. Johnson."

"Thank you, Mrs. Berkley," he answered. "Your husband really made me work tonight."

John shrugged. "You certainly held your own, Dr. Johnson. Dr. Robertson picked a good replacement. I hope his health will improve."

"Call me Warren, please. And thank you. I'll let him know you said that when I see him. He had to leave early."

John directed his attention toward Kate and shook her hand.

"It's good to meet you, Dr. Berkley," she said.

"It's good to meet you too, Kate. Your dad did well tonight."

"So did you, sir."

"Dr. Berkley...Pardon me. Excuse me. Dr. Berkley!" A familiar voice came toward them. John turned around and saw the driver frantically trying to reach them. "We really need to get to the airport so you don't miss your flight."

"We're going," responded John.

Kate looked at Nathan, hating that it was good-bye time again.

"Sorry, Kate. We do have to go. I'll call you tomorrow."

"No problem. Please go, so you don't miss your flight. It was great seeing you. And it was great meeting you, Mrs. Berkley, Dr. Berkley."

"You too," Sandra responded.

John extended his hand to Warren and said, "Dr. Johnson, I enjoyed our discussion. Kate, Mrs. Johnson, Edee, it was nice to meet you."

Nathan shook Warren's hand and said good-bye to Rachel and Edee. He gave Kate a hug, which automatically brought back the memory of their last night in Charleston. "See you soon?"

"You better. Now go, go!" she said, wanting him to do anything but go.

They walked off, with the driver leading the way. Once in the car, Nathan looked at his dad to try to read the expression on his face.

"You did well tonight, Dad. What did you think about Kate?"

"I don't agree with their beliefs, Nathan, but they are pleasant people. Kate seems like a nice girl."

"Mom?"

"They do seem like nice people. Kate is very beautiful. I was glad to meet them."

Nathan had expected the night to be full of drama, an awkward disaster. But it hadn't, and he was pleasantly surprised. The Johnsons had handled the situation with grace, and his parents had exceeded his expectations. The event that could have driven a wedge in his and Kate's relationship had been averted, he thought.

The car sped away toward the airport. Everyone was tired, and no one had much to say. As he looked out the window, Nathan thought about some of the things Warren had said during the debate. He'd been raised with such a different mind-set and had never really had much reason to question it. But so many of the things he'd heard that night somehow rang of truth in his mind. He found himself agreeing with the notion that life was too complex to have just happened by fluke over millions of years. He thought about Warren's composure—the way he handled the tough questions. He also thought about the reactions from the crowd and how Warren seemed to have won over some of them. Something in them, as with him, had been stirred inside.

Chapter 34

AUGUST WAS TURNING out to be a somewhat cooler month than usual in Charleston, which locals and tourists alike appreciated. Warren had enjoyed reliving the excitement of life in the limelight, but he was glad it was just for a brief period. After the debate, he had gotten hundreds of letters and e-mails from around the world with invitations to speak at churches and learning institutions. He and Rachel had agreed that he needed to accept a few for the next several months and then settle back in and focus on their local church.

One Saturday morning, despite getting home late the night before from a trip to Anchorage, he felt somewhat restless and woke up early. Unable to go back to sleep, he decided to do one of his favorite things—fix a fresh pot of coffee and sip on a cup while sitting on the back porch in the still and quiet of the morning. He had always loved that time in early dawn when the crickets' chirping faded into bird sounds. For him, this had always been the best time of the day for crisp and clear thinking, before the craziness of the day invaded and overtook his mind.

The last few days in Alaska had been great, and traveling certainly had its rewards. But all the trips seemed to be running together with little to no time to stop and get reenergized. This, what he was doing at that moment, he wouldn't trade for anything. Within an hour, the effects of long nights and flight delays took their toll, and he fell asleep on his chair.

A distinct sound of car brakes shrilled in the cool air and awoke him. Warren realized he must have fallen asleep as the sound of the brakes replayed in his mind. Wondering if it might have been just a dream, he put his cup down and listened quietly for a new sound. He didn't have to wait long, as a loud thump from a closing door broke the quietness. He got up and walked around the house to the driveway.

A gentleman dressed in a Marine uniform was walking away from a sterile-looking black car with tinted windows. "Are you Mr. Johnson?" he asked when he saw Warren.

Warren's heart dropped as his worst nightmare played back in his mind. "Yes, sir. I am."

The front door opened, and both Rachel and Kate appeared in their pajamas.

"What's going on, Warren?" Rachel asked as she and Kate went to stand by his side.

The Marine officer took off his hat. "Mr. Johnson, madam, madam. I am Colonel Ned Smith. May I have a few minutes of your time?"

Warren extended his hand toward the front door. "Yes, certainly. Please come in the house."

"Thank you, sir," responded the colonel in a matter-of-fact tone as he walked to the door.

Rachel threw Warren a panicked look, and her eyes were teary as they walked toward the door, her hands shaking in his. Warren took her and Kate in his arms and held them tightly as they walked behind the colonel. Afraid of the worst, Kate felt a rush of fear shoot through her entire body.

After getting the go-ahead from Rachel to have a seat, the Colonel sat down, dwarfing the couch with his enormous frame. Rachel and Kate sat on the love seat beside the couch, and Warren stood beside them.

"I'm sorry for such an early visit, but I felt I needed to come as soon as possible and speak to you in person." He paused for a moment, trying to find the right words.

Rachel gave him a reaffirming look. "That's no problem, Colonel."

The colonel looked Rachel in the eye. "Your son, First Sergeant Austin Johnson, has been missing in action for two weeks. He was leading a small group of men on a mission into an undisclosed location when he encountered a group of militants. Two of his men were killed; Austin and two other men haven't been seen or heard from since."

"So what does that mean?" Kate asked, almost screaming.

"We've been in daily contact with our intelligence on the ground, madam, and we don't have enough information to know what's happened to them."

Warren put his arm around Rachel as he tried to sort through all the possibilities in his mind. "What are the other two men's names?" he asked.

The colonel looked surprised by the question but answered quickly. "Um, Corporal Jason Harper and Corporal Robert Jimenez."

"Thanks, Colonel. What's next?"

"We wait, sir. We wait, and we pray. You will be the first to know when we find out something. I wanted you to hear it from me before you heard something on the news and made the wrong assumption." Warren nodded.

Rachel mastered up enough strength to speak. "Thank you, Colonel, for coming to see us. Please, keep us informed of any development, no matter how small it may be."

"I sure will, madam. You have my word." He said good-bye to everyone, and Warren and Rachel walked him to the door.

They were stunned, and they felt completely helpless. They would've done anything to change the situation, but it was completely out of their control. With tears in his eyes and a broken tone in his voice, Warren tried his best to comfort his wife and daughter. "All we can do is trust in God's plan. I don't know what He's doing, but I trust Him." The thought of never seeing Austin again was unbearable to him. He felt drained of all his strength, but he faked whatever he could for their sake.

Kate was speechless as she gazed at a picture of Austin in the living room. The picture was so Austin; he was wearing plain jeans and a T-shirt, and his hair was all messed up. Seeing the look of joy and peace in his eyes reminded her of who he was, and she knew that no matter where he might be, Austin had the wisdom and maturity to put things in the right perspective and make it through. This encouraged her a little, but she was terrified.

For the next hour, they sat holding each other, crying, and praying.

⋆⇒ ⇐⋆

Nathan got home around eleven thirty at night, from an evening outing with Jake. Then his cell phone rang. It was Kate, and he got a little concerned because she never called that late. She usually went to bed before then because she had to get up early for her shift at the hospital.

"Hi, Kate. You're usually on dream two or three by now. To what do I owe this honor?"

"Hi, Nathan. Sorry to call so late. I just needed to talk to you."

"It's no problem at all. I'm thrilled you called. What's going on?"

Kate took a moment before she spoke again; the pause caused Nathan to think that something was wrong.

"Is everything okay?" he asked with more intensity in his voice.

"No. It's not. My brother is missing in action, and they don't know where he is or whether he's even alive," she said, crying.

"I'm sorry to hear that, Kate, but that doesn't mean he's not okay. What are they doing to find him?"

"They're going to continue the search and keep us up to date. I can't lose my brother, Nathan."

Nathan let her cry for a few moments. "Listen. You can't think that way right now. I can only imagine how hard this is because I know how much you all love each other, but you have to hope for the better. No matter what!" He paused for a moment and then said, "Austin could very well be fine. You know?"

"I know," she said, sounding relieved to hear him say that. "You're right."

"I'm here for you, Kate—just stay hopeful."

"Thank you," she said. "I'm so glad I got to talk to you."

"Me too. Please try to get some sleep and call me whenever you need to talk."

"I will."

She thanked him for his time, and they said good night. Nathan felt her pain and wished there was more he could do to make her feel better. He wanted more than anything to be able to take care of her.

Chapter 35

THE JOHNSONS DECIDED to still have their yearly farewell-to-summer barbecue the next day—an event they all looked forward to because it allowed them to reconnect after the craziness from everyone's summer schedule. Edee was there with her husband, Jeff, and the boys. Joshua and Caleb didn't know anything about Austin. There was no need to worry them until they had more concrete information. Kate welcomed their playfulness as soon as they walked through the door because it helped take her mind off where Austin may be. The colonel had already called that morning to let them know they still had no news. This, he had explained, still offered hope that Austin could be alive.

After the meal and cleanup, the adults sat around the living room to talk while Joshua and Caleb wrestled on the floor. Edee was telling them to be careful so they wouldn't get hurt. Jeff was telling them to be careful so they wouldn't break something.

Kate sat back and watched the boys be boys and Edee and Jeff be parents. Their life seemed so normal in comparison to hers and Nathan's. Not only did she and Nathan come from very different backgrounds, but their fathers had debated each other in front of the world. She wondered if Edee and Jeff knew how blessed they were to have such a normal life.

A loud knock came from the front door, and they all stopped what they were doing. It was after nine o'clock, and they were not expecting anyone. Everyone except for the boys froze and looked at each other—a quick shot of fear hit all of them at the same time. Was it the colonel again with news about Austin? Nobody seemed to be able to move. If it was the colonel, it might be very bad news, or could it be good news? Nobody wanted to go to the door and find out. The next round of knocks came quickly, and Warren sprang to action.

He went to the door, and everyone's eyes followed him. They couldn't see the person's face when Warren opened the door, but they could all make out the shape of a man. Warren was noticeably surprised as he swung the door open to let the man in. "Well, I'll be. Nathan! Come in, son!"

Everyone in the living room turned to Kate, who was already halfway to the door in a mad dash.

She reached the door and exclaimed, "Oh my gosh, Nathan! It's you. What in the world are you doing here? Come in!"

Everyone was standing up, and they all had looks of both surprise and relief on their faces. Joshua and Caleb had stopped their fight and were wondering just what Caleb asked: "Who is Nathan?"

Kate brought Nathan into the living room, and Edee was the first to greet him with a big hug.

Rachel stood up, wiping a tear of pure joy. "It's so good to see you, Nathan," she said when he reached over to hug her.

"Nathan," Kate said, making eye contact with him and pointing at Jeff, "this is my brother-in-law, Jeff."

Jeff extended his hand toward him. "It's good to meet you, man. We've heard a lot about you. Actually, we've heard about nothing but you, thanks to Kate." Jeff smiled, knowing she was looking at him with a special look she had for him when he picked on her.

"Don't listen to him, Nathan. He ain't got much sense," Edee said.

"Good to meet you too, Jeff," Nathan said, laughing at the banter.

Jeff called the boys to come meet Nathan, but they both ignored him.

"The bell hasn't rung yet, Daddy, and I almost have him beat," Joshua said with a tone of urgency.

"You'll meet those two knuckleheads when the bell rings, Nathan. Unless," Jeff said, raising his voice and looking at the boys, "I ring their bell first!" The fight automatically ended, and Joshua and Caleb got up to meet Nathan. After the mandatory handshakes, the boys got the okay from Jeff to go play, and within seconds they were out of sight.

Warren joined the group and patted Nathan on the back. He smiled over at Kate, who looked shocked but was smiling ear to ear. She grabbed Nathan's hand as if to make sure he was real.

"I can't believe you're here. This is the best surprise ever. What brought this on?"

"Should we leave you two alone?" Jeff piped out, followed by a stinging elbow to the side from Edee.

Nathan had a concerned look on his face. "You sounded very upset last night. I wanted to be here. Have you heard any more news?"

"We haven't heard anything else," Warren said. "They're not able to tell us much, but we do know that a special missions team has been sent to find them."

Nathan nodded. "I felt like I needed to be here with you, Kate. I couldn't just stay in New Haven knowing you were going through this."

Kate teared up and put her arms around him. "Thank you so much. This means a lot."

After a few moments, Jeff threw his arm around Nathan and said, "Buddy, you just scored a gazillion points. Anyway, are you hungry?"

"Starving!" Nathan responded.

"Okay then! You've never had a burger like this guy can fix," Jeff said in a loud, matter-of-fact tone, pointing at Warren, who rolled his eyes. "Ain't no way y'all's burgers can be that good up 'ere. Come on. Let me show you what a good ole southern burger is. I'd advise you go ahead and loosen your belt though."

Nathan knew he was going to like Jeff.

Kate looked around the room and could tell how much what Nathan had done meant to her family. It had brought unexpected relief during a very difficult time. Nobody she'd dated before would've done something like this. She knew right then and there that her feelings really mattered to him and that he would not sit idly by when she needed him. Kate felt as if he would do whatever it took to make her happy. Jeff was right—Nathan had just scored a gazillion points.

Chapter 36

As the days turned into weeks, the calls from Colonel Smith came with less frequency. Austin had not yet been found, and despite the colonel's sympathy toward the family and his desire to help, he didn't know how to say the same thing over and over again.

Nathan hadn't returned to New Haven. He wasn't sure how helpful he was being in Charleston, but it seemed to make a difference in Kate's life. Their relationship was deepening, and the longer he was there, the more he thought he'd never be able to leave. Thankfully, money was no object for a Berkley, and he could afford to live in a hotel until he figured out what he was going to do. Soon he would have to decide if he was going to go back to New Haven or stay in Charleston to be with Kate, but it was too early to make such a big decision. In the meantime, he started putting out some feelers for job opportunities.

He could sense that Kate and her family were heartbroken, but somehow they had not lost their ability to have fun and care for each other. If anything, they seemed to be getting closer as a family. Despite all the time that had gone by without concrete news about Austin, the Johnsons still maintained hope and refused to give up. The first few days, Nathan thought the Johnsons were probably just putting on a happy act. But the more he got to know them, the more he realized it was who they were.

His time with Kate and her family also did something unexpected: it brought back memories of the one person in his childhood who had ever made him feel safe and happy. And with all the good memories also came a reminder of the most devastating thing that ever had happened to him and his family.

Uncle Lance had always been the life of the party; he was full of joy and positivity almost to a fault. Nathan was only ten years old when his uncle died, but even though Nathan was so young, Lance had been able to make a strong impact in his life. Even after all these years, Nathan smiled as he remembered how, when Lance came to their house, the place became better. Despite Sandra's pleas that he be careful with Nathan, Lance would always lift him up and fly him around the house as if he were some kind of superhero. He tried to do it even after Nathan got too big, but Lance would give up and make a big deal about what a big young man he was getting to be. Hearing a grown man say this to him made Nathan feel invincible, and he never tired of listening to him go on and on about it.

Another reason for the ten-year-old to adore his uncle was that he took him to get ice cream almost every week. John would go with them sometimes, but it was usually just Nathan and Uncle Lance. Nathan loved listening to Lance's stories while managing to get ice cream all over himself, something that didn't bother Lance in the least.

Uncle Lance often told stories of men and women who lived a long time ago in faraway places—stories of men forced into caves with lions and of a man who caught a ride in the belly of a whale. He had a unique way of bringing these stories to life in Nathan's mind so that they meant something. Nathan could hardly wait until the next time they would be together and get to hear more stories. Uncle Lance had a hunger for life that was contagious; he seemed to enjoy every minute of it, and Nathan loved that. He also had a way of bringing out the best in people, especially in John.

The news of his lung cancer devastated Nathan. Lance had insisted on telling Nathan himself, and he had done so at their favorite place, the ice cream parlor. He could still remember the look in Lance's eyes as he carefully and gently broke the news to him. He had a way of talking to him and explaining things like no one else.

As the dots connected in his young mind, Nathan was overwhelmed with fear and sadness. Lance filled a place in his life that would be replaced only with loneliness. The cancer was spreading quickly, and there was nothing the doctor could do, Lance had explained.

As the memories came back, Nathan could still feel the warmth with which Uncle Lance had wiped the tears from his eyes, and remembering that moment broke his heart all over again.

"You and I can be together forever one day, Nathan, so this doesn't have to be good-bye. It can just be a see-you-later. As you grow up, I want you to remember the stories I've told you. I want you to remember who made a difference in the characters' lives, and I want you to think about putting your trust in the same person they trusted. Do you trust me, Nathan? Will you remember?"

Nathan could still remember the lack of fear in his uncle's eyes as he nodded. He hadn't really understood his uncle's words, but he had believed it was possible that they might meet again because his uncle Lance had told him so.

When Uncle Lance died, he left a void in all the lives he had touched. That day, something also died in John. Although John had always been the more serious of the two brothers, Nathan could remember his father laughing more and wanting to be more personable when Lance was a part of their lives.

Dressed in black, standing in front of the casket that held his best friend, Nathan felt an overwhelming feeling of loss and emptiness. Over the next few days, months, and years, he looked for John to take Uncle Lance's place in his life. But that never happened.

John Berkley clenched disappointment and anger and renounced all things having to do with the God for whom his brother had claimed to live. If death was what an ever-loving God had to offer, He might as well not exist. His brother Lance had, a few years past, dedicated his life to God, and now he was dead. A whole lot of good, John reasoned, it had done his brother to place his belief in a God who let him die. How could a God who was supposed to be so good and loving, he had screamed at the top of his lungs at home that night, have allowed his little brother to die and break their hearts? If such a God existed, he wanted nothing to do with Him.

John resolved to denounce all things having to do with God and focus his efforts to provide a humanist, secular alternative to religious faith. He would prove to others, and himself, that God didn't exist. Maybe, he thought, he could spare others the pain and disappointment he felt. John was sure that Lance had believed a lie and put his faith in something that hadn't saved him. John's pursuit became his obsession, and he withdrew and became distant. His rage fueled a motivation that was intoxicating to him and those he influenced.

Nathan realized there were intriguing similarities between the Johnsons and Uncle Lance. They certainly had the same effect on him in that he felt comfortable relaxing and being himself around them. One day while sitting in the Johnsons' living room and looking at a picture of Austin, Nathan noticed something about his eyes that reminded him of Uncle Lance's eyes. Even though their eyes were different colors and the two of them looked nothing alike, there was an undeniable similarity. They were full of life, and Nathan could feel their inner joy.

Nathan hadn't felt the safety and trust Lance kindled in his life for a long time, and he realized now just how much he'd missed his uncle. He lamented what his life had lacked all these years. Despite Sandra's and John's efforts to do what they considered their best for him, they had not been able to give him the love he needed most. To them, providing correction, material wealth, and a reputable name showed him their love. But Nathan would've traded all of that for time spent together, laughter, and important life lessons. He was beginning to understand that it wasn't that they didn't want to love him like that—it was that they didn't know how. They didn't have what his uncle had—the ability to love someone without regard for self.

The pieces to the puzzle that is life were coming together as the days went by. He was starting to see more and more of the big picture. He was also finding it easier to understand why Kate was the way she was. Whatever she had, he also recognized it in Warren, in Rachel, in Austin, through a picture, and in the memory of his Uncle Lance. Whatever it was, he knew it was real and didn't come from them. It was as if there was something very powerful changing them from the inside out.

The thoughts and feelings going through his mind bewildered Nathan. They felt real but made no sense. The more he tried to push them aside and think about something else, the more he realized something was missing in his life.

Chapter 37

TREVOR'S WAS A restaurant that was well known not only to a local like Kate but also to returning tourists. And it was just as busy now in September as in any other summer month. It was where Nathan and Kate ate the last night he was in Charleston during his first visit. As Kate browsed through the menu, she wondered how they ever made it through their meal that night. That whole night seemed like a blur now.

"You're not leaving in the morning, are you?" Kate asked, pointing her knife and fork at Nathan.

"Well, I wasn't planning to. But it's not looking like a bad idea now."

"Excuse me," Kate said, her eyebrows raised.

Nathan pulled back on his chair and lifted up his palms, waving in defeat. "Never mind. I'll hang around."

"I thought so." Kate put her utensils down and confidently picked up the menu without looking back at him. Neither of them said anything as they looked through the menu.

"Thank you for bringing me here tonight, Nathan. The last time we were here was the hardest night of my life."

"Tell me about it," Nathan said, his face registering relief. "Glad we don't ever have to do that again."

Kate seemed perplexed. "What do you mean by that?"

Nathan laid his menu on the table and looked into her eyes. "Well...I want to talk to you about something, and I can't think of a better place to do it. This night is, or at least I hope will be, very different from the last time we were here." He paused for a moment to let what he had just said get the wheels turning in her mind.

"I've been thinking a lot about us the last few days. Actually, I've done practically nothing but think about us since I left you the last time. I love you, Kate. And, well, leaving you is not something I can do again. When I went back to New Haven in May, I was a wreck. If it'd be okay with you, I'd like to hang around here a few more weeks and see where all of this goes."

Kate couldn't hide her smile. Her eyes lit up as she struggled to fight back tears of pure joy. "This is the best thing I could've heard tonight, Nathan." Overcome with emotion, and not caring what anyone would think, she stood from her chair and hugged him.

"Just one condition," she said as she wiped tears from her eyes.

"Okay…"

"Don't get a minivan while you're here. Not cool."

Nathan laughed. "I thought that was what sealed the deal the last time."

"Not!"

Nathan took a letter out of the right pocket of his jacket and handed it to her. "And this is?" she asked.

"Just take a look," he said, pointing at it. "I got it today. This was the third company I interviewed with. They all came back with an offer, and this seemed like the best one."

"Wow," she responded, her jaw slightly dropped. "I guess that four point oh from Stanford is well appreciated around here."

"You could say that."

"So that's what you've been doing while I was at work the last few weeks. What a sneaky fella. Have you ever been a project manager?"

"Sort of. I did an internship with a software company for six months in Palo Alto. Between my schooling, the internship, and other jobs I've held, they decided to give me a shot. A business degree is a great asset in any management role, and this falls right in line with my desire to one day be part of developing strategy and helping a company grow. Teksoft is a software company that is growing fast, and there should be room for advancement."

"That's great. I'm so proud of you. Have you accepted the job?"

"Yes!"

"A little presumptuous of you, wasn't it?"

"I knew how irresistible you find me and thought that tonight would be a breeze."

"Well played. When do you start?"

"In a couple days."

"Awesome!" she exclaimed, grabbing the menu and opening it back up. "I'm eating good tonight!"

Nathan shook his head, with a big grin.

They spent the rest of the evening laughing and cutting up. For the first time in their relationship, they felt relaxed enough to enjoy one another without the fear of getting too close. The cloud of pain they had felt hovering over them since Nathan left Charleston the first time was finally lifting.

Kate knew she was in love with Nathan, and her feelings were irreversible. One way or another, he would always be part of her life. Nathan felt like the luckiest man in the world. Just a few weeks ago, it had seemed impossible for their relationship to survive—first the distance, then the debate between their fathers. Now, their future felt secure.

Nathan found an apartment quickly. He was glad because he wanted to make it on his own, and it was much cheaper than staying at a hotel. As soon as he'd gotten the job offer, he had called John and Sandra and told them he wanted to make Charleston his home for the foreseeable future. Things with Kate were going well, and he wanted to be close to her. John had wished him well but hadn't said much more than that. Sandra had teared up over the phone, but she understood.

Nathan thanked them for all their support through the years, the opportunities they had given him, his Stanford education, everything. He told them that from that moment on he would support himself; he wanted to work hard and make it on his own. That attitude would be important to Kate, he knew, because it showed he was serious about their future together. He wanted to do everything right.

Chapter 38

As FALL SETTLED in Charleston, a stunning variety of brown, orange, and yellow leaves replaced the flowers and greenery. When the sun began to disappear below the horizon every afternoon, its rays had a way of bringing all the fall colors together into a beautiful glow that was almost palpable in the air. Charleston looked like a completely different place, though no less beautiful than in the spring and summer.

Nathan couldn't help but wonder how all this beauty was possible. He had been raised to believe that everything he saw was there by sheer coincidence. But since the debate, he found himself stopping to think more about the why and how of things. That some things just were, or just happened, had become harder to believe. There seemed to be more of a purpose to things—their complexity and interdependence fascinated him.

One Sunday morning, Nathan was taking in all the beauty as he made his way to the First Baptist Church of Charleston. He'd gone there a few Sundays when Warren was in town, mainly to make a good impression on Kate and her family. Avoiding a potential conflict with Kate and her family was worth two hours of his time every week. Maybe that was good enough for them; he hoped it was.

Nathan was still amazed by the number of churches in the South. One in particular got his attention as he neared Kate's church. It was small and quaint, and the whole congregation appeared to be outside. They were all busy at work pulling food out of cars and placing it on folding tables. He stopped at the red light right in front of the church and noticed a group of twenty or so people seated around the folding tables. From what he could tell, the people sitting down looked different from those preparing the tables. The clothes of those sitting were torn and dirty, and most of them had long, unattended hair.

The faces of the people sitting around the tables were full of desperation. That much he could tell from where he was. Many of them looked around aimlessly at the floor or the tabletops until someone walked by them. They would then nod and force a smile before returning to their thoughts. To the side, Nathan saw a man and a woman unloading winter clothes from a large van and organizing them, probably by size, on another table. He figured they were giving the clothes away to the people sitting down. Another man was getting boxes of books from his car and placing them on a table.

The light turned green, but Nathan didn't realize it because his focus was on two women walking around making conversation with their guests. Their smiles were full and genuine, as if they were thrilled to be there. Their demeanor was intoxicating to those around them.

The car behind Nathan honked. Startled, he pressed on the gas to get out of the way, his gaze following the scene as it continued to unfold. Nathan had never seen anything like it, and he was intrigued. He had always thought that kind of thing only happened in the movies or a long time ago.

Within minutes, he arrived at Kate's church. He was ready for his favorite part—the time when, as soon as she spotted him, she flashed a big smile and signaled for him to rush to sit by her side. He loved it when she smiled at him. With a series of *excuse-me*s and greetings to people he didn't know, he hurried to her side.

The music minister got up and led the congregation in a few songs. When the singing was over, Warren walked up to the stage from the front row and arranged his Bible and papers on the pulpit. This image always reminded Nathan about the night of the debate—when Warren had done the same once he reached his lectern. He thought about how that night Warren had been just a man about to debate his father. Now, he was someone who had started to mean something in his life.

As with every other Sunday he had attended, Nathan would try to listen, but his mind would quickly drift away to think about a thousand things that had absolutely no relevance to church.

Attendance had almost doubled since the debate, and the services were now also being broadcast on television. Warren and his staff were grateful that his messages could be heard by many more people, but they had gone to great efforts to make sure his church didn't turn into a big show. His style and the content of his messages hadn't changed, and his goal to keep the focus on Jesus Christ had certainly not changed.

Warren took off his glasses and laid them on the pulpit as he began to address the congregation. "It is my sincere honor to speak with you today. I am thankful beyond words for each of you here and those watching on television and the Internet. It's my prayer that the Lord will speak to you today, and that you'll respond to Him." His eyes smiled at the congregation. His body language, and the way he seemed to really care, reminded Nathan of the night of the debate.

"You know," Warren started, "you look at the people around you and think they have the perfect life. Maybe what they drive, where they live, or what job they have makes you think they have something figured out that you don't. It may be someone who, when you speak to him or her, sounds so spiritual. In your mind, you're convinced they have arrived somewhere you haven't. You may start to wonder what they do right that you do wrong. Well, have you considered that the same people you think have it all together may be looking at you and thinking the exact same things?" He paused to let the question sink in and to give people a chance to think.

Nathan was somewhat intrigued by what Warren was saying, but his mind was already starting to drift into mindless matters about the week coming up. He had woken up late and rushed to the church, and he hadn't had time to make his customary stop to get a coffee, so his main concern was where they might go to eat later.

Warren put on his reading glasses and opened the Bible. "Please open up your Bible to Matthew 11:28." A short silence was interrupted abruptly by the converging sound of pages turning. Warren read the verse out loud.

"'Come to me, all you who are weary and burdened, and I will give you rest.' So what does this have to do with how we see others, how they see us, how we see ourselves? Listen to what Jesus is saying here. He tells us to come to him—when we are in need, when we are tired from the fights life brings us, when we don't know where to go or what to think next.

"He's not saying, 'Look at others to see if you measure up.' He's not saying, 'Look inside you and figure out the solution.' All he asks us to do is come to him. That's all, to just come to him so he can give you the rest that he alone can give you. Every single one of you!" Warren raised his voice. "Every single one of you is in need! I don't care how good you are at pretending to others you have life figured out. I don't care how successful you think you've been in lying to yourself that you can do life on your own—that your knowledge and wisdom will get you through, that you will be okay not living life with Christ."

Nathan snapped out of his daze as Warren's words hung in the air. His mind raced back in time and remembered what the poor man in the streets of New Haven had said to him: "Son. We are all in need."

After that day, he hadn't thought much about what the man had said to him. He'd felt it was kind of ironic, though. If anyone looked to be in need, it was the man, not Nathan. But all of a sudden the man's words had meaning, and they brought a palpable sense of urgency Nathan had missed that day in New Haven. "Son. We are all in need." The words played over and over in his mind.

Nathan wondered about what the man had seen in him that prompted those words. That day he really had just dismissed the man as drunk or crazy and moved on. But not today—now the words had an undeniable ring of truth. He was reminded again of the many people he knew who looked practically perfect on the outside—people who seemed to have it all. He realized he was one of those people. Maybe the poor man in New Haven hadn't been drunk or crazy after all. Maybe he had seen right through Nathan's facade.

Nathan remembered feeling sorry for the man that day. Today, he felt sorrier for himself. He could feel the energy from his body draining as the realization of how helpless and alone he had always been came to the surface. The pretenses of the past, he realized now, had only made the degradation on the inside worse.

Kate sensed something and looked over at him. He seemed somewhat distant, if not disconnected. Nathan noticed and smiled at her.

As the intensity of his realization grew, Nathan thought about the small church feeding the homeless that morning. *Those people look so messed up*, he'd thought to himself as he drove away. He had been so glad not to be one of them. Now, he felt as much in need as they were, not for food or shelter, but for something he knew he couldn't provide for himself. He could see his pride and arrogance. His pride had blinded him to who he really was; his identity was ugly and based on lies and pretension, and he was disgusted by it.

"Come to me…" The words played over and over in Nathan's mind. "Come to me, all you who are weary and burdened, and I will give you *rest*." His heart felt heavy with a conviction that had never been there before.

Warren flipped a few pages back in his Bible as he talked. "Dear friends, the first step to fixing any problem is to realize there is a problem to fix. Wouldn't you agree? Once you've seen what the problem is, you have to look for its source so you can figure out the right path of action to resolve it."

He found the verses he was looking for. "David is one of the many people in scripture whom you could definitely say had problems. King Saul and his men chased him to kill him, and many times he found himself desperate and alone. I want you to hear what he wrote in Psalm eighty-nine, verses fifteen and sixteen. 'How blessed are the people who know the joyful sound! O Lord, they walk in the light of Your countenance. In Your name they rejoice all the day, And by Your righteousness they are exalted.'" He paused to let everyone think about the verses.

"David chose to walk through this life with God, for God's purposes and not his, and what you hear from these verses is the result of what happens to someone who has decided to do that. Listen to this from Hebrews twelve, verses one and two: 'Therefore, since we have so great a cloud of witnesses surrounding us, let us also lay aside every encumbrance and the sin which so easily entangles us, and let us run with endurance the race that is set before us, fixing our eyes on Jesus, the author and perfecter of our faith.'

"In these verses Paul tells us what the problem is: the sinful nature we are born with and the encumbrances that oppress us day after day. Paul experienced the same struggles David did. And like David, he found the solution was yielding his life to God and relying on him. That's the only way we can win this race we call life, folks! What comes next can change dramatically based on what we decide about our relationship with God and our obedience to Him. We have to keep our eyes on our creator, not on others."

These words, coming from a book Nathan had been raised to think was nothing more than a collection of superstitious fairy tales meant for people who were paranoid, weak, or insecure, now seemed to cut right to his core. They brought to the surface a condition Nathan recognized as his own. They rang true in his soul and offered a way out—a path to a more meaningful life, a solution to a problem for someone in need.

A gentle tap from Kate, followed by a stronger one, startled him. He looked around and noticed everyone was standing and singing the closing song.

As he stood, Kate gave him a look of concern. "Are you okay?"

"Um, yes, fine. I'm fine," Nathan responded, acting natural. Kate laughed, shaking her head. Within a few minutes, the service ended, and they walked outside to wait on Warren and Rachel.

Nathan needed to sort through the morning's events, so after lunch he told Kate he needed to fly solo to get a few things done. He spent the next hour driving around. He had no destination, just the need to keep driving. Eventually, he parked his car at the Battery and walked around for a while.

He was trying to busy himself with everyday thoughts as he looked at the water and the stately mansions that lined the Battery, but his thoughts kept coming back to the events of the morning. It was as if a complex tapestry was taking form in his mind. Thoughts, feelings, and realizations were weaving into the tapestry like threads revealing a picture. He was awestruck by the clarity of his thoughts.

Nathan sat on a bench and looked out at the sea, shaking his head and wondering if he was going crazy. The words from the service's closing song played over in his mind. It was a song he'd heard a thousand times before, but one he'd never really paid attention to. "Amazing grace, how sweet the sound...I once was blind, and now I see." *Have I really been blind?* he asked himself. These words were packed with meaning now.

The ocean breeze felt so good on his face. He let his shoulders relax and decided to sit there awhile. After a few minutes, he took out a pocket-sized New Testament someone had given him to take to church and found the verse in Matthew. "Come to me, all you who are weary and burdened, and I will give you rest." He read it five times. The sixth time, he decided to read the next verse,

11:29, "Take my yoke upon you and learn from me, for I am gentle and humble in heart, and you will find rest for your souls."

The breeze picked up in intensity. Nathan sat back and closed his eyes, thinking, mystified by how sure he was that these words were meant for him. He now understood what "rest" meant in the passage. It was the rest he had been looking for since Uncle Lance had died, when hope began to fade. For many years, he'd tried to ignore it, buried it in the busyness of constructing a perfect Nathan the world would approve of. But he knew it had never been resolved, that the need for this type of rest had always been right under the surface. How could he have been so blind? How had he missed something that now seemed so obvious?

From an early age, Nathan had tried to get his parents to provide answers to the bigger questions in life, asking, "What is the point of going through life?" But they didn't seem to have any answers that resolved the issues in his mind. As the years went by, the questions grew larger, and the frustration led him to stop asking or caring so much about the reasons. To him, looking for answers seemed futile, and the only solution was to stop caring. But that was something he could only pretend to do.

He wanted to know more. He had to have answers, and unlike in the past, he wasn't going to put the questions off until later. An unexplainable sense of excitement as to what all of this might mean came over him. He had to share this with Kate. And who better to talk to for answers than Warren himself?

Chapter 39

A COUPLE OF hours had passed since they got home from another epic Sunday lunch at Nawlin's. Warren settled in his big chair, making it clear he had every intention of taking a nap until it was time to go back to church that night. Kate sat on the couch across from him, thinking the idea of a nap didn't sound bad at all. She wondered what Nathan might be doing and made a mental note to check on him after a long nap.

As Warren started to doze off, Kate flipped through channels, wondering how come, with over one hundred channels, there never seemed to be anything good to watch. Her cell phone went off, and unfortunately for Warren, she had turned up the volume earlier to make sure she didn't miss Nathan if he called. Warren, startled away from his light sleep, pretended to give Kate a mean look.

"Hi, Nathan?" Kate answered the phone, looking apologetically at Warren. She could hear only what sounded like a strong wind and a small voice in the background.

"Nathan, I can't hear you! Where are you?" She raised her voice, hoping that would be enough for him to hear. Warren, his hope for a nap dashed away, sat up in his chair with a groggy look on his face. Kate spoke into the phone again. "You need to cover your mouthpiece or go somewhere inside so I can hear you. Are you okay?"

"I'm fine. I'm at the Battery walking around. Would this be a good time to come over and talk to…" A gust of wind came through and muffled the rest of what he said.

"You cut off, Nathan. Tell me again."

Nathan waited, wondering if he was doing the right thing as a streak of panic shot through him. But his mind was made up. "Kate, I want to come speak with you and your dad." He paused, feeling overcome with emotion but not wanting to get upset.

Warren noticed the look of bewilderment on Kate's face as she listened. "Everything okay?" he whispered.

"He wants to come talk to us," she whispered back.

"Dad is right here, Nathan. Come on over."

"Okay. Thanks. I'm on my way."

"You okay?" she asked, both concerned and curious.

"Yes. I'll explain when I get there."

Kate hung up the phone and cast Warren a deer-in-the-headlights look; she could sense that something important was going on with Nathan. He sounded different, and she couldn't help but worry about him.

Twenty minutes later, she heard a knock on the door. She rushed to it and flung it open, welcoming him with the smile to which he was so addicted. Warren greeted Nathan and led him to the living room. Rachel had gone back to the church to help with some preparations for the evening service, so only Kate, Warren, and Nathan were in the house. This was still too big a crowd for Bully, so he mustered the energy to get up and walk out of the room.

Nathan took his jacket off and sat down. "I'm sorry for disturbing your afternoon. I know Sundays are quite busy for you, and, well, I appreciate you being available to me."

Warren leaned back in his chair. "It's my pleasure, son. You know you're welcome here anytime."

Kate came back from the kitchen with a glass of water and handed it to Nathan as she sat beside him. Nathan thanked her and took a small sip. He could feel his emotions welling up inside, and he was afraid his eyes would tear up and he might look weak in front of them. After he finished his sip of water, he dropped his head and took a long breath.

Nathan looked up at Warren. "You know my background, where I come from, who my dad is. I really appreciate the respect you've shown me since the day I met you at the debate. I know that was a hard situation for everyone."

Warren smiled at him and nodded in agreement.

"What you have based your life on is very different from what I was raised with, and somehow, you found a way to love me anyway." He could feel his hands shaking, so he paused for a moment before he continued.

"I'll be honest with you that I didn't get that at all for a while. It was very strange to me, and I really wasn't sure if you all were even for real. I just wanted to be with Kate, and"—he looked over at Kate, and she grabbed his hand—"nothing else really mattered that much, so I was willing to go along with it as long as I could be with her. I guess that's always been my problem, that I pretend to get what I want. The truth is that I've lived in a reality I created for myself, one that worked for me—or so I thought.

"I've never lacked for anything, and for the most part, life has been easy. My parents have always provided everything materially, and until about a year ago, I thought that was all I really needed." He paused to try to collect himself as the truth of his words struck him in a deeper way than before. He didn't know if he might start crying at any moment, and at this point he couldn't care less if he did.

"What you said this morning in your sermon, about everyone being in need, hit me like a ton of bricks. I don't know how to explain it, but it was as if the words were spoken by a familiar voice I've heard before. The voice was so personal, like it came from someone who has always known me—someone who knows me better than I know myself." Nathan looked over at Kate for affirmation that he didn't sound crazy. She nodded, encouraging him to go on.

"I swear I've heard this voice before, and the love I felt from it was incredible. This morning I came to realize that there's so much to this life I'm missing, and it became so clear that I can't do it on my own. I don't want to be miserable anymore. I want to live with purpose, like you all seem to live." He felt the grip of Kate's hand tighten, and he looked at her again. The tears from her eyes revealed a connection between them they'd never had before.

Warren leaned forward in his chair with the reassuring look of a loving father. "Son, God has very unique and personal ways he chooses to show us who we are and who He is. He speaks to all of us, in one way or another, so we can all have the same chance to either accept or reject Him. Some people choose to accept Him—others choose not to. Proverbs 14:12 says, 'There is a way that seems right to man, but in the end it leads to death.' I believe you have seen this truth come alive.

"We have to see for ourselves who we really are—to understand which beliefs we allow to guide our thoughts and our lives. But only God can show us who we are without Him, and that's when we can see our need for Him. He then offers us a chance to choose Him so He can remove the blinders that keep us from missing what life is really about."

Realizing that who he was would never bring him true meaning and happiness, Nathan felt as if he'd been broken open and was being put together as he was supposed to be. He felt hopeless and weak if left to his own devices but strengthened by the prospect of an almighty being who could save him from himself and restart his life on the right path. It was as if he had reached a point of no return in some other dimension, one that applied to reality but somehow transcended it.

"What do I do?" he asked, looking at Warren and squeezing Kate's hand.

Warren's tone was soft but firm. "You choose, Nathan, to live for yourself, the same life you've always lived, or to give your life to Jesus and live for Him. Do you want Him to save you, Nathan, from yourself so you can start anew?"

Nathan placed his elbows on his knees and closed his eyes as he considered the question. Kate glanced at Warren and then fixed her eyes on Nathan. A few moments passed, and Nathan lifted his head. He looked Warren in the eye for a few seconds before he spoke, tears flowing from his eyes.

"I've been so blind, so stupid! I can't do this on my own anymore. I am so exhausted." He paused, the tears flowing more intensely now. Warren placed his right hand on Nathan's shoulder and took Kate's hand with his left.

"Nathan, is this something you believe in your heart, son?"

"I do."

"Will you pray with me?" Warren asked, tightening his grip on Kate's hand and squeezing his shoulder. Nathan closed his eyes and lowered his head.

"Dear Lord," Warren said as he got off his chair to kneel by Nathan. "I thank you for your redeeming work. I praise you for your grace and mercy. You never give up on us despite ourselves. Thank you for your manifestation in this young man's life and the love you have shown him by calling him to be part of your family. Only you can see the state of our heart and mind. Search deep within Nathan's heart and lead him accordingly.

"If you believe in your heart, Nathan, please pray with me now.

"Jesus, I accept your work for me on the cross as forgiveness for my sin. My way of doing life has not worked, and I'm ready to do it your way. I've been blind, but now I see you in a new, real way. Please forgive me. I turn my life over to you and ask you to be my Lord and Savior."

Kate pulled Nathan close and hugged him as they finished praying. They held each other a few moments and cried together. As Warren stood up to leave the room and give them some privacy, Nathan reached up to shake his hand and thank him. The look in his eyes was different from when they first sat down to talk; the heavy burden he had carried for so long had been lifted, and the effect was notable.

Nathan felt like a new man. Free.

Chapter 40

AFTER A LONG applause and the usual congratulatory handshakes, John could feel the exhaustion from the intense travel and the adrenaline rush that had kept him going the last few weeks. He'd lost count of how many cities and countries he'd been in since the debate with Warren, and he was tired. His popularity had increased exponentially, and there was no shortage of requests for him to speak, to write new books, and to appear on interviews. It had become impossible for him to keep up with it all.

John had gotten a lot of attention before, but it had never been this intense. At first it was great fun, but as of late it had gotten to be too much. The stress was taking a heavy toll on him and Sandra, whom he had barely seen in the past few weeks. She joined him on some of his travels, but eventually she felt drained and made the decision to go with him more sparingly. This trip, they had promised each other, would be the last one for at least a month. He had arranged to take a sabbatical—a request the university granted without any reservation. Because he was a celebrity in some circles, and great for the university, there probably wasn't much they wouldn't do if he just asked.

John and Sandra knew they couldn't stay in New Haven and expect to be left alone, so the plan was to get out of town for a few weeks. They had discussed an Alaskan cruise, but after looking at weather reports, they decided to go somewhere warm with a slower pace. Sandra had been missing Nathan, and she suggested they go down South, so they decided to fly to the Florida Keys. After a few days, they would take a rental car through Georgia and South Carolina. Their last stop would be Charleston, and in between they would go to some of the places they had always wanted to visit, places like Savannah and Hilton Head Island.

Part of them, too, was curious about the place that had captured Nathan's heart. His call to let them know he was going to stay there had come very unexpectedly, if not as a shock. They both thought he had rushed to the decision too quickly because of emotion, but it was obvious they would not be able to change his mind.

They were not sure what date exactly they would make it to Charleston, so they decided not to tell Nathan about their visit quite yet. Once they had more definite plans, they would call and let him know.

Chapter 41

TWO WEEKS HAD passed since Nathan prayed with Warren and Kate. During this time he had started to notice some subtle changes in himself, and he was surprised by how much more clearly he was able to look back at his life and see who he had really been. He questioned how much substance there had been to him. Now, he felt as if he was on a new path—on a ride to a destination he was not sure of, but a destination that felt right. For the first time in his life, he knew he wasn't in the driver's seat. And for the first time, that was okay.

In the past, being in control had been a requirement for success. Now that didn't seem as necessary to Nathan. The release of control gave him the freedom to enjoy a peace and a joy he had not allowed himself to experience before. He quickly realized that life was so much easier to understand with God in it. There was more of a point to his existence, and he didn't want to waste any time.

⊷⊷⊚ ⊚⊷⊷

Nathan and Kate spent every moment they could together. He loved telling her about the positive ways the faith they shared was affecting him, and this allowed them to connect at a deeper level. His previous inability to see things from Kate and her family's worldview had almost disappeared, and this enabled their relationship to grow even more quickly than before.

One of their favorite things to do together was go hiking. Early one Saturday morning, Nathan called and asked Kate if she wanted to go on the Awendaw Passage hike. At first she kidded with him, asking why he couldn't have called a little later in the morning, as opposed to six o'clock. But right away, she gladly accepted the invitation.

They stopped to rest halfway through the hike. Sitting on a large rock, Nathan noticed Kate looking at him.

"What is it?" he asked. "Is it too hard to keep your eyes off of me?"

"Well, yeah, as a matter of fact, it is. I do find you quite handsome."

"Understandable," he replied.

"And humble, too," she said with a playful sigh. "I was just noticing the smile on your face. I didn't see that a whole lot a couple weeks ago."

"So you're saying I was a sourpuss?" he asked teasingly.

"No, not at all. You just usually looked preoccupied with something. I love seeing this new look on you."

"Well, thank you. I didn't even know I was smiling." He picked up a stick and started fiddling with it. "I just don't feel overwhelmed by all the what-ifs anymore. Not like I used to. Having God in my life makes me want to be happy and do something meaningful. It's like He has given me potential and confidence, and for the first time ever, I'm excited about what the next day may bring."

"That is so good, Nathan. I'm really glad to hear that."

He pulled her to him and rested his cheek on her head. "I owe you and your dad a lot, for pointing me in the right direction."

"Please don't mention it. God did that, not us."

"I really love you. You know that? I really don't know what I would've done if I hadn't met you." He kissed her on the lips. "You're the best thing that's ever happened to me."

"I love you too, Nathan. And I'm so glad you're in my life. Please don't ever leave me again."

"No way that's ever going to happen."

As they resumed their walk, they both felt as if now, more than ever, they were going in the same direction in life.

Within a few days, Nathan felt strongly that there was no sense in waiting to do what he felt they both wanted. As soon as he hung up from making reservations at the Parlour in downtown Charleston for the special event, he felt the enormity of what he was about to do. And he couldn't remember ever being so nervous. After all, it was not every day he asked someone to marry him.

Chapter 42

THE RESTAURANT HAD the look of a great room in a Victorian-style Charleston mansion, with white columns, large mirrors, and windows that went almost from floor to ceiling. The low lighting from ornate chandeliers carefully brought out the beauty in each detail of the décor. Music from the piano in the corner of the large room reached them at just the right volume, clearly audible but low enough that they could talk and hear each other.

When he picked her up, as soon as she got in the car, he wanted to chicken out. But once she settled into her seat and looked at him with her adoring gaze, he found himself at ease and full of the confidence he felt when they were together.

Throughout the evening, Nathan found himself watching Kate's every move, unable to stop. He could so easily get lost in her beauty. It was still beyond him how he had gotten to this point with her, and he knew there was no one else in the world he would want sitting across from him. The lighting in the room seemed perfectly set to accentuate her facial features. Nathan found himself lost in the moment, wanting to capture it somehow, as if he would never again experience something so amazing.

He couldn't wait another moment. Kate was looking at the busy movements of the waitstaff as they took care of their customers, and he used the opportunity to reach inside his coat pocket. He withdrew a small box and laid it under the palm of his right hand so she wouldn't see it. As Kate looked over at him, he could feel his heart beating with an intensity he'd never felt before.

She quickly noticed something was going on with Nathan. The nervous look on his face was giving him away despite his attempt to look calm and collected.

"Everything okay, Nathan?" she asked with a slight turn of her face, eyes squinted as if to peer inside him to find out what might be going on.

"Sure," he answered, trying to be cool and gripping the box tightly against the table. His heart was beating faster now.

She stared at him for a few seconds, her eyebrows dipping slightly, conveying a feeling of suspicion. *What if she says no?* he thought. But there was no turning back now. It was time.

He felt the soft warmth of her hand on his. "You haven't said much the last few minutes, Nathan."

"I do have something to say, Kate." He slid his hand away so hers would rest on the box. "I have a question to ask you."

Kate gripped the box and turned it over. She shot a quick look at him, her eyes welling up.

Nathan took the box from her hand and opened it so she could see what was in it. Her eyes opened wide, and her whole face lit up.

"Kate, I can't imagine a day of my life without you in it. Will you please marry me and make me the happiest man on Earth?"

Kate looked very surprised. There had been almost no doubt in her mind he would ask her at some point, but it hadn't even crossed her mind it might be tonight. She could feel a swell of emotion, and for a moment, she was speechless.

"Yes! Of course. Yes! I will marry you, Nathan," came her enthusiastic reply as she leaned forward to kiss him on the lips.

Nathan laughed as sheer happiness and relief took him over. A couple in the table next to them realized what was happening and smiled.

"You turkey! When did you plan this? I didn't have a clue," Kate said gleefully.

"I've been planning this since the moment you spilled food on me at Nawlin's."

"Love at first sight, huh?" Kate smirked.

"You could definitely say that," Nathan said with a serious look. "By the way, your dad gave his blessing."

"You asked him?" she asked, pleasantly surprised.

"Sure did. I even did it in person."

"I'm impressed. So, how did it go?"

"I told him I wanted nothing more than to see to it that you be happy and that I would do whatever it took to make sure you were. Then I promised him that I will always take care of you and asked him for your hand. Your dad was amazing. He gave me his consent and assured me that he and your mom would always be there for us. It was just us, so I started asking him questions about faith, and we ended up talking for about an hour."

"Thank you for asking him first. I know that meant a lot to him. I can't wait to spend my life with you."

"I'm going to make you really happy. I promise," Nathan said as he picked up the ring box and put it in his pocket.

"I know you will. Will you promise me one thing, though?" Her face took on a more serious look.

"Sure, Kate. What is it?"

"No minivan, *ever*!"

Nathan laughed, knowing there would never be a dull moment with her.

⊷⊷ ⊷⊷

As Nathan drove to work the next day, he couldn't believe where he was in life. So much was changing so quickly, and in ways he couldn't have imagined possible. He was living in the South, he had a career, and he was engaged to be married to the perfect woman. Nathan didn't feel deserving of so many blessings, and he was very thankful. But everything paled in comparison to the decision he had made a few weeks before. His becoming a Christian was still hard to believe at times, especially given who his father was and how he had been brought up.

He had yet to tell his parents about his new religion. He tried to figure out the best way to tell them, but no way seemed better than another. It was going to be a shock no matter what. And as if that were not enough, the next time they spoke, he was going to invite them to his wedding, where the man marrying them would be the same person John had debated on national television. The irony of everything that was happening seemed at times too much to take in. *Oh Lord*, he prayed quietly as he approached his office building, *I'm going to need you every step of the way*. It still felt strange to speak with dependence to a person he couldn't see. But somehow, he felt someone was really listening.

Chapter 43

NATHAN AND KATE had decided to marry soon. Neither of them wanted a big wedding, just something small and quaint with close friends and family. Most of her family was in Charleston or in the surrounding areas, so getting them there would be easy enough. The date was set for December 10. Soon thereafter, in the same month, people would be busy getting ready for Christmas, so the beginning of December seemed ideal.

One of the first calls Nathan made when they had a date was to Jake, to ask him to be his best man, but unfortunately Jake was going to be in Europe for the holidays, and he wouldn't be able to make it. Nathan was very disappointed that his best friend couldn't come, but he didn't make a big deal about it because he didn't want his friend to feel guilty. Jake promised to make it up to him by coming to see him and Kate as soon as he could.

Rachel and Warren were very happy for them, and they offered their full support. Warren was growing very fond of Nathan and already considered him part of the family. He couldn't help but admire the young man for having the courage to make a decision to give his life over to God, knowing the issues it may cause with his parents.

⊷⇥═⇥ ⊜═⇤⊷

Early one morning, Nathan arrived to work before anyone was there so he could call his parents and tell them about the engagement. After four rings, there was no answer, and the answering machine came on. He thought that was unusual. John and Sandra were early risers, and by that time they were already up. He left a message asking them to call his cell phone, without telling them why he was calling. If they didn't call soon, he would try John on his cell.

Shortly after five that evening, as Nathan started to get ready to leave the office, his cell phone went off. Kate usually called him around that time, so he answered the phone without even looking at the caller ID. "Hey, sweet thing! How goes it?"

There was a moment of silence on the other end, and it soon felt awkward. Suddenly, Nathan heard two people start laughing. Their voices sounded familiar, so he looked at the caller ID and saw the number for his dad's cell phone. He shrugged, embarrassed, and then started laughing too.

"Okay, okay. I thought it was Kate," Nathan said as John and Sandra kept laughing. The response was unusual for them, he thought. They sure were in a good mood.

"What's up with you two? Have you been drinking?"

"No..." Sandra answered, still laughing. "Sweet thing, we have not."

"Yeah, yeah...Where have you all been? I've been trying to call you."

"Sorry we're just calling, Nathan. Your dad and I are not at home. He's taken a month off from work for a much-needed break. We are in Key West, left about two days ago."

"What?" Nathan was shocked that they had gone on vacation and hadn't let him know. It was not like them.

"Your dad needed the break. Our plan is to drive up the coast and visit a few places between here and...well, if it's okay, come see you in Charleston."

Nathan was speechless. He did some quick math in his head, and there was a very high probability that his wedding was going to be around the same date they were planning to come to Charleston.

"What day do you plan to get here?"

"Well...we've not decided for sure, but we were thinking around December first."

Nathan started laughing.

"Everything okay, Nathan?"

"Yes. Fine. Just fine. Can you make sure you're here on December tenth?" he said, chuckling.

Sandra and John looked at each other wondering why he was asking about a specific day. "John? Yes? Sure, Nathan. We'll be there. But why the tenth?"

"You're not going to believe this," Nathan said as he closed the door to his office and kicked his feet up on the desk. He was almost enjoying this. "Well, that's my wedding date. I asked Kate to marry me, and she said yes. We know it's fast, but we just don't see the reason to wait. That's why I tried to call you yesterday, to invite you to my wedding." John and Sandra said nothing for a few seconds. Nathan could see them looking at each other wide eyed, talking in silence, completely baffled.

Sandra took the phone off speaker just in case John said something out loud that would be best for Nathan not to hear. He wasn't one to always think before he spoke when he was caught by surprise. John was pacing, already trying to wrap his mind around what December 10 might be like. Nathan was marrying into a family who stood for everything he didn't. Warren had been his adversary in the debate, and not only would it be somewhat uncomfortable to be around him again, but they were going to be family.

Warren was the reason he was taking a month off from work, and now he was going to end his time off with him. The thought of it made him furious. He wondered what had gotten into Nathan, how he could be so irresponsible. John turned around to look at Sandra, and right away she knew how he felt about it. His face had turned red, and she knew better than to try to get him on the phone. Regardless, she knew there was only one thing to say.

"Congratulations, Nathan. We're happy for you. Of course we'll be there."

"Is Dad still there?" Nathan asked, wondering how his father was reacting to the news.

"Yes, Nathan. He's fine."

"Let me talk to him."

"You want to talk to your dad?" Sandra said this out loud to see how John might react. John waved his hands, making it clear he was not going to get on the phone.

"Nathan, um...Can he talk to you later?"

"He's mad?" Nathan sounded both hurt and defiant at the same time.

"No, Nathan, but can you guys talk later?" She didn't sound convincing. Nathan could tell she felt bad, and pushing her to get John on the phone wouldn't be fair.

"Okay, Mom. See you on the tenth?"

"Yes," she answered, looking at John. "We'll be there a couple days before. Do you need us to do anything before then?"

Nathan was disappointed by his dad's childishness, and he didn't hide it in his voice. "No, but thanks anyway. It's going to be a small ceremony. Just bring yourselves. I love you. Bye."

"We love you too, Nathan. Bye."

He hung up the phone and threw it on his desk. He didn't think there was anyone left in the office, so he decided to stay there a few minutes. A rush of negative emotions and resentment toward John rushed to the surface unexpectedly. He tried to keep them at bay, but they were too strong to control. These feelings were not new, and they taunted him to spew hate and to despair. He could feel himself going down that familiar road again, but before he went too far, he caught himself.

With his head bowed and eyes closed, he asked God to do something he couldn't do for himself: he asked Him to keep the negative emotions back and to not let them get the best of him. Within minutes, he could actually feel a release from the stronghold of the thoughts and emotions. They weren't as binding now. A new, healthier perspective came over him, allowing him to clear his mind and see things for what they were. And to his astonishment, he felt a sense of grace toward his dad he'd never felt before. He knew John was alone in his world and in his mind, without the ability to ask God to rush to his aid.

Pleasantly perplexed by what had just happened, Nathan bowed his head again. Humbled by the almost palpable presence of Christ in his office, he found himself praying for John and Sandra.

Chapter 44

RUSHING AROUND TO get ready for the wedding day made a month fly by, and with just two days to go, it felt as if there was still so much left to do. It was the day Sandra and John were coming to Charleston, and they were supposed to be there in less than two hours. The plan was for Nathan, Kate, and her parents to meet them for supper once they had a chance to get settled in their hotel.

Nathan could feel the pit of his stomach knot up at the prospect of the dinner. They were last together at the debate, which had been awkward enough—but at least with all the commotion of the event, there had not been the intimacy of the coming night. Nathan was also still mad at his father for the way he had acted when he told them about the wedding, and he didn't want either of them to lose his temper during the evening with the Johnsons. He was pacing back and forth in the Johnsons' living room, feeling that familiar pressure he had felt all his life, to please everyone, to impress, to appear to be in control. He didn't usually feel that around Kate and the Johnsons, but knowing his parents were coming brought it all back.

He had last spoken to his parents two days ago, and it had been just a quick conversation to firm up the plans. Rachel, who was in the same room as Nathan, had overheard them talking about what they might do their first night in Charleston, and she had suggested they all meet for dinner, offering to then show the Berkleys around the city. Nathan had felt the sudden need to swallow his tongue so he couldn't mention the idea to his parents. But out of respect for Rachel, a person he had really grown to respect and like, he had passed the invitation on to them. After a few seconds of indecision, the Berkleys had accepted.

Cesar A. Perez

Nathan's phone rang; it was Sandra telling him they had arrived at the hotel. She said they knew where the restaurant was, and they would meet Nathan and the Johnsons there at seven.

"Was that your parents, Nathan?" Kate asked.

"Sure was."

Knowing how his dad had acted when he'd told them about the wedding, Kate said nothing and smiled at him with her eyes. She had prayed often that he would be able to relax and put things in perspective, but he was having a hard time with this one.

Warren put down the mail he was going through and took off his glasses. Looking right at Nathan, he said, "Sit down, son, please." Nathan complied.

"I know you're a little anxious about tonight." Nathan nodded in agreement. "I want you to know it's okay. We're looking forward to spending the evening with your parents."

The statement was just matter of fact, and Nathan knew Warren meant it. The events leading to today hadn't been what usually happens in the lives of most people, and Nathan knew this would be an uncomfortable situation for everyone. He knew where the Johnsons' strength came from, but he couldn't figure out why he wasn't getting the same results from his faith as they did. Not on this one. They were by no means perfect, but they could deal with whatever life threw at them better than most people. He had seen them stressed, sad, and worried plenty of times because of Austin's disappearance—but still, they were able to snap out of it quickly and get on with life.

"Thank you, sir. I'm trying to relax. It's just hard for me."

"It's okay, Nathan—completely normal."

Nathan shifted in his seat. "I wish I could be more like you all. If anyone here has any right to be freaked out, it's you. To be honest, I'm just really angry that we even have to do this tonight. My dad doesn't deserve to be treated like you all are treating him."

"We are great with it, so don't worry about us. Is it a little uncomfortable? Sure, but many things in life are. Let me tell you something I figured out many years ago." Warren narrowed his gaze. "This is something I knew but didn't practice very well for a long time. Yesterday is gone. You will never get *now* back. And tomorrow is not here yet."

Nathan squinted his eyes and attempted not to look puzzled as he tried to get the nugget of wisdom out of what Warren had said.

"Don't live in the past, Nathan. Make the most of the now. And don't worry about tomorrow!" Warren paused to let the words sink in. "I know this isn't easy to do, though. You can only do it by asking God to help you. But it is a timeless truth. If you practice it every day, you will save yourself much pain and be blessed. Otherwise, you will fall into a pit of worry and despair of your own digging."

Nathan sat back and nodded to acknowledge his agreement. There was no need to reply—a simple nod was enough to let Warren know he understood. He looked at Kate and noticed how she was looking at her dad. He could tell she respected her father's wisdom and his desire to help Nathan, and he wished he could feel the same toward his own dad.

Kate appreciated Warren's love for Nathan, for his desire to invest in his young life. She knew he was doing this for Nathan but also for her, so she would have the best husband possible. She made a mental note to give him a big hug later and thank him.

⋆⊱⊙ ⊙⊰⋆

The Johnsons picked Trevor's for dinner. Warren had suggested Nawlin's jokingly—something Nathan had been quick to accept just to see how his parents would react. But the women had more sense than that, and Trevor's it was. They hadn't been waiting more than five minutes outside the restaurant when they spotted the Berkleys walking up the street toward them. Kate felt a surge of nervous feelings rushing to her mind and squeezed Nathan's hand without meaning to. Nathan had been nervous all day, but feeling the squeeze from her hand somehow gave him a sense of confidence and courage. His anxiety seemed unimportant if she needed him to be strong. He loved the feeling of protecting Kate.

Nathan walked up to meet his parents and gave them a hug. "Hi, Mom, Dad. It's good to see you." He put his arm around Sandra and led them to Kate and her parents.

"You remember my dad, I'm sure," Nathan said jokingly, looking at Warren.

Warren extended his hand to shake John's. "Dr. Berkley, it's great to see you again. Thank you for joining us. Did you have a good trip?"

John shook Warren's hand with a good firm grip and offered a courteous smile. His eyes quickly scanned everyone to extend his greeting to them.

"Yes, thank you, Dr. Johnson." John said, withdrawing his hand so he could shake Rachel's and Kate's. "Charleston certainly is beautiful."

Kate shook John's hand quickly and then gave him a hug. "Thank you for coming, Dr. Berkley. I'm so glad y'all are here."

"It's good to see you too, Kate. Sorry we didn't get to speak any in Salt Lake City, but we had to catch our flight."

Rachel hugged Sandra as they greeted each other. "No Doctor So-and-So tonight—just John and just Warren. Okay?" she said to Warren and John, smiling at Sandra.

"And there will be no debating, gentlemen," Sandra said.

Everyone laughed, nodding in agreement as the hostess called, "Johnson, party of six!"

They started moving toward the door, and Kate invited John into the building with a smile. She gave him the impression of being genuinely glad he was there, and right away he could feel himself at ease around her.

Even though the gathering was awkward at first, the ice was quickly broken as they talked about what they were thinking the night of the debate. There was a lot brewing under the surface, especially between Nathan and John, but they were able to relax and have a few laughs.

Nathan felt guilty for all the resentment he harbored toward his dad, and he wished things didn't have to be as they were—but at least John was behaving tonight. He remembered what Warren had said to him earlier, that his reactions were a choice. So he decided to make the best of the situation and not make himself miserable.

The most uncomfortable moment of their evening came when Warren asked the group if it would be okay for him to ask God to bless the meal. He wasn't willing to compromise on this, even if it may cause some discomfort. John and Sandra complied and played it off as if they expected it. They didn't close their eyes during the prayer; they just looked down at the table and felt awkward. What they both did notice was that Nathan had bowed his head and closed his eyes.

All things considered, the experience served to make the Johnsons and the Berkleys seem less abnormal to one another. No matter how different they were in their worldviews, they learned they could relate to each other at a personal level. This helped reduce Nathan's and Kate's anxiety about the future relationship between the two families. They may not become the best of friends and spend every holiday together, but at least there should not be constant animosity and friction.

There were a handful of loose ends to tie up before the wedding, so they decided to take a rain check on the city tour and go get things done separately. As John and Rachel walked toward the Harbor Inn, the place Nathan had recommended, John couldn't help but be impressed by the way Kate had treated him and Sandra that night. He had felt a genuine kindness from her, something he wasn't used to seeing in the people he met day in and day out.

Kate seemed to care about people. She reminded him of someone from his distant past, a person who he knew had truly loved him no matter what—a person he had tried hard not to think about but had never been able to forget. He tried to chase the memories away, but it was impossible. The memories of Lance were not meant to go away. Because somehow, they represented something important that was missing from his life.

Chapter 45

AFTER TWO YEARS of marriage, Nathan had kept his commitment not to buy a minivan. Because of his success at work, he was able to drive an expensive German import he often wished he could push to its limits on the autobahn. Tonight that dream was almost becoming a reality. Whether the light was green, red, or yellow, Nathan kept whipping through the streets. His car couldn't go fast enough. But there was no thrill to this drive; there was only sheer panic.

As the glow from the traffic lights above glided across his windshield, he looked in his rearview mirror to check on Kate. Her pain got worse by the minute. Seeing her in such agony scared him, and he felt helpless. The thought of her suffering struck him at his core, and he wished there was something he could do to take her pain away.

His mind flashed back to the look on her face as she walked down the aisle two years earlier. He could still hear the sounds from the photographer's camera and the laughs of joy from their family and friends that day. Everything had been perfect, even the goofy look on Jeff's face when he tried to make Nathan laugh before he could say his vows. He had felt as if in a trance that entire day, overwhelmed by a peace and joy he'd never thought possible before. Kate's eyes had been completely fixed on him as she walked toward him, smiling and adoring him with her whole being. Her complete love and devotion to him were engraved in his soul that day. Her love had, once again, changed and transformed him.

"You're going to kill me before we get there!" Kate yelled from the back seat. Nathan snapped back to reality, his eyes rushing back to the rearview mirror to check on her. He found her staring back at him, with both a smile and a look of slight concern on her face.

Within minutes, he drove past the hospital's side entrance in a mad dash to the emergency-room door. Kate couldn't hide her pain. She was gasping for air and groaning. Tires screeching, and almost taking down one of the support columns of the emergency-room entrance, Nathan brought the car to an abrupt stop. He looked at the parking lot and saw the truck that belonged to Warren, who was the first person he had called when Kate woke him up just thirty minutes earlier. Knowing he was there made Nathan feel better. He needed someone to help them through this, and he could not think of anyone he would rather have there.

A doctor and an orderly rushed to the side of the car and carefully helped Kate onto a wheelchair. Nathan urged them to be careful with her. A feeling of panic surged within him as he read a look of concern on the doctor's face.

He felt a strong, confident hand on his shoulder as he followed them through the door. It was Warren, who had spotted them and was now walking beside him.

"It's okay, son. She's going to be fine. These guys know what they're doing." Nathan could feel some of the weight of his anxiety lift off, and he thanked God for a good father-in-law, but mostly for a good friend.

"Hey, hon," Warren said, reaching for Kate's hand as they all rushed through the next set of doors. She was in so much pain at this point that all she could offer was a faint smile.

Kate was very familiar with the layout of the emergency-room area, and she knew that soon the staff would not let Nathan and Warren continue to walk with her. Nathan was visibly concerned and nervous, and she knew the doctor would have already noticed, which meant he wouldn't let them know they couldn't go in with her until the last possible moment. This was to eliminate time for arguments and unnecessary stress on her.

As the ceiling lights overhead went by faster and faster and they pushed his precious Kate through the emergency room, Warren also thought about another of his children. Austin. There had been no news about him for years, and the military had declared him missing in action. The thought of where he might be, or if he was even alive, was unbearable at times.

Warren felt a squeeze and a tug from Kate's hand, just as she had always done when she needed his attention. He looked at her and smiled with a confidence he didn't really feel inside. She smiled back at him, unable to speak but wanting him to know that she didn't want him to worry about her. Kate pointed at Nathan with her eyes, asking Warren to look after him. He nodded with a reassuring look, and that was all she needed.

⊷⊶⊙ ⊙⊶⊷

The forty-five minutes following the moment they took Kate into a private room were the hardest in Nathan's life. He and Warren sat down in the waiting room and watched as different hospital staff came in and out. They had spent the first few minutes in prayer, eyes closed and heads bowed. At first it had felt awkward because they were around other people. But within a few minutes of being led in prayer by this man whom he admired and trusted, Nathan could not care less what others thought.

Rachel and Edee had been there for a few minutes when the doctor came out to speak with them. Nathan noticed slight traces of blood on the doctor's scrubs as he and Warren walked toward him. He felt as if his whole life hung in the balance. Whatever the doctor said in the next few seconds could change his life for the better or for the worse.

"Good evening. My name is Dr. Alvarez. Are you the husband?" the doctor asked, looking at Nathan. His tone was forthright and matter of fact. It was obvious he was used to speaking to families and had perfected the art of showing no emotion.

"Yes," Nathan answered.

Chapter 46

DR. ALVAREZ FLASHED a big smile and said, "Congratulations, sir! You have a very healthy baby boy. He's perfect!"

Nathan still had a serious expression on his face. The news was great, but he wanted to know about Kate. "How is my wife?"

"She's resting now," the doctor answered as he patted Nathan on the shoulder. "She had a placental abruption and lost a lot of blood. I hope you understand that's why you couldn't be in the room." Nathan nodded, and Dr. Alvarez continued. "It's a good thing you got her here so quickly or she may have been in real trouble. As soon as we were able to get the bleeding under control, your son decided he was ready to check out what all the fuss was about and come into the world."

Nathan felt a strong pull from Warren to hug him as he sighed with relief. "Oh, thank God. Is she going to be okay?"

Dr. Alvarez nodded. "Yes, sir. Your wife is going to be just fine. We'll want to keep her at the hospital a couple of nights to monitor her closely and let her regain her strength. She will need plenty of strength to take care of your handsome son."

"Thank you, Dr. Alvarez," Nathan said. His voice broke up slightly as he spoke. What could have been the worst day of his life had turned out to be the best. When Kate woke him that evening, she told him she was in severe pain and was worried something might be wrong with the baby. Nathan was terrified he might lose her and their child that night. That would have turned his world completely upside down. But instead, everything had turned out fine and Kate and his son were going to be okay.

In the room that night, lying beside Kate and holding this brand-new life they had created, Nathan felt as if he had just gotten another big break in life. The feeling of almost having lost her was a strong reminder of what she meant to him. It had taught him that sometimes a great blessing could only be fully appreciated after a traumatic event. It also taught him that he wasn't in control. Through this, he had felt a need and a reliance on God he never had experienced before. Their family was a gift, and he vowed to do everything in his power to protect and provide for them.

⋅–⊨⊙ ⊙⊨⊰⋅

Nathan had fallen in love with his son the moment he saw him. And he knew that moment would be engraved in his heart because it transcended the here and now. The new journey he and Kate had embarked on was very exciting, and they couldn't wait for the days ahead.

Every day felt brand new. Little Luke had turned their lives completely upside down as they quickly realized how little they knew about caring for a baby. For the first time ever, they knew what true responsibility was. Nathan wanted to do everything right, and the thought of doing anything wrong scared him.

The days turned into weeks and the weeks into months faster than they could keep up with. Emma came unexpectedly a couple of years after Luke, and Nathan and Kate held on for dear life as the reality of being a busy family seemed to change their perspective on almost everything. They had begun the involuntary, yet very natural, transition from a young couple who drove sporty cars and slept in on Saturdays to a life at the beck and call of their children.

Like many other resolutions they had made when they didn't have children, soon after Emma arrived, they became the proud owners of a new minivan. And Nathan couldn't care less, especially after Kate had assured him she would be the primary driver of their new vehicle.

Regardless of what they drove or what they did, every day was a memory in the making for their young family. Doing the small things together, such as going to the store and cooking a meal at home, was what meant the most, and they wouldn't trade their busyness for anything.

Nathan marveled at all the selfless ways in which Kate took care of their children, and he couldn't help but fall more in love with her as time passed. They were building a life as a family, and the result was what seemed to be an inseparable bond that would last forever.

It seemed impossible that he would have such a deep love for Luke and Emma. The children had been in his and Kate's lives for a short period, but Nathan felt in his core that his life could never go on without them. He depended on them for happiness, for well-being, and for a sensation of wholeness. He knew what he felt toward them went beyond anything he had ever experienced. It was something that came with being a father, a privilege and an honor of which he didn't feel worthy. The unpardonable sin, for Nathan, would be to fail them in any way.

Chapter 47

NATHAN ADJUSTED THE rearview mirror to check on Luke and little Emma as they drove from grandma's house after celebrating one Christmas Eve. He laughed as Luke harassed his sister by taking on and off a John Deere hat Nathan had received when he bought a new lawnmower that summer. Emma loved to wear the hat. She wouldn't leave home without it, and Luke had quickly figured out that the best way to get her attention was to take it away from her. Nathan looked over at Kate, who was laughing to herself as she organized the little projects Luke and Emma had busied themselves with creating that night. They looked at each other and without words recommitted to their mission—get home quickly and get ready for Santa to come that night.

Around six the next morning, Kate rolled over to check on Nathan. Their look conveyed agreement that they needed to get up, but neither of them liked it one bit. They were tired from the night before, and getting up seemed both inhuman and impossible, but the excitement within them finally made them spring up from the bed. Amid shushes to each other to be quiet and not wake the kids, they rushed to the living room to make sure everything was just right before Luke and Emma came in anxious to see what Santa had brought them. Kate turned on the Christmas tree's lights, and Nathan rushed to put a new tape in the video camera to capture every moment.

As he turned the corner from the kitchen to the living room, camera in hand, Kate signaled from the other side of the room that she was starting to hear some noises, pointing to their rooms. The lighting was dim, and her hand gestures were not very clear, but he interpreted three things: he needed to be quiet, to turn the camera on, and to step closer. As Nathan started to walk up, she held up one hand to stop him. The noise from Emma's room was getting louder, and she knew it wouldn't be long before the children came into the living room. Kate started flapping her hands forward, trying to get Nathan to step back to his original spot. This startled him, and he rushed to retreat to where they wouldn't see him.

Nathan struggled to walk backward in the dark room. All of a sudden, he felt an acute sting of pain on the bottom of his bare foot. The pain quickly turned into an unexpected jolt backward as his foot launched forward. On his way down, he saw the culprit speeding across the hardwood floor toward Kate. It was one of the little cars Luke liked to push around the house. With a less-than-graceful landing, Nathan found himself on top of some of the presents by the tree. As he looked up in the midst of his shock, he noticed the top of the tree rocking back and forth. Kate came rushing to it, her eyes wide open and arms extended. The tree was already tipping forward when she got there, but she reached it in time to stabilize it.

Kate got on her knees to check on Nathan, who was still lying on the floor with a stunned look on his face. She was fighting a strong urge to laugh while maintaining a look of quasi-concern on her face. She wanted to make sure he wasn't hurt, but as the last few seconds played in her mind, the urge to laugh was getting harder and harder to resist.

"Oh, honey, are you okay?" she whispered.

Nathan nodded, embarrassed but also mad at his luck. "I'm fine. The presents broke most of my fall."

She patted his chest as she kissed him on the cheek, and they both started laughing. Their chuckling was interrupted by the sound of tiny steps and hushed little voices coming down the hall.

"Oh, how sweet," Kate said to Nathan. "Get the camera rolling."

"It's been rolling this whole time," he answered.

She chuckled, nodding her head at him. "Can't wait to watch that one later." She paused and put her index finger on her mouth, telling him to be quiet, although he wasn't the one talking. "Here they come."

Nathan stood up and made sure the camera was still recording. He pointed it at Kate and zoomed in. She looked so excited, so happy and complete.

The little steps and hushed voices were getting closer. "Emma, shhh…he might still be heo," said Luke as the leader of the little escapade.

"Okay," came the sweet reply from Emma. Kate bent down, trying not to laugh out loud as her heart filled with joy.

"Come on, Emma. We are almost theo. Be vewy quiet, now. If he is still heo and heos us, he will take our toys with him."

Seconds later when they felt there was no risk, after having waited for this moment an entire year, Emma and Luke came through the door hand in hand. Nathan zoomed in to their faces. They both had looks of pure excitement. He and Kate would never tire of seeing that joy. Their eyes were full of wonder as they walked through the room taking in all that Santa had brought them. Nathan loved their ability to get lost in the wonder of the moment.

Christmas had always been just another day for Nathan, but now each year was better than the one before. The images of Luke and Emma walking to the tree in the living room wearing their pajamas, hair all messed up and eyes full of wonder as if they were about to walk into a treasure, would always be some of the most precious memories for Nathan and Kate.

Kate couldn't wait another moment, so she jumped out from behind the couch and took the children into her arms.

Chapter 48

HARD WORK, DEDICATION, and a great attitude during Nathan's career at Teksoft had been impossible to ignore, and management had long been taking notice of his tenacity and ability to turn tough situations into successful outcomes. The position for the director of professional services came open. And although there were people who had more seniority than Nathan, management decided he was the man for the job. Kate was so proud of him, not only for being rewarded for his hard work, but also for doing his best and providing for them. Nathan loved the feeling he got when she was proud of him, which had been a huge catalyst driving him to work even harder the last few years.

The desire to succeed and make others proud quickly became a powerful driver in Nathan's life, and his career took off at breakneck speed. But with every promotion there was a price to pay: long hours at the office and time away from home. Teksoft was growing rapidly and gaining a lot of market share, and he knew that if he didn't overperform, there were plenty of people champing at the bit to take his place. One by one, the moments he tried to protect, like church and family time on Sundays, became critical times to get work done so the company could keep its competitive edge.

One early spring afternoon had all the right ingredients for family time at home. It had been a stressful week at work, and Nathan vowed to keep his phone turned off and his laptop closed. After a great lunch together, Luke made a mad dash to his room to watch a movie, and Nathan took Emma to play in the backyard.

They'd had a lot of rain, and the grass and flowers were bursting with vivid colors as the sun shone brightly on them. Nathan sat on a chair in their back porch and watched Emma run to the swing set, marveling at the beauty of the rays of sun glistening through her blond hair. He couldn't believe she was almost eight. Time was flying by, and he wished he could somehow slow it down. She had a beaming smile on her face, just for him, as she swung back and forth.

There was so much joy in his heart as he took it all in. He knew he had it all, certainly much more than anyone could ask for. But unfortunately, the pressures of work, and the now-familiar worry and anxiety that came with it, interrupted the moment he had so desperately needed. The weight of his responsibilities caused him to want to buckle under sometimes, which made things seem exponentially worse than they really were. He shook his head and wondered if he had allowed himself to take on too much.

Emma looked as if she was having the time of her life. She was completely carefree, unconcerned about yesterday or today—only the current moment mattered. Nathan wanted the same. He longed for the joy he had seen slip through his fingers lately. He knew in his heart that there was a lot to enjoy right where he was, but he had allowed his mind to get too overburdened. As he had done often lately, he felt like a kid in a circus unable to enjoy the wonder and fun around him.

He heard a loud noise, and before he could wonder what it was, Luke flew past him. "Hi, Daddy," Luke said hurriedly as he ran toward the swings. Kate came out to the porch moments later. She smiled at Nathan and without saying anything sat down between him and one of the large columns in their back porch. There it was, he noticed right away, that joy on her face she'd always been able to maintain. Nathan found himself envying her disposition, almost resenting it. He knew that was wrong, and he had tried to make himself stop, but he couldn't.

The giggles got louder as Emma chased a butterfly through the backyard, getting their attention. Nathan returned Kate's gaze with a smile he wanted to feel but couldn't. He realized how wonderful the moment was, but enjoying it seemed to him as unattainable as a dream.

Nathan tried to pray his thoughts and feelings away, but to no avail. When at first he realized he was going down this path, that his mental life was being consumed by worry and anxiety, he had turned to prayer successfully. But as the demands and responsibility of life increased, he found less and less time to stop and pray. He had many things to take care of and very little time in which to do them. Soon, he developed the habit of putting off prayer and time with God until sometime later when things might calm down. But things never calmed down.

His cell phone rang. It was John calling, which was highly unusual since they hardly ever talked. "Excuse me," he said to Kate as he went into the house to take the call.

Nathan would have preferred to ignore John's call, but he figured it might be something important since calls from him were rare. He decided to be as pleasant as possible. "Hi, Dad. To what do I owe this honor?"

"Hi, Nathan. How are you doing?" John responded.

"Pretty good. How are you and Mom?"

"We are good. Thanks for asking. The reason I'm calling is that I'm getting a lifetime achievement award next week, and I'd like you to come up and be here for it." Sandra had put John up to making the call and saying he wanted Nathan there, and John was trying his best to sell it in order to appease her.

But Nathan had no desire to be there. "I'm very sorry," he said. "Right now is not a good time for me to take off work and come up there."

"It figures," John said, dismissing Nathan.

"What's that mean? I really am busy at work, and our family has a lot going on. I am happy for you, though. Good job," he lied, "but coming up there on such short notice is not possible."

"What it means, Nathan, is that you act like Mr. Perfect in front of Kate's family. But when it comes to doing something for your family, you don't feel the need to be quite so perfect. I know the real you, son, and you can't pull the wool over my eyes like you can theirs."

Stunned by John's words, Nathan was getting very angry. He almost hung up but decided not to. He looked around to make sure neither Kate nor the kids were in the house before he said anything else. "What in the world are you talking about? Where is all this coming from?"

"I don't buy your little Christian act, Nathan. I never have. I've known you all your life, and you never believed any of that crap. Then you meet a pretty girl, and all of a sudden you are one of them? Please, I know better. I know who you really are. What you are is a great pretender, but you're not fooling me. And you're not fooling yourself. You are the same as you've always been and will always be. So don't waste my time or your mom's with the good-guy act!"

"You are a pitiful excuse for a man," Nathan said to John. "Don't bother calling me again." John slammed the phone with every intention of doing just as he had been told.

At first, Nathan dismissed everything John said as the rantings of a failed father and someone who needed God in his life. But in the days that followed, John's words led to a lot of inward reflection, which caused him to question his beliefs and his motives. Nathan was taking his eyes off God and trying to deal with this on his own, which ultimately led to a lot of anxiety and self-doubt.

He knew the effects of all of this. He had dealt with minor bouts of depression before, but this time it was coming with an insatiable hunger to consume him. There was a lot more at stake in his life now and much to lose, and Nathan was terrified to mess up what he had.

He knew what he had to do as a Christian—stop worrying about everything and put God first. But as time went by, things got away from him, and the downward spiral seemed to be getting out of control. He told Kate about the conversation with his dad, but he didn't tell her about what the strain was doing to him.

Even though Nathan knew he was self-destructing and quickly getting to the point of no return, his pride kept him from reaching out to someone to get help for fear that he would look weak. Instead, he put on a facade and tried to act as if everything was normal.

What broke his heart the most was how quickly he lost his patience with the kids. As much as he loved them, he couldn't figure out how he would at times get so angry so quickly. Nathan still knew God was there to help him figure out what was wrong. But at the same time, he felt helpless, as if he were someone on the outside looking in while some unstoppable force he couldn't control was taking over. In years past, he had always been able to gain some type of perspective that helped him get through a tough time. This time was different—his feelings of depression wouldn't go away. They were slowly overtaking him. They were replacing the peace he had known with doubt and unrest. They were changing him from the inside out, and he hated the person he was turning into.

He knew he had it all—an angel for a wife, two perfect children, a career that seemed unstoppable, their dream home, and the best support system possible in her parents and family. But on none of that could he rest. It was the opposite—the more he realized he had to be thankful for, the more desperate and hopeless he felt because he was afraid he would lose it if he didn't snap out of his depression. God seemed more distant every day, and he was no longer able to rest his mind or experience joy.

Talking to Kate about it was the last thing he wanted do. He didn't want her to think he was weak, much less that he was going crazy. He preferred her to see him as strong and always in control, and he knew he couldn't handle the embarrassment he would feel if she could see who he was becoming. So he pretended to be okay in front of her and everyone around him, but inside he was horrified as he quickly spiraled out of control.

Chapter 49

THE CHANGES IN Nathan had at first appeared subtle to Kate. In the last couple of weeks, however, he had been more distant and disengaged. She could tell he was unhappy, and she was getting concerned about him. His enthusiasm was almost completely gone, and she couldn't remember the last time he had rolled around on the floor to wrestle with Luke or dropped by Emma's room for a tea party with her stuffed animals.

Kate had no doubt he loved them and was fully devoted to them, but she knew that whatever this was, it was getting worse. At times she casually asked how he was doing in hopes that he would open up, but he just pretended to be fine. If she pressed, he claimed to be tired or busy to avoid talking. Nathan hated lying to her, but he felt he had no other choice. Guilt overtook him, making him feel she deserved more than the man he was being reduced to. He was terrified he would lose her and the kids if he didn't get it together; this haunted his thoughts and eventually took away his sleep and appetite.

One Friday night, Kate arranged for Warren and Rachel to take care of the kids so she and Nathan could spend some time together. She thought that this might cheer him up. They would actually have a chance to talk, which was rarely the case when the house was buzzing with all the activity. Nathan had suggested they go out to eat, but Kate insisted he let her cook them supper. She promised to make his favorite meal, and he immediately agreed.

As soon as he got home from work, she greeted him at the door. Dinner was almost ready, and she insisted he relax on the couch and watch TV until everything was on the table. It suited him just fine to get all of Kate's attention, so he offered no resistance. Kate offered little conversation over the next few minutes because she was trying to get him to relax. They would have plenty of time to talk while they ate. He could hear she was busy at work in the kitchen. And by the sound of things, this must be some meal they were about to have.

"Nathan, are you ready to eat?" Kate asked when everything was ready.

"Sure am. It smells great," he said as he got up from the couch.

She watched him walk toward the table and felt saddened as she noticed once again how much weight he had lost lately. She poured his glass as he sat down and put the napkin over his lap.

"This looks great. You must have been at it all day," he said with a forced smile. Kate looked over at him and smiled but said nothing while she poured her glass. Nathan was looking at everything she fixed, and she followed his movements without his noticing. She could tell he was trying hard to look excited, but she knew him well enough to realize his mind was somewhere else. His thoughts were being taken captive by an inner struggle she was desperate to understand so she could help him.

Kate picked up a large serving spoon. "Let me serve you, Nathan."

"I'll get it. Don't worry."

She stopped her hand in midair, still holding the spoon, and took a deep breath. "Nathan! Are you even hungry?"

He looked at her and smiled. His gaze seemed to focus somewhere beyond her.

"What's wrong with you, honey?" she asked with a hint of desperation in her voice.

He shrugged. "There's nothing wrong with me, Kate. I'm just trying to decide what I want to eat."

Kate placed the spoon on the table and grabbed his hand. "I'm not talking about the food, Nathan. You've not been the same the past few months. I want you to talk to me and tell me what you're feeling. I need to know what's wrong so I can help you."

He stopped smiling and stared at her as she pleaded with him.

"You hardly talk to the kids anymore, or to me. When you're at home, it's like you're not really here. What's going on?"

Nathan sat back in his chair and looked down at the table. He felt caught, embarrassed that his attempts to hide his struggles had failed. He didn't want to talk about his feelings of depression, but he knew there was no way out of doing so now. His eyes shifted from side to side as he fought the urge to break down.

Kate grabbed his other hand and tugged at it. "Look at me, Nathan," she said. But his gaze stayed on the table as he took a deep breath. She looked to the side and felt the urge to cry as the pain she had borne the last few months came to a climax inside her.

"Look at me, Nathan, please." This time her tone was more direct. Nathan looked up, and her heart sank as she saw the full measure of his torment in his eyes—a pain he seemed to no longer want to hide. "Talk to me, Nathan. What's wrong?"

He withdrew his hands from hers and rubbed his face. He could feel the anxiety building up inside, and with every second he felt himself caring less what he might say to her. *Dang it!* he thought, regretting his inability to get it together and avoid this situation.

"I want to help you, honey. The kids and I need you. I really need you back."

"Okay, okay," Nathan responded after a few seconds. His voice quivered as a wave of emotions suddenly rushed to the surface, dredging up all the pain that had built over the last few months. He wanted to get up and postpone this conversation, but he knew things couldn't continue this way, and Kate deserved answers.

"I've wanted to talk to you, Kate. You just don't know how badly I've needed to talk to you—how much I've missed you."

Kate felt a numbing fear come over her as she realized something was seriously wrong with him.

"I just didn't know how to talk to you about it. I love you all so much." His eyes teared up, and he struggled to keep talking. He felt so frustrated by his state of mind that he slammed his fist on the table. The dishes bounced up and landed in unison, making a loud noise that filled the room. Kate was startled, but she didn't let it show.

"Sorry. I didn't want to do that. I just feel so overwhelmed."

"What are you struggling with, Nathan? You can tell me anything. Whatever this is, we'll work on it together. We'll get through it. Please trust me with whatever it is."

Nathan knew she meant what she said, but something deep inside told him that, as wonderful as it sounded, it might be too late.

He looked at her, and he saw both pain and confusion on her face. She nodded at him, telling him to go on. There was no doubt in his mind that she would stick with him through anything. He wanted more than anything to get back to the amazing life they'd always known. But there was something ugly and powerful inside him, something he couldn't control. It was taking all he loved and cherished out of reach.

He looked at her again, his eyes blood red, and he clenched his fists as he realized he was about to lose her. "You've got to know that I love you, Kate." She nodded.

He continued. "I don't want to believe it, but I'm afraid my father might have been somewhat right when he said I was living a lie. I was desperate to believe my transformation was real, that I could actually experience true peace and joy. But when push came to shove, when things got hard, I reverted back to the same Nathan as before."

Kate reached for his hand as tears began to flow from his eyes.

"I was spending so much energy protecting my life and my self-esteem that I got away from everything that made my life beautiful. My guilt led to insecurity and depression, and my fear of being weak eventually made me weak. I've felt like such a pretender. What a lie I am."

"Nathan, those feelings are normal. You have a lot of pressure to support our family, and that's not easy. You're an amazing man—the real deal—and we are all so proud of you, especially me. What your father said to you wasn't true. Don't let all of this get to you. Every day, for you, for me, is a battle. It's how we choose to react to circumstances that makes the difference. Why didn't you tell me this was going on?"

Her words rang true, but a voice inside him said, *Not you. That's not you, not anymore. You've gone too far.*

"Oh God, Kate. I know you're right. But I am exhausted, and right now nothing seems possible. I feel like I'm going crazy. And I'm so afraid to lose you and our kids." He was convinced she now thought he was weak and not worth wasting her time on, but nothing was further from the truth.

"Listen to me, Nathan," Kate said, looking him in the eyes. The expression on her face conveyed both compassion and conviction. "You can't give up. Life is hard. Not just for you but for everyone. I love you. The kids love you, and they need their daddy. We will work through this, but you have to know that it can be done. There is nothing we can't do if we let God help."

Nathan's first reaction was to shrug, which took her aback.

"Have you been praying about this, Nathan?"

He gazed up at her with a look of resigned desperation and said nothing.

"Nathan, honey, when life is too much to handle, God is all we have. He will get you through absolutely anything, but you must let Him. You have to ask Him to help you."

He knew what she meant. And he knew she believed it because he had seen her and her family live this out. He nodded at her, acknowledging he understood.

As he nodded, however, he realized for the first time that their faith was much more real to them than it had perhaps been to him. The realization that he didn't have the faith to rest on God when he was completely helpless shot chills through his entire being. He did not believe in God enough to trust with this.

Chapter 50

Am I a fraud? Nathan asked himself as Kate kept her gaze on him. *Was all of this just in my head? Why can't I experience what they can?* When things were going well, it had been so easy to believe in God. But now that everything felt out of control, his doubts were as real as his fears. He felt as if the weight of the world were coming down on his shoulders.

Kate sat back, unsure of what to say next. She thought about the day he'd come to talk to Warren and prayed to receive Christ. His eyes had been full of excitement then, ready to take on the world. That fire wasn't there now. He looked like a completely different man.

"Do you still believe that? You know you can trust God. Don't you?" she asked, but Nathan didn't look up.

"I think I do." He struggled to speak as a look of frustration filled his face. "It's not that easy, Kate. God seems so distant right now. He must have given up on me, because He's just not there right now."

She chose her words carefully. "God is always there, honey. Always. We can get in the way, which causes us not to feel Him, but that doesn't mean He's not there. He can use hard times to draw us to Him in a new, deeper way. Don't waste this chance, Nathan. Trust Him with all your heart, even if you don't understand or feel it right now. If you walk in faith right now, you will one day see what He was doing. You will be able to see a whole new side of Him you may not have seen otherwise."

He put his hands in his pockets and felt the coin Kate had given him, the one engraved with the barley leaf and fixed with the mirror. He remembered her explanation, but at that moment the coin had no discernable meaning. It was just metal and glass. "I wish it were that easy, Kate. None of that seems so real now."

"Are things okay at work? Please help me understand what all is going on so I can try to help. This is starting to scare me. Are you still upset with the whole Charles thing?"

He said nothing for a few seconds, the battle raging inside him becoming more obvious in his expression. He shook his head as he fiddled with a fork. "A lot of things have happened, not just at work. Them giving the stupid VP of operations position to Charles was just par for the course. What a moron anyway! Attend a meeting with him, and even you would probably say the same thing."

Kate was taken aback by the tone of his voice, but she didn't show it. "Nathan, I'm really proud of you and what you've accomplished in such a short period of time. We all are. It's incredible. So what if you didn't get that promotion? You'll have plenty of chances. Do you feel like you should go somewhere else or do something different?"

"I don't need to run away. I can handle it just fine, Kate!" His tone was raised and irritated. "I may not be the great Warren Johnson or Austin the hero, but I've done pretty well for myself. And how dare you question what I do or don't do. Of all people, I thought you would believe in me."

"I do believe in you. I always have, and I always will. But you're not happy. And I want you to be."

Nathan sat up and put both hands on the table, the look of desperation now replaced with one of anger. "So where is God now, Kate? Where is He?" he screamed, startling her. "I sure as heck don't know."

Kate said nothing. She felt tears start to flow as she struggled to understand what was unraveling before her. The candlelight shone off her tears, and Nathan hated seeing she was upset. But the anger that had built up inside him was too strong, and he couldn't bring himself to comfort her.

"I love you, Nathan. I just want to help you because I care."

"I know that," he responded, trying to calm the rage he felt inside. "The reality of life has just sunk in."

"This happens to everyone. We think we're invincible, and then life comes at us with everything it's got, and we start to get all self-conscious. You have a lot to be proud of and don't need to feel insecure. Nothing has been lost, Nathan. Nothing. We can fix this. You need to listen to the spirit of truth. Don't let a spirit of deception tell you it's impossible."

"I'm sorry about this, Kate. You've been so good to me, and the last thing I wanted to do was to upset you. You are the last person in the world that deserves this. I just have to get it together somehow. Please pray for me. It's not working for me right now, but I know it does for you." He looked into her eyes, with tears in his, and said, "I have no idea who I am anymore. Maybe I don't deserve you and the kids. Maybe you'd all be better off without me!"

That night, Kate prayed for hours as the distant look in his eyes haunted her. She couldn't understand how this had happened. Over the last few years, he had gotten very involved in church activity, and just over a year before, he had been ordained as a deacon in the church. She remembered the obvious joy in his eyes then, void of the fear of failure and feeling of insecurity that had taken him hostage. How did he get so off course? Her questions overwhelmed her, and all she knew to do was pose them to God.

After their conversation, Nathan got in his car and drove to the Battery. He told Kate he needed some fresh air and a chance to think. The place brought back memories of the Sunday afternoon when he had gone there for a walk after hearing Warren preach. What a wondrous day that had been. His whole life had changed in a matter of hours, and he desperately wanted that feeling to return. That day he had felt blessed and invincible—now he could see everything leave his grasp. With every step, he felt the anger and disappointment of the past few months gain a stronger foothold in his mind.

He stopped and looked out to the dark sea. What he had experienced that Sunday afternoon was now like a distant dream. He wanted to stop this craziness, but he had nothing to use in his fight against it. Nathan buried his face in his hands and surrendered to the deafening quiet of the night as he came to realize his greatest fear. He was lost and alone. Again.

Chapter 51

Four years later...

The young man and his son came back from a second trip to the dessert bar. Jamie's eyes were fixed on his plate, full of excitement and anticipation as he looked forward to attacking the banana pudding. Nathan smiled at them as they passed by.

The young man got a cup of coffee and watched his son eat dessert. "You don't want any dessert, Dad?" Jamie asked, obviously baffled as to why anyone would say no.

"I'm fine, son."

Jamie paused, spoon in midair. "You don't wanna get fat, Dad? Like Mom?"

Nathan started laughing. The young man turned around, shaking his head. "They just say what comes to mind. You know?"

"Yes, I know," Nathan answered, nodding.

The young man looked at his son and then back at Nathan. "I'm sorry you've not had a very peaceful dinner because of us."

"Oh, no," Nathan said. "I'm glad you were here. I needed some company tonight."

The young man sensed he was being honest and continued the conversation. "Do you come here often? We used to growing up...a good bit, actually. My dad loved this place, and it just sort of became what you would call a family restaurant to us."

"I used to come here a lot myself, but the last time was years ago."

The young man looked around to see if anyone could hear him and in a hushed tone said, "Yeah, I can see how you may need to stay away if you used to eat here a lot. It's easy to pack on a few pounds, this stuff is so good. Might even avoid a heart attack."

Nathan laughed, and so did the young man, who turned toward his son to help him wipe his mouth.

"No, it wasn't because of the food. I've lived somewhere else the last few years. Are you from here?" Nathan asked.

The young man nodded. "I was born and raised in Charleston, but I was away for a while myself. The whole time I was gone was not by choice. Let's just say I was very thankful to get back home. Where are you from originally?"

"I'm from up North, Connecticut. After college I came here to see what the South was all about, and I fell in love with it."

"I can understand that," the young man responded as he repositioned his chair to face Nathan.

Nathan continued. "I didn't just fall in love with Charleston. I fell in love with the most beautiful person I'd ever met. I couldn't help but to move here so I could be with her." He paused and sighed as the familiar feelings of loss and guilt made their way back.

The young man could sense sadness and regret in Nathan's voice, and something rose within him, causing him to want to reach out. "Go on!" he said, encouraging him to continue. "This is a great story. Don't leave me hanging now."

Nathan felt energized by his interest and managed to dismiss all the negative thoughts. "We got married the same year we met. Those were the happiest years of my life. How about you? Are you married?"

"Yes, sir, I am. I married my childhood sweetheart about four years ago, just a few weeks after I got back. And that little fella right there..." He looked over at Jamie with a playful shrug. "He ruined our peace and quiet three years ago."

"You're a lucky man. I hope you know just how much," Nathan said, pointing at Jamie.

"I do know. Do you have kids?"

Nathan felt a surge of emotion, a deep sense of longing, rising up. "Yes, I do. We had two kids. Not a moment goes by I don't think about them."

"I don't mean to pry," said the young man as he checked on Jamie, who was now focused on getting a small toy car to stay on an imaginary road on the table. "But do you get to see them often?"

Nathan sighed. Shaking his head, he said, "I would like nothing more. I miss them terribly. Can't live without them, but it's better for them this way."

The young man leaned forward. "I really doubt that."

"They deserve a lot more than me."

"Oh, come on," said the young man with a cheering tone. "I think they would love to see you."

"Not after the way I acted. Not after what I became." Nathan paused and looked around the restaurant, wondering why he was sharing something so intimate with a complete stranger, but somehow talking about it was helping. He figured he'd never see the guy again anyway, so he continued. "We had a great marriage. But life got hard, and I got scared and selfish. My wife would've stuck through anything with me—that's just the kind of person she was—but I couldn't get it together. The home environment was changing negatively because of me, and I couldn't bear the thought of staying around and making everyone miserable. They deserved so much more than what they were getting with me there.

"So I convinced myself that the best thing for them was to be without me, and one day I left. I stayed away because I was a coward and couldn't face my failures. Whenever I thought about going back to them, it always felt like it was too late. Not a day goes by that I don't regret what I've done."

Nathan took a sip of his coffee and thought about Kate. His sadness and melancholy were almost palpable. Talking about the past reminded him once again of how much he still loved her. She and the children were a part of him he had never been able to live without.

He looked up at the young man, switching his thoughts back to the conversation but wanting to change the subject. "My name is Nathan, by the way," he said, extending his hand. "We've been talking for a while now, and I just realized we never introduced ourselves."

The young man laughed in agreement. "It's a pleasure to meet you, Nathan," he said in a genuine, almost familiar tone. "My name is Austin. Austin Johnson."

Chapter 52

NATHAN'S HEART NEARLY jumped out of his chest as the name registered in his mind and he recalled the picture in Warren's living room. There was no doubt he was the same person as in the picture.

"You are Austin, Kate's brother? Your dad's name is Warren?"

"Wow! You're good!" Austin replied, smiling but perplexed at the same time. "You're either some kind of psychic, a CIA agent, or—"

"I'm Nathan, Austin. My last name is Berkley."

Austin threw his hands on his head, and now it was he whose eyes were wide open and whose jaw was dropped. They both sat there speechless for a few seconds, looking at each other in amazement.

"This is too much! Nathan? Really?" Austin excitedly reached over and shook his hand. "What are the odds? Wow! It's nice to meet you."

Nathan was relieved at his reaction. "It's great to meet you, Austin. I can't believe you're here. Not just talking to me, but back home. We didn't know what had happened to you, if you'd ever come back."

Jamie looked up to see what all the sudden excitement was about.

"What happened to you? Where were you all that time?" Nathan asked, not trying to hide his excitement.

"My unit and I were on a mission that turned very ugly. We went into this little town where a group of insurgents was waiting on us. Without going into a lot of detail…man, they unleashed hell on us." The memories were obviously hard on Austin, but he continued to smile.

"I lost great friends that day. Those guys were real heroes. I was one of the few lucky ones who got captured. We spent years as POWs, and we didn't know from one day to the next if that was the day they were going to kill us. I was with three other POWs."

"Your family was very concerned for you. They never lost hope, though. It was amazing to watch."

Austin smiled and nodded. "As hard as it was, I couldn't help but feel a sense of purpose being there. I knew I wasn't there by accident. Two of the POWs were not Christians when we got captured, and I saw Christ transform their lives in the worst of circumstances. Man, I saw God do things that flat out blew me away. Eventually, a couple of the guards befriended us. They were badly mistreated by their superiors, and they started to be very attracted to the way we related to each other. They allowed us to share God's love with them, and one of them actually became a Christian. It was so wild. One day, they made it possible for us to escape. As a matter of fact, they escaped with us."

Nathan nodded as he listened intently.

"A couple days later, we all got caught. But as they were taking us back to their compound, after quite a beating, might I add, special US forces came out of nowhere raising total hell. They were popping shots right and left to get to us. Those guys are something else. I'm convinced they would've gone to the pit of hell to come rescue us. They were successful, and within a couple of months, we were back home." Austin paused a moment as his countenance went from an intense grimace to a warm smile. "You should've seen Kate the day I got home. She was so happy to see me, it made it all worth it. And Dad...man, when he hugged me, he couldn't let go."

Nathan smiled and nodded, agreeing that was just how they would be. He couldn't help but admire Austin's optimism, especially after having gone through something very few people could survive, not only physically but also emotionally. In his own case, Nathan knew, when life got a little hard, he had acted childish and selfish. He had wasted a lot of time and caused too much unnecessary pain.

"Your dad was so proud of you," Nathan said as he remembered how Warren talked about Austin. "They all were. I was amazed every day at how they never lost hope despite the obvious pain they felt."

Austin nodded and smiled. "Wow, Nathan Berkley. In the flesh. I'm blown away. Where have you been all this time? When did you come back?"

Nathan looked down and exhaled. He felt such shame and guilt to even talk about it. But there was something about Austin he trusted; the way he looked at him and asked the question made Nathan feel as if he really cared. He couldn't help but see Warren in his son, and he thought about how much he had missed their talks all these years.

"When Kate and I separated," he said, "I quit my job and went back to New Haven. My relationship with my dad was pretty bad, but we patched things up enough to tolerate each other somewhat. It was weird, but even though they'd never been to New Haven, everything there reminded me of Kate, Luke, and Emma. One day I just took off to travel the world, to get as far away from my troubles as possible. I was gone for years, coming to New Haven from time to time. But no matter where I went or what I did, I came to the same realization every time—that the problem was not in New Haven or Charleston or anywhere. The problem was with me.

"The memories chased me relentlessly, and the pain got more and more unbearable. I visited a lot of beautiful places, but I couldn't enjoy a single one. I was my own curse." He welled up with emotion and fought tears for a few seconds before he continued. "I've been such a coward. I came back to the States a few weeks ago and didn't really know where to go. Eventually, the only place I could think of going to was here. I can't explain why, but coming back here was the only thing I thought could bring some relief."

Austin's eyes perked up, which surprised Nathan. He had figured that after hearing how messed up he was, Austin might grab his son and run for the door.

"I see," Austin said. "You know? I'm really surprised I didn't recognize you earlier. When I first came back, every time I went to visit Kate, Emma would always bring me a picture of you from Kate's bedroom. 'This is Daddy,' she would say proudly. I saw that picture so many times that it was engraved in my brain."

Nathan said nothing and kept his gaze on Austin as his eyes teared up. He wanted nothing more than to hold his family in his arms and tell them how sorry he was.

Austin could see the pain and regret on Nathan's face. "I can't think of anything that beautiful young lady would love more than to see her daddy."

"I'd like to see her too," Nathan whispered. "I really screwed up."

Cesar A. Perez

"When I first got captured," Austin said as he checked on Jamie, "I really thought that was it for me. I was terrified, and my first reaction every day was to give up. Those feelings are normal. If you're human, they are normal. We all have them."

Nathan looked over at the spot where he had first met Kate. How many times he had returned to that moment in his mind, wishing he could somehow go back and start all over. "So what did you do?" he asked.

"I had a pity party for weeks. I couldn't even talk to the other POWs, I was so depressed. But as the weeks went by, I started to sense there was a reason for being there. I'll be honest with you—I didn't have a clue what that was, but it was becoming obvious that there was more to my circumstances than what I could see. What really became obvious, quite honestly, was that I wasn't in control.

"So you asked me what I did. Nothing, because there was nothing I could do to change my circumstances. All I could do was trust that God was who He said He was. I believed His words through the prophet Jeremiah, where He told us He has a plan for us and His plan is to prosper us and not harm us—that His plan is to give us hope and a future. These words made absolutely no sense in my circumstance, but I knew who God was and how He had come through for me in the past. So I chose to believe them, and I saw them come true in my life. It was extremely hard, but I chose to trust God, and He came through for me in unimaginable ways."

Nathan nodded in agreement, with a look of humility on his face. "I had the exact same choice to make, and I chose wrong. I took God out of the equation and made a selfish choice that hurt a lot of people."

"Nathan, your failures don't have to define you. At any point, you can make the choice to leave the past behind, work on the present, and move ahead. I'll share something with you if I may." Nathan nodded, and Austin continued. "Like with most teenagers, high school didn't start so good for me. I wasn't making the best choices at first, and I started getting in trouble. My actions were affecting everything and everyone around me, and they were influencing my outlook on life very negatively. I'll never forget what my dad said to me one day. He said, 'Yesterday is gone, you'll never get *now* back, and tomorrow is not here yet! Translation: Don't live in the past, make the most of now, and don't worry about tomorrow!'"

212

Nathan smiled as he heard the familiar words.

"I chose to believe and trust in what my dad was saying instead of in what I thought I knew at the time, and I reaped the benefits the rest of my life.

"This is a choice we have to make every day, and it's only when we trust in our heavenly father that we can not only survive but thrive. But life can't be about what we want it to be. It has to be about what God created each one of us specifically to be. If we're not willing to sacrifice our needs and wants and exchange them for His plan, we can never become the person He intended. And so the result, then, is that every day is a confusing struggle.

"Man, so many people go through life self-destructing, and they don't even know it. They don't see it because they haven't allowed God to open up their spiritual sight. It's when we have a relationship with God through Jesus that we can see things from His point of view. But we must let Him work in our lives, and to let Him we first have to trust that He is who He says He is and He can do what He says He can do."

There was a flurry of activity in the restaurant as three servers and a manager worked to pull together a few tables for a large party of people who had come in the restaurant. Jamie paused his game, enthralled by all the activity.

Nathan sat quietly, and Austin wondered if he had overstepped his bounds with him. They had just met, after all. But he offered one more thought: "Life gets crazy at times, especially when you have the responsibility of a family. Doesn't it? It gets overwhelming, happens to all of us. I promise you that. We can quickly get insecure and take the reins ourselves. That's when we start to lose control."

"That's what I did," Nathan said, sighing. His eyes raced from side to side as he tried to collect his thoughts and hold back his emotions. "I let it get out of control, and now it's too late."

Chapter 53

THE DAYS AFTER Kate had confronted him came to Nathan's mind. He knew she had prayed for him every day as they became strangers living in the same house, and he remembered how she had tried to hide the pain and stay positive for Luke and Emma. The distance between him and his family grew by the day, and every attempt to make the situation better seemed to make things worse for everybody. Kate knew he loved them because she could see it in his eyes when he looked at her and the children, but it was obvious Nathan was overwhelmed by his depression and had lost control. His life was consumed with himself.

Kate had confided in Rachel and Warren what was happening, and that had validated their concerns that something wasn't right. Nathan had always gone everywhere with his family. But in the previous months, when Kate brought the kids over, Nathan had only been with them a handful of times. He had also stopped going to church with them. At first, he gave excuses of being sick or too tired, but eventually he offered no excuses. It broke Warren's heart to see Kate and the kids sitting by themselves on Sunday mornings.

Warren went to visit Nathan the Sunday before he left home. Nathan still had a deep love and respect for Warren, but their conversation was very short. His reality had gotten very distorted, and he could not be talked off the ledge. He was down on himself and had gotten very negative toward people and life in general. As they talked, Warren could feel his heart breaking for a young man he loved like a son.

After they prayed together, Warren hugged him and said, "I love you, son. I know God is not done with you. He's with you right now, even if He's the last thing you feel. By His very nature, He will never leave you. But you need to turn back to Him, Nathan." These words from Warren would be engraved in Nathan's heart, and he would recall them many times in the years to come.

Ever since the day he left home, Nathan had wished he could run away from himself and back into Kate's arms. He yearned to hold Emma in his arms and have her feel his strength and protection. There was nothing he wanted more than to wrestle on the floor with Luke and hear his laughter and joy. He wanted to lose control to God all over again but seemed to be at the point of no return. He hated himself and the idea of allowing who he had become to ruin his family's precious lives. There was only one choice in his mind. He had to stay away.

"It's not too late, Nathan," Austin said, bringing him back to the conversation.

"The first months as a Christian, life felt as if it was on rails," Nathan said, smiling, almost laughing. "I felt so good. Things made so much sense. At some point, I don't really know when, I got comfortable and put my relationship with God in cruise control. I think that made it possible for the old Nathan to take over."

Austin smiled because he understood exactly what Nathan was saying. "I know, man. We all live a double life, and we don't even know it most of the time. Especially as Christians, we somehow live both in this physical realm and in the spiritual realm. God uses the physical-realm experiences to change us in our spirit, though. It's when you realize this, when you see it's not something you do but something you trust God to do, that He will transform you. He will make you new."

Nathan nodded, agreeing.

"I'm sure you've heard this verse before. Dad referred to it often in his sermons. He lived by it. It's in Proverbs. 'Trust in the Lord with all your heart, and lean not on your own understanding; in all your ways acknowledge him and he will make your paths straight.' If you will cling to those words, regardless of what you feel, eventually you will see that God is at work in your life. Otherwise, if you only live by what you see, you will lose yourself. You will construct a false reality based on yours and the world's wisdom—a reality full of riddles and misguided understanding."

"Your dad had such an influence in my life. Did you see the debate he and my father had?"

Austin nodded, almost laughing. "That had to be a wild time for you and Kate, huh?"

Nathan could see the same expression on Austin's face he had seen on Kate's, a look of respect and love for their dad.

"Yes, that was something else," Nathan said. "But I'm so glad it happened. Hearing your dad that night stirred something inside. He helped me see I had not been looking at things, and thinking, like I should have. It set me on a path of seeking that led me to an understanding of God I don't think I could've gotten to otherwise. How is he, your dad, by the way?"

Austin looked startled by the question. Nathan took a sip of his coffee as he waited for him to respond, but the response didn't come right away. The look on Austin's face was both joyful and sad, and he seemed to struggle to find words to answer Nathan's question.

"Dad passed away a year ago. I guess that's when you were overseas, so you didn't hear about it."

Nathan put his cup down, sat back in his chair, and let out a deep breath. He didn't want to scare his nephew, so he held his emotions as best he could. Austin could clearly see how much Nathan had loved Warren and what a blow this was to him.

"Dad loved you, Nathan. The day I came back from overseas, we all had a big meal to celebrate my return. Afterward, we sat down and talked for hours. Dad talked a lot about you. He never gave up on you, you know. I'm sorry to have to give you this news."

Nathan nodded as he regained his composure. "I loved him too, very much. He had an enormous impact on my life. I wish I'd had a chance to tell him that."

"Don't worry. He knew how much you cared for him."

"You remind me a lot of him. It looks like you became your dad and I became mine. I defaulted to my upbringing instead of trusting God, and that is the last thing your dad would've expected of me. I guess I didn't know what God expected after all."

"Don't beat yourself up. You need to remember all God wants from us is that we know Him. What we do is not as important." Austin's whole countenance lit up with passion. "Knowing Him, having a relationship with Him. Man, that's worth everything. It is worth losing ourselves to Him, all that we are and all that we have. It is then, and only then, that we can find who we really are. That is when true joy and peace are possible."

Nathan nodded in agreement, but this was something he really struggled with. "Faith was easy at first. Then it got too hard," he said.

"You're not kidding," Austin said as he put his arm around the back of Jamie's chair. "But we both know that God created us with the capacity to believe in things we can't see. Like, for example, me knowing that Jamie trusts me even though I don't see that trust. If there's one thing I have learned to be true, it is that God speaks to us often, guiding us through life, decisions, relationships, everything. But if we're not rightly related to Him, we miss how He is trying to work in our lives. We make it way too complicated.

"We often look for people to be a wolf in sheep's clothing, but where we are deceived is that we don't look for ourselves to be that. We need to work on ourselves first, before we can look at others. I love the following from the book of Ezekiel: 'Moreover, I will give you a new heart, and put a new Spirit within you: and will remove the heart of stone from your flesh and give you a heart of flesh, and I will put my Spirit within you and cause you to walk in my statutes, and you will be careful to observe My ordinances.'" Austin paused, letting the words sink in.

"The natural mind can't reason the things of the spirit, and we can't construct ourselves into who we want to be. Only God can help us understand and make us into who we should be if, in faith, we let God do it."

"I wish it were really that easy," Nathan said.

Austin felt a tug on the back of his shirt. He turned around and saw the obvious signs of a sleepy little boy. He checked his watch to see the time, and to his amazement they had been talking for over an hour. Jamie had been very patient, and he knew it was time to go.

Austin picked Jamie up and turned around to face Nathan. "Jamie, there is someone I want you to meet." Jamie lifted his head up from his dad's shoulder and looked at Nathan with sleepy eyes. "This is your uncle Nathan. He is Luke and Emma's daddy."

"Nice to meet you, uncle Nathan." As soon as he said this, Jamie laid his head back down and continued to look at Nathan with a faint yet sincere smile.

Nathan could feel his heart swell. "It's good to meet you too, Jamie. It's really good to meet you."

Austin checked his pockets to make sure he had his keys. "Nathan. Man! It blows me away you were here tonight. It was so good to meet you. Please know this. He who began a good work in you will be faithful to complete it."

Nathan nodded and stretched out his hand. Austin noticed that his eyes looked different from when they'd first met. They seemed less resigned.

"Thank you, Austin. You are your dad's son. Before you leave, can I ask you something?"

"Of course."

"How is Kate?"

Austin smiled and looked at Nathan. "She still loves you, and your children would love to see you."

Chapter 54

NATHAN FELT THE Charleston breeze he had missed so much as he took a night-time stroll. He had been to so many places in the last few years, but nowhere else felt like this. He thought about the old saying "home is where the heart is," and he had no doubt this was home. As the conversation between him and Austin replayed in his mind, he felt something stirring inside. He knew he had felt God's love through Austin's words, a love he realized transcended the time that had passed and the emotions he felt.

His heart shattered into a million pieces as he thought about what he'd once had. Tears began to flow as he remembered his friend Warren—gone from his life before he had a chance to say good-bye.

"I hope I'll see you again one day so I can tell you that you're the best person I've ever known," he said to himself as his emotions got the best of him. Heaven suddenly felt like a real place, and an inexplicable sense of confidence told him one day he would see Warren again.

A smile emerged as he thought about the day he'd met Kate at the very place where he'd eaten tonight; he could almost feel the hot food from her plate as it spilled on him. His heart skipped a beat as he felt himself falling in love with her all over again, but this time with even more intensity. He felt the pain from the night they'd had to say good-bye. He felt the magic of her touch the night of the debate.

There was nothing Nathan wanted more than to be with her, Luke, and Emma. Austin's words had hit their mark, and he knew beyond the shadow of a doubt that God had spoken to him that night. He could see what a lie he'd bought into; it had taken years of pain and failure, attempts to do things on his own, for him to realize that God still loved him and wanted to redeem him. But this could only happen if he truly trusted God with his life.

Nathan felt God's presence, telling him He loved him and asking for his trust. He thought about one of the last things Warren had ever said to him: "Son, I've done a lot of things wrong in life. If there's one thing I can tell you for sure, though, it's that God never stopped loving me. He never stopped waiting on me to come back to Him. I want you to remember this. No matter what and no matter when, He will be ready to give it all back to you."

Nathan understood now where he'd been wrong. There was no doubt in his mind he had been honest when he asked God to save him and come into his life. But he had missed a critical part: he had not made Jesus the lord of his life. He took the gift of salvation but tried to do life on his own. He regretted more than ever the pain this had caused him and those he loved most.

The wind picked up, and Nathan put his hands in his coat pockets. In the right pocket was the coin Kate had given him years ago, which he'd kept with him ever since. He pulled it out and looked at it as guilt and self-hate tried to creep in.

"Not tonight," he said out loud. What Kate was trying to communicate through the barley leaf in the coin finally made sense: no matter what, if a person trusted in Christ, he was meant to thrive and not perish.

He had missed this truth all these years, but he knew tonight things were different. For the first time, Nathan was able to allow God's mercy and grace to cover him. For the first time, feeling vulnerable was good, and he knew he could trust God to take care of his future no matter what it may bring. He realized he no longer needed to appease himself. Only God could reconcile him with himself.

He took his cell phone out of his pocket and prayed out loud. "Dear Lord, I'm so sorry I took over. I don't blame you anymore for the last few years. I did that, not you or anyone else, and I want you to please forgive me. No matter what happens next, I will praise you. I'm ready to trust you and live the life you want for me. My life is fully yours."

With tears in his eyes and a shaky hand, he typed "Home" into his cell phone. His heart beat like never before as he hit the call button and the phone started ringing. After four rings and no answer, he decided to hang up. Disappointed, he started to walk back toward the hotel.

Within minutes, he reached the front door of the building and took the key out of his pocket. He dreaded going back into that place, where he had experienced so much pain. His phone rang as he started to open the door, and he looked at the caller ID.

Home.

"Hello?" he answered.

"Nathan?"

"Yes, it's me. I'm sorry I called so late. I wasn't thinking about the time."

"It's fine," Kate said, surprised that she was talking to him. "Where are you?"

"I'm in Charleston."

There was a long pause. "You are?"

"Yes, I've been here a few days." Hearing her voice was amazing. "I really need to talk to you, Kate. You don't have to talk to me if you don't want to. I wouldn't blame you, but there's something I need to say." She said nothing, and he continued.

"How I acted and what I did can't be excused. I let life get the best of me, and I threw away everything that meant something to me. I know I caused you, your family, and our kids a lot of pain, and words can't express how sorry I am. I realized tonight that my insecurities and my ego had kept God from doing in my life what only He could do, and for that I've asked His forgiveness." He struggled to keep his composure, but he persevered because he understood that she needed to know he could be strong.

"Kate, I want to ask for your forgiveness. A lot of time has passed since I left, and I wouldn't blame you if you have already moved on, but I really need you and the kids in my life. I will do whatever it takes to have you back, to earn your trust, and this time I will let God have control no matter what happens. I've never seen things so clearly as I do tonight, Kate. I wouldn't blame you if you didn't take me back, because I really do want what's best for you, Luke, and Emma. I just want you to be happy, and—"

"Nathan!" She broke in. "Come home."

Made in the USA
Monee, IL
31 January 2021

59240085R00125